The Sex Lives of Sorcerers

2nd in the Sorcerers and Magi Series

by Soror ZSD23

kult ov kaos
publishing house

Published by

kult ov kaos publishing house
P.O. Box 2939
Sioux Falls, SD 57101
ISBN-13: 978-0615694689
ISBN-10: 0615694683

Cover art: William Blake (1757-1827). Illustration from *Paradise Lost: Satan Watching the Caresses of Adam and Eve.*
Cover design: Dee Rapposelli

"The Dragon dieth not unless he be killed by his Brother and Sister; not by one only, but by both together, that is by Sol and Luna."

—From the *Rosarium philosophorum,* an alchemical pictorial text first published in 1550.

Love does not end, but gifts of prophecy do as does the gift of communicating in mystical languages. Knowledge will ultimately fail us too. For our knowledge is imperfect, and our prophesies are imperfect, but when what is perfect comes, what is imperfect ceases.

When I was a child, I spoke, acted, and reasoned like a child. Now that I am mature, the ways of children are behind me. Now we see as if looking at a dim reflection in a mirror; then we will see face to face. Now my knowledge is incomplete; but then I will know as completely as I am known. Ultimately and in brief, only three things last: faith, hope, and love, and the greatest of these is love.

—Epistle of Paul, I Corinthians 13:8-13

CONTENTS

0
[The Fool]
A Fallen Fairy

Anderson watched Michael approach the woman. The impulse was to call after him, but Anderson restrained himself. He and Michael had been watching the damsel struggle to get too many grocery bags though the back entrance of the condominium.

She was in her prime and of average height, with a lustrous mop of hair that seemed to be made of gold and copper filaments. She was well-formed for a Commons, with a lithe and airy physique and no doubt an airy and angst-ridden temperament from the way she was making the simplest and most ordinary task so difficult for herself. It was painful to watch in the way observing comically pathetic things are.

Her arms were weighted with plastic bags—four to five clutched in each fist. The weight made her waddle and walk with strained steps. Anderson watched her shift all the bags to her left hand to open the door with her right, but there was no way she could accomplish this. She set the bags down and seemed to be attempting to wedge an elbow or an ankle in the door, grab the bags, and scrape through. She dropped the keys and couldn't maneuver the wedge in the door before it slammed shut.

She was standing, as if helpless and slighted, in the slosh of plastic bags from which vegetables and toiletries were escaping when Michael broke away from Anderson and approached the woman. She had one hand braced against the building and the other against her brow. She was weeping. The sight made a dull, throbbing pain invade Anderson's left sinus. It snaked up to the outer rim of his eye socket and then his temple. It was her; she had a headache. Anderson huffed. He wasn't up to feeling her pain—or fixing it. Michael would do it, he thought wearily.

Michael's intention, of course, was to be rakish but courtly toward some pathetic Commons woman. Upon nearing close enough, he abruptly turned back to Anderson. His face was marked by sharp surprise; his mouth parted in astonishment. Upon getting a hold of himself, his eyes lit up and his expression became impish.

"What?" Anderson mouthed.

Michael gloated and turned back to his self-appointed task.

Anderson watched Michael place his hand in the space between the woman's shoulder blades and brazenly wriggle a finger into a ringlet of her hair. He opened the door and smiled consolingly such that the tears in her eyes welled over and dribbled down her face. All Anderson could gather when she spoke was that she had had "a bad day." He tediously sighed and rolled his eyes.

"It's past you now," Michael said in a pitch that was sugary and loaded with a bass timbre. Anderson imagined that the vibration of it shot straight down to the woman's pubic bone.

Michael waved his hand over the woman's head and across her face. She seemed taken aback by it and said something that was excited and weepy but inaudible to Anderson. He wasn't sure whether she had noticed that Michael had relieved her of her malaise or whether it would take time for her to realize that her headache was gone.

Watching Michael in the act made Anderson feel weightless; he couldn't imagine what the woman might be experiencing besides the sappy trap of infatuation—the

"Sweet Surrender maneuver," as it was called in the Inner Plane. Michael thought he was an expert in it, but if he was, why did he use it on Commons so often and hardly ever on his own kind?

Anderson bristled and glared at the woman when she caught his eye. He knew she lived on the fifth floor. He had shared an elevator ride with her once soon after Michael had moved into the building. Anderson had remembered that even though something about her felt chaotic and out-of-sorts, she was unusually "bright" for a Commons. Her eyes had a certain provocative gleam that one generally only saw in Commons when they were on the last legs of evolving from the Outer to Inner Plane. That the woman had this characteristic should have been inspiring and congratulatory but it was unnerving for Anderson. He wasn't sure why.

The woman grasped her grocery bags and sidled through the door. She muttered thanks and coyly gazed at Michael until the door between them slammed shut.

Michael lingered there, fixated on the door.

"What are you doing, Michael?" Anderson remarked in a chastising tone.

The younger man turned. With an astonished look, he exclaimed, "I think she's a fairy."

Anderson grimaced as if he had bitten into something bitter. "I don't think so," he said.

Michael simply nodded contrarily.

Anderson glared at him before saying, "Let her be. Don't start this again. If she is one, she's fallen, and we've had enough of fallen fairies for this lifetime, haven't we, Michael?"

The woman's name was Bellaluna Drago. She lived in a cluttered but spacious one bedroom apartment on the fifth floor of a mid-rise condominium complex in the rather compact-city part of a sprawling pedestrian New England town called Stamford, a half-hour drive north of Manhattan.

The way of life was suburban. If you were looking for culture or intellectual life, you had to find a demimonde or travel to other cities. But then Bella Drago didn't really know what went on in the world. She kept to herself, solitarily dawdling in a nearby woodland park when she wasn't working or else dabbling in obscure and singular interests.

She was a speech therapist. She served stroke patients and others who were rendered mute by neurological injury. She trained them to speak again through a technique called melodic intonation therapy. That is, she taught the mute how to sing; first how to drone and intone and then how to turn sounds into words. It forced brain cells to form new neural pathways and compensate for brain parts that were blighted by injury. In time, patients would be able to sing conversation and then speak more or less normally.

Bella worked in this way several hours a week. Otherwise, she picked up freelance work as a medical writer, hustling for accounts and working long nights and weekends when a job came through. But on the other side of her life, she fancied herself an occultist and "kitchen witch," educated in the mystical lore of plants and minerals, charms, folklore, and superstition. She engaged in solitary meditations and ritual work and in the manufacture of fanciful ritual objects such as magical wands and talisman.

On that particular day, the usual melodrama called Life began early, earlier in fact than the part where Bella was lingering in her car, having arrived for work at a stroke rehabilitation clinic. She was lingering because a certain song had begun on the radio. The doleful beginning-part of it went nicely with Bella's mood. She didn't drone along with it as she usually would've. She was preoccupied. She watched condensation make tear trails on the windshield, which made her feel even more melancholic.

She had checked her email moments before departing for work. Her "special friend" Wayne had sent her a message. In it, Wayne, told Bella that an amazing and inexplicable thing had occurred over the weekend about which he hoped Bella would understand. He said he had met and fallen in love with someone (else). He therefore wouldn't be seeing Bella on the upcoming Saturday as planned.

Bella read the message twice, clenched her jaw, and marked the email—and every saved email from Wayne—as spam so as to block any additional messages that the bastard might send. Then she got red-eyed, weepy, and pent-up with anger for playing along for so many weeks.

She was a nice-looking woman—the kind who appeared deceptively younger than her age. She had a youthful, almost growth-stunted manner that never matured past that of an ingénue. She had warm, Mediterranean skin and large, shiny hazel eyes, but the wild golden brown hair was the attention-getter. And she tended to dress all arty and bohemian instead of like a lady.

Bella had been christened Bellaluna Marie Drago, which—except for the perfunctory saint name in the middle—meant "Beautiful Moon Dragon." When Bella was old enough to determine this, she mentioned it to her parents who, in their distracted pedestrian way, squinted and pointedly told her that she was not a "dragon" and that she should sharply rebuff anyone who said so. The child never mentioned the issue about her name again although she always wondered why her folks chose Bellaluna of all the crackpot monikers.

Even though her name was problematic, especially during childhood with the razzing and accompanying grief throughout grammar and secondary school, she took pride in it in adulthood. After all, Moondragon was the name of an eroticized femme-fatale interstellar comic book heroine. The early 16th century geomancer and theologian Cornelius Agrippa had mentioned it, too, in De Occulta Philosofia. It referred to a mostly auspicious ancient astronomical symbol that related to when the planet Jupiter was directly overhead in the sky.

Within occultism, the dragon sometimes symbolized raw energy—the prima materia—or primeval chaos. The moon symbolized the divine feminine, creative potential, the soul, embodiment, and time, space, and cycles. Joining with the male divine principle, symbolized by the sun, the raw energy of the feminine principle was transformed into perfection and power. In Eastern mysticism, this integration might be called the "diamond body"; in Western occultism, it might be called the "philosopher's stone."

In homage to this trivia, Bella kept a small green bean-bag toy dragon in the shadow of her computer display in her bedroom. The dragon shared its space with a translucent piece of red Lucite that resembled a crystal. Bella had written the words "before" and "after" on tiny Post-It paper and placed the "before" near the dragon and the "after" near the chunk of plastic (which was supposed to be the philosopher's stone). Bella found inspiration in it although she did throw the dragon across the room and then pelt it with the plastic "crystal" (while screaming "Lying-waste-piece-of-shit") after reading Wayne's email.

In any case, the day was shot in the head from its start. Bella rallied by reminding herself that the people she was attending to in the clinic had much worse problems than she did. That she had the power to help them was a very good thing. She sustained herself with this thought.

When she left the clinic, she went food shopping and, returning home that late afternoon, made the mistake of trying to get all of the grocery bags into her apartment at once. She crumbled but was saved by a shining-armored knight.

His name was Michael Paracelsus Solaris. Unbeknown to Bella was that this fellow was not a common man — or a "Commons" one; he was a sorcerer who hailed from the Inner Plane. And he was no ordinary two-bit sorcerer but a doctor of healing arts who also held the high academic degree of Sortiar Excelsis — "High Sorcerer." He was an expert alchemist and passed himself off as laboratory scientist specializing in pharmacotoxicology in his exploits in the Outer Plane. He had a fascination with the medicinal and toxic uses of snake, snail, fish, bat, and spider venoms.

He was not a bad sort per se — even if he had been a double agent and sometime assassin in covert operations for the Royal Dominion of Principalis Central Intelligence Programme in his youth. It was his fated duty, considering the rare magical talents he had come into the world with — talents for transmuting and obliterating things.

Of course, he regretted some of the consequences of his talents and mercenary missions in the service of his terra, but it couldn't be helped. Michael's talents had rendered him into an exploited thing. Part of that exploitation was to be stripped of original personhood and become someone else's idea of a person. Most everyone suffered this fate, but in Michael's case, it meant transforming a shiny, bright, new person into a spy and a killer.

It was ruthless, certainly, but it was not ignoble to be a soldier. It was in the interests of the welfare of the many and, of course, the State. Michael would solace himself with that passage from the Bhagavad Gita in which the incarnate deity Krishna tells his mortal comrade-in-arms Arjuna, who was suffering a crisis of conscience:

It is your fated duty. Thus, you must not falter. There is no greater good for a warrior than a righteous war. Be happy and consider it an open gate to heaven. If you do not participate, you will incur sin, fail in your duty, and ruin your reputation.

It was as it was, and having happened, it could not be undone.

Michael's other less-than-stellar life event that placed his integrity in question—this one indeed ignoble—was that he had been the third person in a lovers' triangle that had left his mentor Anderson Albright, who was a particular kind of sorcerer called a mage, in ruins some years ago. Anderson didn't blame Michael so much; he blamed the woman—a fairy—a harpy or strix was more like it.

The men recently had reconciled. After all, Anderson had been Michael's mentor since Michael's adolescence. He had trained him in how to maintain dispassion, and discipline in his responsibilities to the State however much the mage was averse to violence and intrigue. Michael knew that the mage regularly performed mystical rites of atonement and absolution for him so that he would not find himself trapped in the payback that fate had in store for him after making him what he was in the first place.

Anderson was an academician. He also was a specialist in healing arts. He held a Magus Celestus degree. It was the equivalent of a Sortiar Excelsis degree except that the discipline of magianism, as it was called, took a more mystical direction than the discipline of sorcery, which was more focused on practical magic.

Anderson, in his own academic work, had done extensive research on interaction between otherworldly beings (e.g., fairies) and ordinary persons (magical, and even more "ordinary" mortal people, or "Commons"). The subject of incarnated otherworldly beings—"fallen fairies" in particular—had been of special interest to him.

At the height of his work on the subject, Anderson held the radical idea that fallen fairies weren't "fallen" exactly. He argued that fallen fairies chose to forget who they really were and then chose to incarnate into challenging human experiences to be that much more beneficent and compassionate after slogging through the ordeal. Their powers were hidden like toys in the attic. They had strategically made themselves a little lost and martyring in pursuit of transcendence. A skilled magician, thus, could save a fallen fairy by initiating her into her own power (and thus gain her favor) or else he could sap her, like a vampire.

It was pure romanticism and pure theory. Anderson's view was shot through when his own liaison with an alleged fallen fairy left him whirling in the delirium of an enchantment. It sapped him of power, and, as mentioned, he was ultimately cuckolded by her and his then 27-year-old apprentice Michael Solaris. Eight years later, it was water under the bridge, but Anderson did not want to get anywhere near another fairy — fallen or otherwise — again.

Fairies — fallen ones especially — had peculiar, sometimes melodramatic, ways of operating. For example, the first thing that the just-now sighted fallen fairy Bellaluna Drago did upon alighting to her apartment after her encounter with Michael was to gather the elements of a witchy little love charm that she had been dabbling with. Anderson wasn't aware of all of the specifics of her activity, but he shuddered nonetheless when he noticed her gazing out a window to the parking lot. He knew she was up to something. But her amateur sorcery had nothing to do with Anderson or Michael; she had issues with a Commons man who had spurned her.

She placed the remnants of her charm — parchment, rose petals and herbs macerated in aromatic essential oils, and the melted candle wax — on a dainty, floral teacup saucer. She glared at the stuff. Flecking a wand she had made from driftwood, copper, menstrual blood, and chips of coral and hematite, she forcefully announced that the spell was broken.

The pronouncement startled her. It was as if the world had become very quiet—hushed and aghast. The resolve, steadiness, and peculiar silence in her mind were mildly frightening. But maybe the sensation was closer to awe than fear. Bella reasoned that the uneasiness she felt was merely what could be expected from an abrupt shift in consciousness. At least she didn't sulk and sob as much as she otherwise would have under the circumstances.

In a gesture of disdain for the love spell gone awry, Bella scooped up the magical debris and, maintaining the attitude of ceremony, threw it in the kitchen garbage pail. Doing so had a certain fiery resoluteness. It was scary, too, because she wasn't sure whether it was okay to dispose of magical objects that way. There was no telling what the blow-back would be.

It was important to remove the trash from the apartment then. Bella took it out to the chute in the hallway. Then she sprinkled salt around because doing so was supposed to repel bugaboos and negative energies. She could've muttered a prayer or two but she was too angry. She wrested a bottle of cabernet from her wine fridge a bit too urgently. With a shaking hand, she poured too much of it into a tall water glass.

As she gulped the drink, she realized that her shining-armored knight and his snotty friend were still standing in the parking lot. Bella ventured onto her balcony with its "scenic view" of the condominium parking lot and the lots of two adjacent apartment complexes. Her water glass of wine was in one hand and her "magic wand" in the other. She impulsively watched the men, hoping that her new nice neighbor would glance up at her. She wondered whether the older man was his jealous boyfriend and whether he was a rich, class-conscious snob even if he had smiled at her and made her feel validated as a woman.

He seemed to be nearly 30. He was fit and carried himself like a gentrified man, but his face was delicate — more beautiful than masculine — and he sported a rather voluminous mop of golden curls as if he were a rock star or a 17th century nobleman. When he had gazed at Bella while they stood at the back entrance of the condominium, he had done so with bright dark eyes that were penetrating, pitying, and saccharine. He spoke with what almost sounded like a British accent.

"Mister Knight's" friend was an older, lanky, well-groomed man who sported round copper-rimmed glasses. Bella watched him and the knight stand close and speak intently to each other. The older man was speaking forcefully. His right hand was firmly lodged on the knight's left shoulder. Bella was morbidly waiting for the two to sneak a furtive embrace or squeeze each other's asses when the telephone rang. Bella ignored it. The answering machine kicked in. It was Wayne. He was asking Bella whether she had received his email. Crass asshole that he was, he uttered, "I just wanted to check to make sure we understand each other. I hope you can be happy for me and, you know, we can stay in touch, because, well — "

Bella glared at the machine from the tiny balcony of her apartment but her gaze shifted back to where Mister Knight was walking back toward the building. He was alone, as if his companion had sprinted away or else disappeared. The knight looked up briefly without emotion or acknowledgement. Bella nevertheless fantasized that he had made eye-contact with her from five stories up.

As she watched the very top of the knight's head disappear from her vantage point, she aimed her magic wand at the answering machine. She figured she should say something magical but didn't know what, so she saidd, "Get bent" instead.

Bella heard Wayne screech as if he had been stung by something venomous or electric. He cursed the way persons do when they bang their head or a elbow against something. Then the phone went dead. Bella gaped at the answering machine. The word "astonishing" came to mind.

"That's right," she hollered at the appliance. "Don't FUCK with me! Shithead."

She half-hoped she hadn't killed Wayne (that would be bad karma). She cried for 15 minutes and then sat in the gloaming of the bitter end of sunset for another half hour before getting to work on an editorial project. "Multidisciplinary Efforts Emerging for PNES Interventions." She typed the words against the white void of a Word document. PNES was an acronym for "Psychogenic Non-Epileptic Seizures." What she had typed would be the title of an article based on interviews Bella had had with two epileptologists and a psychiatrist. The article would be about how neurologists could convince persons with a psychiatric disorder that mimicked epilepsy that it was okay to be crazy given what they probably had gone through in life and that they would be better off pestering psychiatrists instead of neurologists about their problems.

As for Michael, he knew that the woman who lived in 5C was troubled but he didn't think she was Trouble itself. She was world-weary, and she was displaced, on the wrong planet or plane of existence. That's what he thought when he got close enough to her. He was attracted. He wanted to be attracted. After all, life had become rather boring and lonely. And lo! His impulse to be good-neighborly opened up a serendipitously splendid opportunity. A fairy in the world of Commons! It would be a fine conquest.

Anderson ridiculed the idea. He had become cynical

about these matters. He had been badly burned by a fairy-like creature. Because of her Michael and Anderson had had a falling-out. Because of her, Michael couldn't resist double-crossing him — his own mentor!

Anderson, in his incurable tender-heartedness, insisted that that other creature was a "fallen fairy," but this turned out to be untrue. One, the creature, who called herself Aisa Morae, clearly knew that she was a magical entity and could traverse the Inner and Outer Planes at will. Two, her special forte was to divide and conquer, and in so doing, sap men of vital force, leaving them to languish. She was a siren, and she almost met her end (as sirens were said to be destined to do) when a certain notorious pair of sorcerers known to Anderson turned the tables on her. The two sorcerers, Tristan Lundragon and Jason Paleologos, also might have originally mistaken Aisa for a fairy. Their diabolical aim would have been to sap her. In any case, they were immune to her charms. They dallied with and then spurned her, which took the wind out of her sails for a while.

Michael had ultimately spurned Aisa as well, but doing so did not deter her momentum. In fact, she had taken to stalking him and wreaking havoc in every relationship he attempted to enter since disengaging himself from her wiles.

Michael found himself taking up residence where he had in that condominium complex in sleepy Stamford, Connecticut, because it was a sea and plane away from that noxious entity. The other reason was . . . well . . . this was it: Michael had covert goings on with certain dignitaries and provocative persons in an Inner-Plane locale called the North Atlantic Sovereignty. The site was the hub of a gripping political upheaval in a country called Terra Novit. Michael, although a foreigner, was one of its conspirators. Yes. He was in league with a rebel faction called the Lions of Light. You could say he did consulting work regarding weapons systems . . . in magical warfare, that is.

Soon after night fell, Michael sat in candle-lit darkness and made his own light from the magical projection of a glowing mandala. A rosy glow emanated from his chest and a sharp white-blue light shot from his brow. An image of the blossoming Rose Mystica and relevant sigils danced in space. The cycles of time, marked by the directions, the seasons, the stations of the day, phases of the moon, the zodiac, and a set of mystical Cabalist letters, encircled him. Images of the seven alchemical spheres appeared in descending order along the column of his body: Sol, Jupiter, Mercury, Venus, Mars, Luna, and Saturn. He imagined himself as the mystical grail — the philosophical egg — in which the metaphorical alchemical transmutation from lead to gold took place.

Michael sat poised in this vision as was his usual custom at the end of the day. Before closing the interlude, he contemplated his new agenda with some intensity so that, when he opened his eyes, the image of the fairy was in them. He laid back and allowed himself to feel hot and luxurious about it. He would suck the palm of his hand as if it were the juicy fruit of some part of a woman, lick his fingers and run them over the skin of his neck, his chest, and abdomen. Unleashing his penis from the confines of clothing, he would cup the appendage in a moist grip.

Caress it; vigorously work it into the makeshift interior of his fist, stoking and flaring the fire the activity incites until he was mindless heat and incandescence — but not so lost and self-absorbed to not force a conjuration. He would make that woman who lived five floors below yearn to be plugged up to him at that very moment. She would be restless and burning and would have to stop whatever she was doing to suit herself: put her finger there and obsess on him while she solitarily lit her bit on fire.

1

[The Magician]
A Walk in the Woods

Maybe it was weird but, when Bella . . . um . . . masturbated . . . she thought of being in nature instead of being with people. She heated herself with visions of moss-covered rocks to scrape her breasts and pelvis against and of eddies in streams to sink into where rushes lapped and whipped and tiny fish pecked between her thighs.

She imagined leaf-laden boughs thrashing her and gnarled roots binding her ankles while she felt the world on her skin and moist, swishy, wriggling things titillating her sexual parts. She would come pretty robustly from that actually. She wondered whether she wouldn't try finding a solitary spot to get off in the next time she went for a walk in the woods.

It was weird, but maybe, in the end, it was better not to mix sexuality with men — or people. The reality was always problematic. Bella had been married and divorced, and most of the men with whom she had been in her history as a woman were not particularly erect or otherwise dynamic in the sack.

It was uncanny and tragic. Her women friends thought her confessions about encounters with erectile dysfunction were odd. Bella was sure the gossip was that she was either clueless or frigid, but in truth, most of the penises that had been in Bella's bare-assed presence had either deflated or shot-the-wad as soon as their Cyclops heads got a gander of the divine clit they were supposed to slide past to enter the Inner Sanctum. They chickened out. They just couldn't handle it, which was what Bella had to tell herself to keep from feeling like a total pathetic freak. Penises literally hardly ever made it "in." Their circuits popped like light bulbs that had no business being in the sockets they aspired to be lit upon because of wattage incompatibilities.

But as far as getting-off in nature went, the nearby woods that Bella frequented — although expansive — was pretty much inhabited on any given day. However much a person thought she was alone in it, she could never find a discreet spot to piss in if she had to. Someone and his dog would always find her even if she hadn't seen or heard another soul for hours before squatting behind a rock to empty her bladder. So . . . she probably couldn't go dry-humping logs or writhing against the slimy underside of boulders in streams. People would see her.

The woodland park was about eight-minutes' drive from Bella's home. It stretched for acres. The best part — despite that it was used as a dog run — was a stream where men in fly-fishing attire spent serious hours catching, mutilating, and releasing very small trout that the county put there especially for them. The stream coursed amid witch hazel, beech, maple, hemlock, pine, mountain laurel, and weedy shrubs laden with berries, wild grape vines, and thorn bushes.

The trail along the stream appeared to end at a rusty chain-link fence beyond which — further upstream that is — was a shallow waterfall. A person could bath in it if she dared trespass, but Bella never did. She would sit in the shade of beech and maple trees on a gray boulder in the stream on the border of the posted zone and watch other people cavort in the falls.

Nearly two years went by before Bella realized that the path along the stream didn't end at the fence. A person could follow the fence uphill and then around a blocked-out, caged-in portion of the park in which rich people had built homes. Once past that, a person would come to paths that ran along the stream's edge again. They continued for at least another mile before fading into poison ivy, rocks, and bramble and the sound of a highway.

If a person walked toward the interior away from the stream, the webs of paths wheedled through hillcrests. Bella seldom ventured that way because it was easy to get lost, but she knew of a shallow cave out on the crest of a hill that overlooked a lush gorge of shrubs and trees. An old aromatic pine grew twisted out of the boulders that formed the cave, and dried pine needles were the thresh on the cave's floor.

Bella had other special spots here and there: the rock downstream of the waterfall and further downstream, a grouping of stepping stones that led to a large, flat, blond boulder near a tiny island of shrubs and reeds that made the current choke and twist. Black damsel flies that flashed iridescent green-blue or violet or else had red dots on the edges of gossamer wings flitted in hoards around the witch hazel there. They often gently landed on Bella. She very much liked that. Tiny frogs poked about, and, occasionally, a crane could be seen. Upon being startled, it would leap into the air and soar away with amazingly wide wings.

Way into woods toward the end of the path that ran along the stream was the ruin of a small cottage or perhaps a smokehouse. All that remained on a little hill was the slate floor and a stove-of-sorts that consisted of a fire pit with a metal grill built into a counter. The structure was affixed to a chimney made of slate, stones, and mortar. It had the look of something altar-like and sacred. Bella would often wander there and linger.

She would sit on the slate countertop adjacent to the grill and relax into the natural silence. Deer might approach, sometimes in groups, as if purposefully congregating to meet her. They would stand on the perimeter of the ruin, gaping and frozen except for their lower jaws that warbled and wriggled as if attempting to communicate.

On a day that was warm, sunny, and magically scenic for early October, Bella drove south through modest neighborhoods where families of mid- and struggling-incomes lived; past the golf course, and then northwest along a scenic winding road marked by nouveau riche sprawl: manor-like houses and incessant renovation.

She turned down an easily missed side road that led to a hidden, unpaved lot. When she pulled in, a lanky woman with perfectly straight, glossy, and unnaturally uniform honey-colored hair had just stepped from a shiny black BMW convertible. The car's bumper was brazenly marred by prosaic stickers that read: "I believe in dragons, good men, and other mythical beasts," and "Are you a good witch or a bad witch?" The woman was clad in a black, pleated mini skirt and shiny, beige, spandex running tights that made her legs look naked. She wore a bulky suede waist jacket and pristinely clean hiking shoes. She smiled at Bella as if she recognized her.

"Do you know where the park is? The forest? I've been driving around for 45 minutes looking for it," the woman huffed. Her turquoise eyes, which were very round and large, were made up to look even larger. "The park's-department bitch on the phone who gave me directions — I don't know what she was talking about."

"Well, 'you are here,'" Bella said as if reading words off a location guide. "The trail is up the road on your right."

"Can I follow you there? You're going there, right?" the woman asked anxiously.

"Sure," Bella shrugged.

They walked to the entrance, and then the woman became a hanger-on. Bella wasn't sure whether she appreciated the company, but she figured the encounter would snap her out of the melancholy that gripped her.

The woman said her name was Aisa Morae. She handed Bella a business card. "Pronounced MOOR-ray, like the eel and other things," the woman uttered. She snorted out a loud and grotesque giggle and then said she crafted jewelry from special stones and metals and made a decent living at it. "A man used to keep me comfortable, but I wrecked that," she confided. "The rest were just users. I can't deal with having a man own me. They're all vampires. Energy vampires. You know what I mean?"

Bella nodded because she thought she did.

From beneath her jacket, Aisa pulled on silver- and red-colored silken cords and drew out two amulets, which were examples of her livelihood. "But don't touch them," she said. "They're charmed."

Bella smiled and envied Aisa's magical thinking.

Aisa explained, in a quaintly sincere tone, that the amulet made out of a polished iridescent stone, a rough chunk of amethyst, and oddly shaped fresh-water pearls was her moon-energy amulet, "for healing and psychic abilities and women's mysteries." The amulet on the other necklace consisted of a mass of red coral, carnelian, amber, and a dappled red-green stone. It was her sun-energy amulet, "for protection, passion, and especially vigor," she giggled provocatively. "But we don't have trouble with that—they do," she smirked. She wriggled a bent middle finger to suggest that some of the men she was in a position to "invigorate" had penis problems.

"You, too," Bella said.

"Mmmm," the woman asserted. "'Commons' men," she added blithely.

"Uncommon men must be extremely rare, if they exist at all," Bella replied.

She and Aisa commiserated while they walked even though they were strangers and even though they were talking about the delicate subject of erectile dysfunction.

As they went along, Aisa pointed out all of the defoliating shrubs, the desiccated viney bramble, and spots of ground cover that had yielded wild edibles that summer. She sang to birds that answered her call and was quite agile at hopping across stones as she zigzagged across the stream or strayed off the path to scale hill crests.

Aisa fascinated Bella at first, but the love-affair was short lived. It soon became apparent that Aisa was zigzagging and bushwhacking through the woods to avoid an entourage that included baying hounds. She kept diverting the direction she otherwise seemed set on in accordance with cues set by the cacophony of the animals. Bella simply followed her — haplessly and worriedly — after all, this Aisa moray-eel-person was a complete stranger.

When Bella smelled pine strong in the air, she knew that she and Aisa were approaching the little cave. The damned dogs still could be heard. Bella spotted them in the gorge seen from the crest near the cave. She spied two men. Both were tall, lean, stately, and rather handsome. They were mature, though; perhaps in their early forties. One had dark hair; the other's hair was light. A more unkempt and slouchy but lanky fellow who was perhaps in his mid-20s was in their company. Despite a limp, his romping, hyperkinetic gait seemed to be why the dogs were so frenzied.

The light-haired man looked up and spotted Bella on the crest. He smiled kindly as if to communicate that he thought it fortunate that Bella had found such a nice vantage point. Aisa had retreated to the cave. She was huddled within in it, in fact, despite that glass shards, burnt wood, and other detritus left by others littered the cave's floor. Bella told her to come out; the cave most certainly was contaminated with bugs and infectious bat and rodent droppings, she said. Bella pointed out the cottony masses of exudates from insects and molds that spotted the interior walls of the cave.

"The cave is pretty groovy but I don't think you should hang out in there," Bella stressed. "You could get an infection from breathing in mold spores." Bella mentally recounted the names of infections that persons could get from breathing in certain types of fungal spores that grew in nature: histoplasmosis, blastomycosis, cryptococcosis.

Aisa wasn't listening or else didn't care. She was gazing at hieroglyphic-like graffiti that was chalked onto the interior of the cave with black soot.

"Look at that," Aisa remarked in a wizened tone. She smirked and quipped, "Angels," as if she thought the glyph implied that someone in the area was up to something stupid.

The symbol resembled a trident within a trident. The tines of the tridents were crowned by tiny circles. Bella knew that it was a letter in a magical alphabet that corresponded with the Hebrew alphabet. Indeed, it was a letter in so-called angelic script.

"Samekh," Aisa exclaimed as if responding to Bella's thought. "It's the letter that corresponds with the Devil-card in the Tarot."

"'He caused the letter Samekh to reign in wrath,'" Bella uttered to let Aisa know that she wasn't in the dark about these things. The words were from a passage from a famous Qabalist text called the Sephir Yetzirah. "He" was "God" who, according to the author of the Sephir Yetzirah, created a numinous garland of letters—the Hebrew alphabet—that, mystically speaking, became the basis of name and form. Each letter had symbolic correspondences with celestial bodies, times of the year, parts of the human anatomy, the senses, and certain emotions and activities of daily living. There was nothing sinister about it. It was just that when the 19th century esotericist A. E. Waite drew correspondences between the mystical Hebrew alphabet and popular Tarot lore, the letter Samekh—"Sh," that is—got pinned together with the card in the Tarot deck on which was illustrated a picture of the Devil.

The sound of the jabbering dogs picked up. The animals were rapidly nearing.

"Shit," Aisa squeaked. She anxiously goaded Bella to enter the cave. She looked troubled.

"Do you know those people?" Bella asked.

Aisa simply shook her head and grimaced.

The three hounds had alighted on the crest and were rounding the rock formation that made the cave. Upon reaching the cave's mouth, the creatures jostled and paused. They lingered hesitantly with heads nodding as if taking caution. Their snouts assessed the find. Bella inched closer. She reached out a hand that the dogs vied to sniff and nuzzle.

The men called the dogs away as they passed. Without expression or comment, each fellow peered into the cave to briefly glance at the two women crouched within it. Bella thought that both grown men were very handsome. This thought made her sad and lonely and that much more uncomfortable about being with Aisa, who was clearly crazy. The younger, less put-together man lingered and gaped, with deep-set black eyes, as if fixated on the sight of copulating apes caged in a zoo cell. He was rather rakish looking. He had an angular, alluring face, a faint mustache, a goatee, and an outgrown mop of dark brown hair.

Not knowing quite what to do, Bella flashed an uncomfortable smile and raised a hand to make a slight and unsure "hello" gesture. The young man raised his eyebrows in a leering way.

"Robert." One of the older men called in a tone people use when tempering children. The young man loped off.

"Are they?" Bella heard the younger fellow asked.

"Mmmm," muttered one of the other two affirmatively.

With that, Aisa darted from the cave. "Hunting?" she screeched accusingly. "Go back to where you came from! Fucking vampires!"

The mature men reacted with dismissive amusement. They turned and winked, but mostly at Bella, and continued on. The younger man hung back to gape at the women until Aisa seemed to do something startling that Bella couldn't see because her back was to Bella. The fellow shuddered as he gazed head-on at Aisa. He faltered as he pivoted with his gimping gait and galloped past his guardians toward the pack of hounds. Aisa simply frowned when she turned back to Bella. She made her head shimmy in an exasperated way again as if she couldn't bear explaining the situation.

The women started back from the way they came in their woodland trek. The mood was quiet and irritable at first. Then, in a manic tone, Aisa launched into a delusional rant about an alternate plane of existence inhabited by sorcerers who got off on toying with ordinary people and creating turmoil in the ordinary world. She said the women-sorcerers were witches and that their male counterparts used sex to absorb peoples' vital energies in efforts to become more powerful.

Bella humored Aisa and bided her time. The woman apparently was very angry at men. It was as if her mind had become diseased because of some vicious cycle of abuse that had begun when she was very young and helpless. Bella always had been fascinated by case studies of persons like Aisa Morae, but she found that actually interacting with such a person was creepy.

When they got back to the lot, the golden-haired English nobleman who resided in the condominium complex in which Bella lived was approaching. His bitchy older friend was in tow. The friend walked past the women as if they weren't there. Aisa's gaze followed the older man. It was as if she meant to say something but held back before turning a rabid look at the nobleman.

"Fancy meeting you here," she snarled and added, "There's dogs in the woods," as if it were in the man's fault.

The man looked bothered. His eyes flitted between Aisa and Bella, who realized that these two — or three, including the blond guy's older friend — were involved in some weird way. There certainly was no reason for Bella to linger.

If she were in a brazen mood, Bella might've thanked Aisa for ruining her day, but she merely uttered that it was nice to make the woman's acquaintance and that she had to get going. She faintly smiled at the beautiful blond man and wondered whether she should discreetly let him know that Aisa was off her meds or something. Or maybe this was obvious to him from the look on his face. Maybe he and the other fellow had even come to retrieve Aisa — lock her back in an attic, or whatever. Bella hesitated. Then she thought, "fuck it," and was about to start away.

"Mike," the man announced. "Michael Solaris."

Bella nodded politely.

"Say your name," he remarked. "We didn't get to it the other day."

"Her name is Bella," Aisa grumbled. "Why are you asking her what you already know? 'Bellaluna Drago,' like, you know . . ." she said cryptically with a smirk. "He already knows your name, Sweetheart," she added. "He's a vampire, like I said."

Bella's mouth dropped open because she hadn't told that woman her full name. A feverish burn that might've been terror came over her. She winced and shrugged at the man.

"Say your name," the fellow coaxed as if Aisa hadn't

made sound. The tone of his voice set off a strange flushing and a pulling sensation in Bella's chest.

"Bellaluna Drago," she replied. "'Beautiful Moon Dragon.'" She simpered and uttered, "See you back at the ranch," before running away.

2

[The High Priestess]
The Legacy of Lunaris Dracon

Michael was was peeved . . . but he was a prick. Aisa Morae was never going to let him forget it. No. He wasn't going to get near that Bella chickie. Tough. Aisa let him pine while she looked back to watch Anderson turn out of sight and onto the woodland path from which she and that God-forsaken creature, "Bellaluna—the Dragon's Moon Lady," had just emerged.

"So, how is he?" Aisa asked. A pall of teary redness grazed her eyes and cheeks as she lamented that Anderson was the only man who had ever been nice to her.

Michael glared at Aisa. "You don't care a whit about Anderson, you're simply insulted by the inattention," he said. He told her that he was shocked to see her and tired of her antics.

Aisa flashed a derisive smirk and announced that two high sorcerers, Tristan Lundragon and Jason Paleologos, had been tailing her and her new-found, kindred-fairy friend through the woods all day. "And three dogs and that gimpy idiot kid," she complained. "Lundragon seemed very taken with her," she added smartly. "We know where that's going."

Michael didn't know what to say. He burned a bit with the forbidden wish that Aisa not exist. He tensed as if tightening his body would freeze his thought-stream lest Aisa intuit his sentiments.

"You need to get yourself a mentor who will help you work with your troubles, Ais'. . . because you're going to end up crossing the line someday with someone who will dispose of you, like Lundragon almost did. Perhaps he's been contracted to hunt you down, subdue you, and restore the order of the universe," Michael facetiously quipped.

"Are you threatening me?" Aisa screeched.

Michael fumed quietly and blinked. Then he softly said, "You're operating in a perverse way. You need to look at that."

"Oh yes, doctor." Aisa smirked and rolled her eyes.

Michael shifted past her.

"That was nice of Anderson to take you back," she snapped. "Don't think you're making time with that woman," she added. "She's that prick Lundragon's thing—not yours. Yeah," she snorted spitefully. "Tristan's going to have a time trying to stick it into her. Or maybe he'll just let his friend Jason do it while he watches."

Michael's impulse was to demand that Aisa keep her distance from Bellaluna Drago—and from him, as well—but stating this would only provoke her. Then Michael would have to hear her talk more—and loudly. He hurried on wondering whether it would be immoral to make her go away for good if she wouldn't do it on her own.

Sirens were creatures that were half-bird, half-woman, in origin, perhaps like the Egyptian ba. To the ancient Egyptians, the ba was the surviving part of a person that flew to the Underworld when a person died, but sirens were renegade creatures. According to classical myth, they lived on treacherously rocky isles off the coast of Sicily. They wanted nothing more than to entice passing sailors. Being lured, these sailors, thinking they'd get good head, instead found themselves in listless, dumbfounded stupors from which they languished and died.

It was portended that if a ship passed in which the occupants were resistant to the sirens' song, the sirens, in frenzied dismay, would kill themselves. Thus, it is told in the Odyssey that these creatures leaped off cliffs when the epic's hero, Odysseus, and his crew sailed by.

The sirens descended to the Underworld where they continued to sing, this time in mourning for the dead. Their imagery became mixed up with that of mermaids who themselves, in lore, were the mystical remnants of disposed-of women, who taking vengeance on the violence done to them, lured men to their deaths with the promise of sex through the sweetness of their song.

It all meant something metaphorical about men, women, ecstasy, sense control, and, of course, sex and death. One had to ponder it and trace the theme and imagery across cultures and time. To say that Aisa Morae was a siren — or a fairy — a banshee or strix — was mere convention. No one knew what she really was except that she was something of a Pandora's box that had a thin layer of jewels at the top of its contents under which scorpions rustled.

But being a magical entity more than a person per se, Aisa Morae, it could be argued, was a "thought-form." She was something that someone had imagined that took on form and came to life.

Thought-form–like beings could linger indefinitely, transforming themselves over time. They could become increasingly unstable to the point where they suddenly popped and were done with. Aisa conceivably could go on for lifetimes, becoming increasingly fouler and more erratic. It all depended on the prowess of whoever had set her in motion in the first place.

As for fairies, they weren't persons, technically speaking. They began as elementals, which were energies at work within the natural world. When a person tapped into an elemental energy, he or she not only gained something from it, the elemental did so as well. The attention that the elemental got allowed it to acquire personhood, like a marionette magically becomes a Pinocchio.

In time, the elemental took on that form and those characteristics and purposes imagined by the person who interacted with it, just like a marionetteer carves, paints, and dresses a puppet and then gives it a voice and a drama to act out. As the elemental developed, it could become self-aware. In doing so, it would become its own person independent from the person who had shaped its existence.

The question was whether elemental energies that became persons had souls.They might move and act, live and die, and transmigrate through the dimensions of existence just like real persons did. After a short time — like persons — they would completely forget how they originally came into being and why and would become more grist in the cycle of Life.

Weren't we all fairies and imps, angels, gods, and demons at some point and before that, weren't we elementals and even just elements within primal chaos?

The burning question for Michael was whether Aisa Morae was ensouled or whether she was more of a phantasm. If she were ensouled, disposing of her would be a gravely criminal act. If she were closer to a thought-form in the traditional sense — that is, a mirage of the imagination — especially if she were a troublesome one — then making her go away would be considered a good deed.

It was tricky. Michael already had focused on magical spells to make Aisa go elsewhere to wreak havoc with other persons instead of him, but those spells weren't working. Aisa always came back at strategically inconvenient moments. Michael's thoughts about the situation were becoming sinister and desperate now.

When he caught up with Anderson, he uttered, "Why can't you get rid of her?"

"She's your hell now," was Anderson's bitter reply.

"She ran into Lundragon and Paleologos somewhere

in there." He jutted his head toward the forest before them. "It rattled her up. At least they're good for something," Michael muttered.

The two said sorcerers, Tristan Trithemius Lundragon and Jason Paleologos, were interlopers. They were intruders in this new development about the existence of a fallen fairy. Lundragon had honed in on her from across a continent and an otherworldly plane of being. He had gotten all hot about the fairy's existence because of her provocative name: Beauteous Moon Dragon. Of course, he only wanted to exploit her.

Rumor had it that Lundragon and Paleologos were dark sorcerers whose magical practices involved buggery between them. Once Michael learned of their interest in the fairy, he got it in his head that he especially had to protect her.

The sorcerers wanted to meet with Anderson about the creature. Michael had scoffed but Anderson complied. The mage said it would be better to conference with rather than dismiss and, hence, antagonize Lundragon and Paleologos. He was namby-pamby like that—a mage with his head in the celestial clouds where everything was fine and dandy and where the air was so rarified that Anderson couldn't feel his dick being ripped away by birds of prey or his feet being bitten by springing vipers.

Michael accompanied the mage to his "conference" to protect him.

"Do you know where we're going?" Michael asked.

"It's a ways in," Anderson replied. "Along the stream toward the end of the path."

They did not speak. Anderson was somber and contemplative, as if saving up his mental notes for his confrontation with the sorcerers.

Michael felt a flip-flop feeling of anticipation as he and Anderson neared a rusty chain link fence after having walked about a mile in.

"That's not it," Anderson said and carried on up a steep incline away from the stream and around the perimeter of the fence. The trail became winding and mixed with intersecting paths. Anderson continued without hesitation. He was honed in on the direction like a compass and trekked, sometimes on a trail sometimes off, sloshing through mulch, hopping stones within intersecting brooks and gullies, and striding through gateways blocked out of remnants of stone walls.

After another mile or so, the path along the stream ended in mulch and bramble. Noise from a nearby highway could be heard.

"So where are they?" Michael asked.

Anderson grumbled before spotting a rather picturesque washout where bared tree roots formed step-like structures. The path wound up between gray boulders and witch hazel that framed a clearing where sunlight streamed in and highlighted a beech tree that was growing a bit too diagonally out of the ground. The tree formed an archway that one had to pass under before wheedling further up a winding incline to the cleared plateau. On it was the ruins of a building. It was a small, square patch of territory marked by a chimney attached to a slate, stone, and mortar counter that had a large, rusted iron grill in the center of it.

Lundragon and Paleologos were some yards away surveying a large house on a hill that lay beyond a high chain link fence topped by a voluminous whirl of barbed wire.

With a movement of a finger, Paleologos, a tall, dark-featured, brazenly V-shaped man, seared an ember-red vertical line from bottom to top in the fence and made the structure billow until it tore apart. Again, with mere mental projection, he shaped the breach in the fence into a crude archway, the purpose of which seemed to be to welcome trespassers into the abode of whoever was the king of the hill.

When the two turned and caught sight of Michael and Anderson, Paleologos quipped that it was very brave of Anderson Albright Magus to come out to meet them. He and Lundragon smiled meanly. Anderson maintained an air of quiet disdain.

"Did you see her?" Lundragon asked in an urgent tone.

Michael grunted in the affirmative.

"And what's that other one doing with her," Lundragon barked. "I don't want her around that one, Solaris. Get rid of her already. . . . associating with magi so much; you've lost all sense of practicality," he griped.

"Get on with it," Anderson snapped.

Lundragon shifted into a more civil mood and even admitted to being "rather ungracious." He scrambled for the right words before apologizing to Anderson for his manner. He even gently bowed. He was as tall and refined as Paleologos but fairer, lankier, and less broad-built. In addition, his manner was much more hardnosed than that of Paleologos, who generally came off as gentlemanly despite his behavior that day.

Anderson remained stoic.

"First of all, this is my find and my project," Michael blurted.

"Yes, you can look at it that way, too," Lundragon shot back, "but she's the product of my ancestral lineage. Technically speaking, she belongs to me."

"Conniving," was the only word that Michael could get out. He shot a glance at Anderson who seemed to find humor in the testiness.

"Lunaris Dracon," Lundragon announced.

Anderson scoffed and rolled his eyes.

"It's obvious," Lundragon insisted.

"The historical veracity of what you are alluding to is suspect at best, Tristan," Anderson remarked. Lundragon pouted and glared at the mage for addressing him informally.

Sorcerers were formerly addressed by their surname followed by the title "Sortiar." Mages were addressed by their surname followed by the title "Magus." Those were the respectable forms of address in the Inner Plane. Only familiars and subordinates were referred to by their first names. In addressing Tristan Lundragon Sortiar informally, Anderson Albright Magus had audaciously driven home the pecking order. It was within Anderson's right. He was the senior magical person among them. Besides, Lundragon, like Michael, had apprenticed with Anderson years ago.

"Admittedly, you are a superb scholar and scientist, Tristan, but this egotistical romanticism about Lunaris Dracon casts a pall of incredulity over the whole body of your work—for no good reason except for this unyielding stance about this legendary person," Anderson said—and it wasn't the first time he had said so.

"I have a document," Lundragon protested.

"Of course you do," Anderson muttered. He shook his head but it was more in an attitude of dismay than of derision.

Lundragon explained in a tone that was impressively controlled and sincere that it was true; he had uncovered a document that dated back to the early 16th century. Lundragon said that he had examined the document using chemical, radiographic, and microphotographic techniques and that it indeed bore the seal of Lunaris Dracon, the alleged pseudonym of an historical person named Tomas Ladon.

Ladon might have been an ancestor of the modern-day

Lundragon clan. In March of 1522 at the mature age of 45 years, Ladon was burned at the stake for a string of offenses, including the murder of his wife. Decades after his death, he was celebrated in the Inner Plane if not the Outer as an important and prolific occultist. Anderson, however, was in league with a faction of scholars who did not "believe in" Ladon and who contended that Lunaris Dracon was not Tomas Ladon but the pen name of a group of Outer Planes Renaissance-era magical persons who hid their identities so as not to be jailed, tortured, hung, and burned at the stake for their anti-establishment views.

The fabled Lunaris Dracon was known for penning steganographic tracts, ciphers, and cryptographic alphabets — that is, encrypted documents and their corresponding keys. According to legend, the information was imparted to him by etheric beings such as fairies, elementals, angels, and even rarified adepts residing in very Deep Inner Planes.

Dracon's name and seal coincidentally appeared on a large number of documents dating from 1510 to the year before Tomas Ladon's death. These documents were arcane pictographs and tracts written in otherworldly scripts that said one thing but really meant something else. Many of the documents had primers although many of these primers were now lost.

Dracon's deciphered documents spoke of the nature of elementals and of how to "grow" elementals. Among his works was a protocol for conceiving a fairy. No one besides wizards residing in the Inner Plane of Tibet had yet authentically replicated the procedure, and some magical scholars believed that the document was a "covertext" within which was another encrypted document. Nevertheless, a version of the tract became a standard text among secondary school students in the Terra Novit and the Terra Principalis (where Michael, Anderson, Tristan

Lundragon, and Jason Paleologos had come from) for learning to create magical thought-forms.

Dracon also was associated with an infamous document titled The Beauteous Consorte of the Mirour of Luna. It was a montage of glyphs, sigils, little pictures, and explanations written in a strange alphabet that Lundragon had decoded although the translated text read like gibberish. It was thought to be an example of steganography. This meant that another text with another, more coherent message was somehow hidden within it.

Four persons in the past 500 centuries were said to have understood the message: Dracon's wife, a 17th century mage, a lowly folk practitioner who lived during the mid-19th century, and, most recently, a young patrician academic who fatefully examined the text a few days after giving birth to twins. Each of these persons went into profound ecstasy upon recognizing the hidden text and turned into rainbows before presumably apportating to the Deep Inner Planes never to be seen or heard from again.

This tidbit about Dracon supposedly explained why Tomas Ladon had been pinned with his wife's murder among other transgressions having to do with heresy, sorcery, cavorting with demons, etcetera. But then, the anecdote was more of an urban legend than an historical fact.

Tristan T. Lundragon Sortiar was an archivist of the work of Lunaris Dracon and his contemporaries. He was a cryptographer and a steganographer. Because of the political unrest that was seizing Terra Novit, Lundragon, although hailing from the Terra Principalis, also was engaged in more modern and practical encryption work that had the flavor of espionage. Jason Paleologos, a career academician, historian, and artist, was Lundragon's primary research associate.

Lundragon and Paleologos had just crossed into their

40s and, therefore, were a few years older than Michael Solaris. They were prolific in their discoveries and had remarkable track records for distinguishing forgeries from authentic historical works. Still, some in the magical scientific community thought Lundragon and Paleologos themselves were forgers par excellence who, with every new, cocky "discovery," were tempting fate. These critics anxiously waited for Lundragon and Paleologos to be caught in their duplicity and silenced.

Lundragon knew that Anderson Albright Magus, noble chap that he was, essentially believed that Lundragon and his research partner were—for the most part—on the level: true magicians, scholars, and scientists even if Anderson didn't buy into the idea that Lunaris Dracon was a real historical person and even if he also thought that Lundragon was loathsome. Most noxious to Anderson's sensibilities was Lundragon's less flamboyant but known contention that he was the reincarnation of Dracon. Anderson regarded these notions as a neurotic need to fabricate an identity.

Lundragon had been a student of Albright's for a time. The sorcerer had just turned 20 when he began his magian studies. He was suffering an identity crisis or perhaps a crisis of conscience. Anderson knew that the fellow had been toying with dark and left-handed practices—him and his yet-then companion, Jason Paleologos. Approaching Anderson for instruction perhaps was Lundragon's way of looking for an "out" about what he was otherwise doing. He may have been searching for a way to transform and elevate inner forces and proclivities. Perhaps he was looking for a more profound meaning to his existence . . . aspiring to redemption perhaps.

Excursions into the realms of the wicked and deviant were not uncommon diversions for adolescent magical persons—boys especially. It was a way of establishing machismo and bravado. For some, it was a potent way to establish themselves in the cut-throat, grown-up world of sorcery. Somewhere along the way, fledgling sorcerers had to demonstrate what reckoning with them meant. Indeed, there was a certain type of sorcerer who was perpetually testing and trying to cannibalize other sorcerers — and magi (and lowly folk practitioners and Commons). A sorcerer had to be prepared; young sorcerers wasted a great deal of time and energy wrangling with these bullying types. Then again, power-mongering was the nature of the beast; it was part of the territory of being a sorcerer.

This was not to say that sorcerers, generally speaking, were noxious. Most practiced their arts nobly and respectably. It was just that the detours, off-road terrain, and scenic drives along the path were a little dicier than what one would encounter on a magian trek. In any case, most gentrified and educated magical persons were reasonably skilled in both disciplines of sorcery and magianism. In this way, it was common for sorcerers to apprentice with mages and vice-versa, and the greatest sorcerers and mages often where those whose mentors where expert adepts in the alternative discipline.

Lundragon apparently had a mind to aspire to greatness in this way. He sought higher ground in the fabric of magian studies with Anderson Albright Magus years ago. The mage accepted him into his fold but Lundragon wasn't a very good climber in Anderson's estimation. He was disciplined and very precise but he was a sly, controlling, and paranoid youth akin to someone who had been emotionally warped by early trauma. Something in Anderson kept him from investigating it and from performing healing work for the young man.

Lundragon ultimately lost patience with the mage for keeping him lagged behind the other apprentices. It didn't break Anderson's heart to see the young sorcerer drift away.

In the years that had gone by, Lundragon had made a name for himself as an all-seeing eye and a highly skilled practitioner of coercive magic. He had earned a reputation for being a rather merciless controller, an insidious puppeteer—he and his friend, Paleologos, both.

The two were known to be quite bacchanalian as well: wine, women, and song in excess. All that on top of being provocative academicians and scientists of distinction.

Lundragon materialized—out of the ether—a crisp parchment scroll and held it out toward Anderson.

"This is a facsimile of the document," he told the mage. "It's in code and quite undecipherable."

"How does the document put any claim on Bellaluna Drago, then?" Michael protested.

Lundragon shot a hateful glance at Michael for interrupting his rapport with Anderson Albright Magus.

"It's not meant for us to decipher. It was written for the fairy," Paleologos interjected.

"If she can decipher this, we can verify her speciation and everyone will know that she is my own and that what I am saying—and have been saying all along—is true," Lundragon exclaimed.

"I think you and the 'Moray' Eel-Lady have been drinking from the same bottle," Michael quipped.

"And I think that it was remarkably adventurous of you, being a 'closet-magus' and all, to stick it into an entity who happened to name herself after the death-dealing Fate—or Moerae—of classical Greek myth, 'Aisa,'" Lundragon mused. "The role of this Fate, who with her two sisters sang with sirens, was to cut the thread that her sisters, Clotho and Lachesis, spun and wove: the thread of life. Isn't that how the story goes, Albright Magus? Tell me, did you consider that when you yourself engaged in your tender dalliance with the entity?"

Anderson did not react although Michael called Lundragon a despicable fiend. With that, Lundragon, in rage, materialized a copper- and bronze-encrusted oak staff. He aimed its olivine finial, which was a figurine of a winged creature with the head of a hawk and the body of a lizard (a moon dragon, that is), at Michael.

"Lundragon Sortiar," Anderson exclaimed in an urgent tone. "We'll speak alone you and me. We'll sort it out. Scuffling out here in the open in view of Commons would be . . ." His voice trailed off because the statement needn't have been elaborated on.

Upon composing himself, Lundragon uttered that he always had held Anderson in high regard even if the sentiment wasn't wholly reciprocated. He said that he indeed would very much like to speak with Anderson alone in a civil manner at a site more conducive to professional conversation.

"I will prove myself to you, Sir," Lundragon insisted in a tone trimmed with vehemence. "And in so doing, liberate you from the residual effects of the malaise that has crippled you for too long." He glared accusingly at Michael to let it be known in a glance that his contempt for him, considering Michael's his role in Anderson's melodrama with Aisa Morae, knew no limit.

It was decided that Lundragon and Albright would meet again in two days' time at Lundragon's studio at the Royal Dominion of Principalis Academy of Magical Arts and Sciences back home in the Inner Plane. Then, despite that they were standing in the open in a populated woodland park in the Outer Plane, Lundragon and Paleologos abruptly translocated out of sight.

3
[The Empress]
The Page of Swords

"Albright Magus and Solaris Sortiar found a fairy," muttered Bobby Fludd. "A lost one in the Outer Plane. I saw her with that other one—the 'Evil One.'"

Alba Sandalphon Magus raised an eyebrow.

"You know the story about the other one. Right?" Bobby questioned.

Alba faintly nodded. She was in the midst of making arrangements for magical contraband to be delivered to an underground political operation known as the Lions of Light. She would be dispatching Bobby as the "mule."

"Lundragon Sortiar says she's his." Bobby smirked because the situation implied high intrigue and mayhem.

Alba broke her concentration on her own intrigues to laugh ruefully at the stupidity of the late-breaking melodrama. "What are Albright and Solaris doing skirt-chasing fairies, after all?" she said dryly.

"It supposedly was an AX-ci-dent this time," Bobby explained. "Se-ren-DIP-i-ty. And then Lundragon found out about it because, you know, he's a scrying freak. He claims he knew about the fairy all along—with his Lunaris Dracon shit." Another smirk grazed Bobby's face. "After Solaris moved in on her, Lundragon finally got the balls to take a look at the thing up close. So I went with him and Jason—you know, Paleologos Sortiar."

Alba nodded to assure Bobby that she knew who Jason Paleologos was.

"Lundragon let me handle the dogs but then he got a

little annoyed with me," Bobby griped.

Alba gently nodded again as if in sympathy with Tristan Lundragon's predictable impatience with Bobby Fludd.

"He and Jason arranged to meet Albright and Solaris, but . . . anyway . . . he sent me back, so . . . ." Bobby cringed as his voice trailed off.

"Lundragon wasn't abusive to you in his expression of pique, was he, Bobby?" Alba asked in a plain but concerned tone.

Bobby said no, but Alba suspected this was untrue. Lundragon had a reputation for having a short fuse although in reality, he had a long-suffering, smoldering temperament that blew like an overfilled teapot that was finally at a roiling boil but left unattended.

Twenty-five-year-old Robert Fludd, who had been named after a famous 17th century alchemist and Neo-Platonic mystic, very much wanted to be known as the apprentice of the high sorcerer Tristan Lundragon. Lundragon had repeatedly refused to conduct an initiation ceremony although it was understood by all who knew about the two that Bobby was Lundragon's "nephew," his magical child, the first among any apprentices that Lundragon might take under his wing. Nevertheless Lundragon would not let Bobby publicly address him or behave in any formal way in which, by convention, apprentices and mentors were identified.

"So what was it like seeing two fairies, Bobby? What did they look like?" Alba asked. She was weaving the contraband into books that Bobby would carry in a knapsack. Despite Bobby's banter about fairies and the dick problems and pissing contests of a bunch of cock-strutting academicians, he was carefully studying Alba's preparation of the encrypted stash he would smuggle into an Inner Plane territory called Terra Novit.

The awareness of this attention to detail panicked Alba actually. It did so because it was hard to know what went on in Bobby's mind. He often behaved as if he was intellectually challenged, but he was dangerously brilliant . . . wily. Whether he was principled in his loyalties or swayed according to opportunism was the question. After all, he was the right hand of Lundragon Sortiar, who had a reputation for being brutally devious.

Alba wasn't sure whether these aspects about Bobby were part of a "glamour" — that is, an act that magicians put on to dupe people about how sharp and lethal they really were.

Although troubling on the one hand, on the other, Bobby's manner   made him appealing to Alba — and probably Lundragon. There was something ingenious about him. One wanted to think so.

Alba privately referred to him as her Page of Swords. The Page of Swords was a card within the Tarot that denoted political or interpersonal intrigue, spying, double-dealing, and strategic diplomacy. To have Bobby pampered, tamed, and faithful would serve those of influence who knew him. Alba was hoping that he and she were truly sympathetic to each other and that his risqué work for the Lions of Light was founded in commitment to the Cause and not motivated vengeance or extreme sport. Otherwise, the draw of the card he was to Alba might augur rack and ruin.

Having retired from the presidium — that is, the top ruling body — of Terra Novit, Alba Sandalphon Magus was working as a political provocateur. She was doing so from an English-speaking sovereignty that lay a sea away within the Terra Principalis.

She was a mature, dark-skinned, impressively built lady who always dressed in the formal white attire of certain high-level magi. She wore a tall, impeccably wrapped turban as a headdress and affixed a dainty lace veil to the turban with a bauble made of iridescent moonstone, craggy uncultured pearls, and platinum. The veil and bauble were her only adornments besides a medallion that she wore under her apparel. It was a gold disc on which was embossed the insignia of the Lions of Light.

She held a visiting professorship in political sciences at the Royal Dominion of Principalis Academy of Magical Arts and Sciences, which is how she came to be aware of the gossip about the school's leading academicians, such as Anderson Albright Magus and Tristan T. Lundragon Sortiar. She had only heard about Albright but she knew Lundragon; he had made a point of making her acquaintance.

Lundragon had a need to "befriend" influential people. He suffered credibility issues about his work, which caused him great frustration — not that he confided such things to Alba. He mostly boasted about whatever project he was involved in, which generally consisted of decoding and translating highly esoteric texts.

They never spoke about the Lions of Light. That aspect of Alba's life was secret. But Lundragon apparently knew about her involvement. He had dispatched Bobby, who had expatriated from Terra Novit while yet a teenager, to Alba as a kind of gift. It turned out that Bobby had been dabbling in espionage for the Cause through another underground front and that his parents and an elder brother had been "disappeared" because of their political activism. Bobby barely escaped the raid. The memento of the incident — besides being orphaned — was his leg injury.

"They looked like ordinary women," Bobby said in response to Alba's questions about the encounter with fairies.

"And they think of themselves as women and are just

women. Remember that, Bobby," Alba replied.

The young man appeared dismayed by the response. Alba continued: "If they really looked special or acted as if they thought they were, they wouldn't be," she said. "Beings aren't powerful or special in their own right, but some beings have the ability to magnify the power and specialness of life itself. It happens through them spontaneously and naturally and not by—" Alba grasped for the words—"personal force. Our only work here is to become clear like adamantine crystals through which the source of power and beauty, order and love is magnified."

Bobby smiled appreciatively at Alba. After appearing to reflect on her words, he took a deep breath as if uplifted by inspiration.

"The one that Lundragon and Solaris both want isn't as hot-looking as the Eeee-veal One, but she's not as crazy, I don't think. So, she probably has more juice," Bobby said.

"You'll keep your eye on the developments and keep me informed, won't you, Bobby?" Alba requested.

"Sure," the young man replied.

"The next time you go off to the Outer Plane, why not see if you can talk to her. She might find you fascinating, and you can protect her from the men," said Alba, feeling sinfully mischievousness about the suggestion. She watched Bobby's face light up in response to the directive. It was sweet and satisfying for Alba. Let the little sorcerer flex a muscle or two, she thought.

"Are you prepared for this?" she asked in a voice that nearly trembled.

"Ready and willing," Bobby flippantly replied.

Alba handed him the knapsack and a book. "When you enter the café, a young woman will address you as Henry. She will be with a teenaged boy. The boy's little finger on the left hand will be in a splint with a little piece of yellow tape on it. Put the knapsack under the table when you take your seat and give this book to the young lady as a gift. You'll drink coffee; you'll chit-chat, and then another young woman holding a pink rose will wave to you from the street. She will put a flower petal in her mouth and act as if she's taking a picture of you and your young friends with her cell phone.

"You will run out of the café to embrace her. After talking for a short while, you'll walk off with her — but don't get cute," Alba warned. "Don't take liberties, and do not disclose anything factual about yourself or boast about your connections with anyone. No one cares who Tristan Lundragon Sortiar is over there in the Terra Novit, so don't waste your breath," she admonished. "And do not forget that you are 'wanted' in Terra Novit. You have a price on your head. No one is your friend, even persons supposedly on our side."

"I know what I'm doing," Bobby snapped and crankily added that the rigmarole about passing off a package was idiotic.

Alba continued with the directive: "Your other 'friends' in the café will realize your absence and that you left your knapsack behind. They'll hurry out of the café to return the knapsack to you, but they won't. You need to translocate out of there immediately after this interlude takes place," Alba told him.

Bobby smiled in a goofy manner and winked as he instantly translocated from the office suite of Alba Sandalphon Magus to a major city on another continent of the Inner Plane.

Φ

Even though Sandalphon Magus was shitting bricks about it, it worked out fine. And Bobby took his "liberties" alright. He made sure he stuck his tongue in the mouth of the beautiful girl in the street with the cell phone when he kissed her. He knew who she was. Leela Solaris. She was related to that sorcerer who was vying for Lundragon's fairy.

When Bobby grabbed and kissed her, he mashed his pelvis against hers and it was . . . quite nice. She mostly pushed her arms against him, but she was into it.

When they finished, she scowled at him. Yeah, well, maybe Bobby didn't have his "Sweet Surrender" groove going on. Jason was the one who had taught him how to pull it off. Bobby was 19 at the time. When Lundragon got wind of it, he made a snide comment about it being better late than never.

"Now all you have to do is lose your virginity and you'll be all set," he snipped. "Perhaps Jason can do the honors with that one, too." And he said it with that stupid, dissing thing he did with his rolled-up eyes. He was such a fucking asshole sometimes.

Anyway, Bobby was left telling edgy little Leela, a wild child probably born from an orgy, to be ha!ppy. A light, little laugh came out of her when he uttered, "You're supposed to be 'glam-amour-us.' Hmmm?" He coaxed her for another smooch. She complied. Then he grasped her hand tightly and, with his bad leg, hobbled at a frantic pace away from the coffee shop and down the block with the giddy girl in tow.

They went into a music store at which point Bobby exclaimed, "Oh shit, I left my knapsack at the coffee place!" He pecked a kiss on the girl's mouth and, with a rakish wink, said, "Back in a jiffy," before translocating out of there. Mission accomplished . . . except for the hard-on he was left with for a 17-year-old piece of cake.

He didn't go back home, though. He went to the Outer Plane. He wasn't far from where Lundragon's fairy lived anyway. He just had to figure out where she was exactly.

On the one hand, Bobby thought Lundragon Sortiar was one of the greatest sorcerers around; on the other, there were lighter people who actually had senses of humor in the world. The job of Lundragon's buddy, Jason Paleologos, seemed to be to smooth things over and keep Lundragon from having a stroke or something.

People called them butt-fuckers, but . . . you know . . . people always had something nasty to say. And people said they were . . . oooh . . . into spooky "black magic," but they were just two guys.

They liked the ladies and vice versa. Bobby had seen each in action enough times. It was much less frequent these days, but they liked to make a party of it—orgiastic sorcerer stuff. Then there was the time the two of them were sharing a hot little sorceress in something of a three-way ritual sex-magic routine. They sent her away when she began playing the guys against each other.

That was being heroic, they said. They lectured Bobby about the how, in mythology, men stuck together to resist sirens, nymphs, she-monsters, witches, sorceresses, and stuff. Bobby then made the mistake of telling them that those stories were made by men who needed to blame women for their dick problems. They scoffed and then tortured him with the hallucination that his dick had fallen off and turned into a clit. The phantasm lasted for three days before Bobby came to his senses and broke the spell.

In that women didn't get in between Lundragon and Paleologos (except for when they were doing a three-way), you could say that these men were more into each other than ladies, but whether they were on each other (or other men) was uncertain. Some sorcerers relegated certain same-sex practices to magical Work—Work that typically was potently single-edged and of a dark nature. If that was the deal with Lundragon and Paleologos (as alleged by their detractors), Bobby figured he would know, but he didn't.

Still, if these men were intimate with each other . . . sexually . . . in the interests of affection, magic, or sheer libidinous debauchery . . . it would seem normal kind-of, considering that they had been devoted to each other for years while the women came and went.

Bobby didn't care. Lundragon was Bobby's mentor even if the sorcerer refused to make it official, and Jason was an okay guy. Bobby regarded these men and Sandalphon Magus as his family.

But if Bobby could kind of get in between Lundragon and his fairy, it would sort of be like a little revenge—just like a little way to stick it back for the sorcerer's prickly manner. Sandalphon Magus had put the idea out there, and she used to be one of the leaders of an entire freaking nation—Terra Novit—so that was like getting an order from a political commander or something.

In addition to encryption and code-cracking—which Bobby had a natural talent for—Lundragon had taught Bobby two things really well. One was translocation, which most magical persons saved for necessary occasions because it took a lot of energy to do. It was the art of disappearing from one place and suddenly appearing in another. If you didn't do it right or puttered out in midstream, you were fucked. You could end up lost in the interspaces between one plane and another or anywhere— in zero-gravity outer space or at the bottom of the deep blue sea. But Lundragon had the key to it, and he recognized that Bobby did as well. It was how the young man had saved himself at the tender age of 14 years when the "powers-that-be" came to silence him and his folks for their political transgressions. He escaped by translocating. But having little experience in the art, Bobby sustained an injury. It could've been much worse, though.

In any case, Lundragon could translocate effortlessly and precisely—and, with practice and guts, so could Bobby.

It was one of the things that made Bobby a perfect agent for the Lions of Light.

The other talent that Lundragon had turned on in the young man that also made him invaluable to the Cause was scrying—that is, remote viewing—magical spying. It was accomplished by staring at patterns in a reflective surface such as a black—or even a regular—mirror, a shiny piece of glass, a chunk or orb of crystal, basin of water, antique computer or television screens. It wasn't that an image of the target would appear in the scrying device; it would appear in the mind but the device would help the mind to open out to a place not confined by the body where a new, broader kind of sight could be accessed.

Bobby wandered into another quiet and lonely café set up with little tables and quaint throw-away furniture—this one in the Outer Plane. After purchasing a large cup of mint tea, he flopped his long, sinewy limbs into a big, orange lounge chair. He knew a girl was staring at him but he was staring into his big cup of steaming water that was flushing green from the mint teabag. The hot vapor and medicinal herbal scent pierced his frontal cortex—or at least that is what it felt like with the minty steam digging into his eyes and his sinus passages. He liked it. He liked the burning cool sensation in his head more than what would turn out to be a bloated itch in his groin if he got distracted by another set of nice tits.

He couldn't see—that is, spy—a thing in the cup but when he looked up, he realized that the girl whose eyes had been on him wasn't a girl—it was the fairy-lady. She was sitting at a table a few feet away and was slouched over a laptop computer and a bunch of papers. Of course, she only looked at him when he wasn't looking at her but, anyway . . . It was her.

"Are you writing a novel? An inspirational self-help book? A disser-TA-tion?" Bobby asked. He had to keep jabbering because she didn't seem to hear him or perhaps she didn't realize that he was speaking to her. "A memoir . . . a formula . . . or maybe a uh . . . ."

"Hello?" she finally said in an unsure voice. Her face looked as if she had been rudely awakened.

"What are you writing?" Bobby asked.

"I'm ghost writing an article on Lewy body dementia. It's kind of like Alzheimer's disease and gets confused with it," she replied.

"Neuro-FIB-ril-la-ry tangles," Bobby enunciated. He didn't know what neurofibrillary tangles were. He just knew that they were the last two words in the fairy-lady's head before Bobby had caught her attention.

"People with Alzheimer's disease have a head full of neurofibrillary tangles and people with Lewy body dementia have a head full of little red dots called Lewy bodies — in the brain cells in their heads — until they don't have any room in their brain cells for what's supposed to be there," she explained.

"How do you know if it's one thing or the other?" Bobby asked.

"Doctors don't usually," the fairy replied. "After the person dies, they chop up his brain and stick it under a microscope, and then they can tell. But now doctors are figuring out that the symptoms of the two diseases are a little different. So I'm taking all this crap that other people have ghost written for a certain doctor and making an entirely new article out of it that'll have his name on it," she said and slapped her hand on a disheveled stack of photocopied papers.

"Okay," Bobby said to show that he understood her.

"You were in the woods that day," she remarked.

"You were in the cave that day," Bobby replied in the same tone.

"I was in the cave with a crazy lady," the fairy chirped.

Bobby snickered at the way she played when she spoke. "Yeah. The EEL-lady. We've run into her before," he said. "I was being an instigator. IMP-u-dent."

"Yeah, well, 'vampires' are like that," the fairy quipped, apparently remembering that vampirism was the accusation that the "evil one" had laid on Bobby and his companions. "But you look more like a troublemaker," the fairy grinned.

Bobby's skin flushed because the fairy was being flirtatious. He leaned forward and was about to introduce himself when a hand squeezed his shoulder rather harshly.

"Robert! Taking the day off?" Jason Paleologos said even though he obviously knew everything.

Bobby cringed and sunk back in the lounge chair. "I took an early retirement. Didn't you know?" he snapped.

"Had I known the life of a courier was so leisurely, I wouldn't have bothered spending all that time and money at university," said Jason in his dapper accent. He winked at the fairy before sauntering to the counter to perform the theatrics of buying a latte or whatever. The fairy's eyes followed him. It was obvious to Bobby that she was enthralled with the sorcerer's majestic manliness. It angered Bobby . . . stealing his thunder and all.

Then the fairy-lady turned an amused glance at Bobby and asked him what he did for a living. He told her that he was "an international man of mystery," which was true. He cocked his head toward Jason, saying dryly, "He's 'a man of wealth and taste,' if you're into that sort of thing."

When Jason wandered back, he had a hard glint in his eye for the younger man. He put his hand out to the fairy and asked if he could introduce himself.

"Doctor Strangelove," Bobby blurted, which led Jason to simper and quietly send a very sharp, electrical pang up Bobby's bad leg and into his testicles. Jason then launched into a chit-chat with the fairy about "what a lovely little park" that wooded area "over there" was.

In an abashed manner—and apparently torn between chatting with Jason and expressing concern that Bobby appeared to be in pain—the fairy told Jason that she really didn't know the other woman. She said she had merely encountered the woman in the park that day.

Jason said, with his saccharine charm, that he had run into the other woman before and that she was a talented artist but "quite off her rocker." (Yeah, well, Bobby knew that Jason had had sex with that crazy freaking entity a long time ago. Maybe he fucked her brains out . . . replaced them with neurofibrillary tangles . . . . Fucking bastard. When was he going to leave already?)

"Well, good-day, Miss . . . ?" Jason grinned and made believe he was fishing for a name.

"Bella. Bella Drago," the fairy said and handed Jason a business card.

"'Beautiful Dragon,'" he grinned. "I'll keep that in mind." He winked.

The woman simpered.

Bobby scowled at Jason and blew out a weary laugh. Jason, in turn, pointed a sharp finger at him before departing.

The fairy gazed at Bobby with furrowed brow as if imploring him to divulge what lay beneath the testy display between him and the other man. Bobby simply huffed and shook his head in an exasperated way.

"How do you know each other?" she asked.

"We're 'vampires,'" Bobby sourly replied.

4

[The Emperor]
Lions and Fairies and Snails

Before Anderson Albright met with Tristan Lundragon to discuss fairies and Tristan's curious awareness and ideas about Miss Bellaluna Drago, the mage went to take a look at her again. For one, he thought it serendipitously odd that her name should be "Bellaluna Drago" — "Beauteous Moon Dragon." On that note, he had to give Tristan some credit. On the other, Anderson was concerned that the fairy had done something to Michael Solaris — and Tristan as well: ensnared them in a binding spell. And what was the drive for drawing these two particular and rather formidable sorcerers across not only a dimension, but a continent?

Strife and angst: these were the gifts of fallen fairies, in Anderson's view these days. But was Bellaluna Drago really a fallen fairy or simply a denizen of some other dimension who, being haplessly trapped in the Outer Plane, was unconsciously sending SOS signals that maybe Michael and Tristan had picked up but were reading into instead of just reading. Or perhaps she was a mere Commons whose time had come to cross into the Inner Plane? Anderson had seen it in her eyes, hadn't he? And such transitions could be provocative and disorienting, so why shouldn't her energy be marked by melancholy and angst?

Differentiating the various species of entities that lived within the multilayered cosmos was sometimes tricky. From where they were coming wasn't always clear, so it was hard to know whether they were offering assistance, seeking refuge or rescue, or else were laying a trap. Anderson wondered whether anything in the way of catharsis or redemption would characterize the upheaval that Bellaluna Drago might exact if she were a fairy or some similar type of entity — or could she be expected to operate like that other one, Aisa? Anderson was mulling this over as well as the genius and hubris of his two prodigal acolytes: Michael and Tristan.

Tristan's comments about proving himself and redeeming Anderson from "the residual effects of the malaise" that had been "crippling" him rang in his head. He might have been a romantic or eccentrically deluded, but Tristan . . . well, Anderson was impressed by the sorcerer's intensity. It wasn't the voice of a poseur or even an opportunist. It was that of a man of conviction who was truly frustrated about the credibility gap that plagued him.

Anderson's attitude toward him softened. He considered giving the fellow the benefit of the doubt about Lunaris Dracon. He decided that he would council him on this Bellaluna-Drago situation. Tristan being a sharp and wily man might take heed — more than randy Michael would. Anderson would encourage Tristan to take a more dispassionate approach to what seemed like a potentially dangerous dynamic between himself, the fairy, and Michael. He would advise Tristan not to jump to conclusions however much it seemed that the gold ring he had been seeking was approaching. After all, anxious desperation and expectation left one vulnerable to deception and manipulation.

Anderson was well aware that Tristan had long been bitter about not penetrating Anderson's inner circle of apprentices years ago. Tristan's temperament was ill-suited for magian studies. He had a rather brittle, hypervigilant, and uncompassionate personality. It was not conducive to the higher studies and initiations that Anderson could provide. The prolonged preparatory work that Anderson subjected Tristan to while the other apprentices progressed confused, frustrated, and alienated the young sorcerer. It naturally reinforced a bias that many sorcerers had toward magi: that they were particular, elitist, and had their heads up their asses and in the clouds instead of being involved with the magic of the here and now.

Magi were concerned with intrapersonal and transpersonal processes—rarified mystical experiences and transformations. Their goal was to one day transcend the phenomenological world and merge into the Supreme Illumination. Sorcerers wanted to work magic and revel in the potentials of creativity, consciousness, and experience. They wanted to become an increasingly greater Self— empowered, untouchable, and enrapt in unfettered bliss.

These were broad stereotypes, though. The lines between practical magic and mysticism varied and blurred from one person to the next regardless of whether he or she identified with being a mage or a sorcerer. In any case, adepts of the highest caliber, regardless of persuasion, had no bones to pick with each other. They knew their goal was the same; only the words used to describe the paths and processes differed—like different boats used to cross the same sea.

It was becoming increasingly popular to equally embrace sorcery and magianism—at least it was the trend in Terra Novit. The territory was going through a provocative political and social transition. Something called the Lions of Light—a utopian movement—was afoot. After it took over Terra Novit—if only as a populist weed—it would take over the world.

Anderson didn't know that much about the movement except that Michael had ties with one of its key leaders—an imposing high sorcerer who was named Leo de Lux. de Lux once had been a harsh, self-serving, and patrician politician and a close friend of one Michael's uncles, a debauched and polygamous character named Reginald. Michael had nothing to do with the uncle but did consulting work for de Lux and his mage son, Leonard Junior. Michael's work primarily focused on a certain lethal and rarified charm called the Conus magus. The charm was named after a species of venomous marine cone snails that paralyze and absorb their prey.

It was not a charm that one could learn nor could the charm be transferred except possibly through certain rare and specific circumstances related to the dynamics of interpersonal intimacies. It was a latent but rare power that a magical person was born with in the way a person is born with a genetic predisposition to go bald or have this or that disease eventually.

Because Michael had been born with the potential to perform the Conus magus charm, he was conscripted into the service of the Royal Dominion of Principalis. He was a child soldier made to do what child soldiers do unquestioningly. But Michael was a prodigy, an old soul, and wise man, in Anderson's opinion. The fellow had managed to do his duty and yet grow up to be a compassionate, thoughtful, and more or less admirable person—almost as best as could be expected under the circumstances. After all, only angels were angels.

Michael's mercenary involvement with the Lions of Light was something of a hobby. It was a game he knew well. It intrigued him because it was dynamic and familiar—and he was in sympathy with the cause even if it was a rebellion.

The story about Leo de Lux, as Anderson understood it, was that upon being overtaken by a paradigm shift in consciousness, he doffed the ceremonial attire of a sorcerer (consisting of a dark-colored dalmatic and chasuble and miter or cone headdress) and donned the white dalmatic, chasuble, and skull cap of a mage—at least for a while. He retired from his political appointment as the consul of the North Atlantic Sovereignty of Terra Novit and became a political provocateur counter to everything he stood for during his years as a magistrate.

His consort, a world famous maga who all agreed was the catalyst of de Lux's transformation, doffed her white ceremonial attire to clad herself in red as a symbolic testament to her syzygy—or divine union—with de Lux. de Lux's son, Leonard, was the maga's chief apprentice—her magical child—therefore, between inheritance through the father and the mentorship of the maga, the son was deemed to be exceptionally formidable. He and his followers wore ceremonial garb composed of albs, dalmatics, chasubles, and copes of all crazy mixed-up colors and decorated them with emblems that had nothing to do with the traditional imagery of sorcerers or magi.

The lines between sorcery and magianism were particularly blurred among this group and among many of its wannabes and sympathizers. Some persons thought the eclectic syncretism was wonderful; others thought it was confusing and perverse.

This digression aside, Anderson, through his own magical wiles, managed to appear at the little Outer-Plane condominium complex where the alleged new-found fairy, Bellaluna Drago, lived. He entered the building's foyer at the moment Miss Drago had descended from her unit to visit her mailbox. Anderson lingered there between her and another door that led from the foyer to an elevator bank that shuttled people to and from their apartments.

Some time passed before the woman acknowledged Anderson's presence. She smiled faintly and uttered, "Am I in the way?" as if concerned that she was blocking the doorbell panel.

Anderson twitched his head in a very subtle gesture to

communicate that "no"; she wasn't.

She seemed perplexed by his presence, as if compelled but reluctant to be neighborly. Anderson looked her straight in the eye and said, "Yes. Well, I can see why he wants to tie you to the bedpost."

A pallor flushed over the woman . . . a rank discomfort . . . fear. She bristled, huffed, shook her head, and exited the building even though she was wearing fuzzy green slippers and a rather thin and worn pant and t-shirt assemble.

He watched her dart off. She felt rather light up until then, Anderson thought to himself.

He lingered in the lobby, placidly waiting for Michael to descend from his new digs in Commons terrain. They planned to go for a stroll to discuss how to deal with Bellaluna Drago and Tristan Lundragon. He had a mind to tell Michael, again, to just let it go; leave Lundragon and his buddy to play and leave the fairy to fate. It was time to put aside these dramas and pursue higher aims. Still, an itch of pity and tenderness for the fairy had wheedled its way into Anderson's heart now that he had confronted her in the way he had.

He knew where she had gone. She was loping around the block, shivering from the cold autumn air and whimpering because of it. She also was whimpering because a strange man had menaced her in the lobby of the building in which she lived. Anderson felt a twinge of remorse. It truly wasn't very fair or magian of him to have done what he did.

"Victimized," he heard her say even though she was far out of earshot. Anderson placidly figured that, at a later date in the enfoldment of this escapade, he would have the opportunity to apologize.

When she had done a lap around the block, she entered the condominium through the back entrance, which adjoined the parking lot. By then, Michael had alighted and was lingering in the lobby with Anderson, who had told Michael that the fairy would be passing by momentarily.

When he spotted her slink through the back entrance, Michael said hello in a cheery voice. The fairy didn't know how to respond. She gaped at him and tried not to look at Anderson.

"Are you alright today, Bella?" Michael said in a saccharine voice.

The fairy's complexion flushed and her mouth cringed sourly. "I'm not the one who's 'sick,'" she uttered and dashed into the elevator, pressing her thumb hard on the door-close button.

Michael glared at the sealed elevator door. Anderson remained composed and silent, waiting for the proverbial shoe to drop.

"Did you say something to her?" Michael asked him.

"She seems unnerved by me," Anderson replied.

"Were you harassing that woman?" Michael scolded.

"I was assessing the situation," Anderson responded.

"Get over it and piss off!" Michael hollered at the mage. "I was just as much a victim about what happened 10 years ago as you," he said and pleaded: "Don't take it out on this one. You're screwing her up, and you're fucking me over—and I've already paid for what happened—and I'm still paying—and I don't want to pay anymore. I want to pursue this. Don't wreck it on me."

Anderson exited through the rear door of the condominium complex. Michael, incensed by the reaction, hollered after him, exhorting the mage to go on and coddle his great unrequited admirer, Tristan Lundragon. "I'm sure he's overflowing with ideas about how to help you ruin my life!"

Φ

Michael ascended to the fifth floor and proceeded to wrap his knuckles against the door of 5C.

"Bella, this is your neighbor Michael from the penthouse," he bayed. "I apologize for that man. I'm very sorry. I've sent him away. Can I speak with you?" He had to say words such as "Please," because time seemed stretched out, and the woman wasn't responding to him.

"Enchanted. Enchanted," the words stung his mind. Not that Michael was "enchanted" with Bella Drago—although he clearly was—but that he might be enchanted by her—ensnared in a magical spell. He didn't care, though. That was the problem with enchantments. Even if you knew they were upon you, you didn't care; you were driven—high on a spell like a sailor lulled to his death by the toxic songs of sirens.

The door was hot. The door was exceptionally hot to Michael's touch. It was not burning in a smiting manner but in a way that implied utter longing. "I'm here. I've come. I am your savior," he wanted to say. "I want to save you," he muttered under his breath. "Let me."

He expected Bella to be pallid and scowling when she opened the door, but her cheeks were rouged and hair fashionably tousled. She apparently had made haste to preen herself before answering the door. Nevertheless, her complexion was sulky and blanched. Her big olive eyes were ruddy.

"He's completely harmless," was the first thing Michael said. "In fact, he's a very gentle and thoughtful man."

"Is he your boyfriend?" the woman asked in a dry tone.

The query startled Michael. His jaw dropped, and he flinched. "Do you find me effeminate?" his mind was screaming. He blurted that Anderson was his uncle. "He has issues with women," Michael remarked.

"Obviously," Bella said before Michael added that, unlike Anderson, he did not have "issues," although this was far from true, considering that Aisa Morae had caught up with him again.

A flustered pause ensued before Bella cracked a wizened grin and said, "Good."

Michael asked Bella whether she could step out to take a stroll to share a refreshment or some such thing. She laughed as if the proposal were ridiculous—as if the endeavor might be painful for some reason.

"What could go wrong?" Michael teased, but her expression was quizzical.

"I fancy you. I want to know you," he said and exuded a subtle hint of a Sweet Surrender maneuver; that is, a subtle and coercive love spell.

After collecting herself a bit more, the fairy emerged from her apartment dressed in a long embroidered skirt made of khaki and a thin mauve sweater with extra-long sleeves. A mismatched red but equally interesting embroidered jacket was in her grip. She looked a bit like a bohemian—the lovely Mimi from La Boheme. She was wearing a rather grateful and contented smile. Indeed, when she was cheerful, the energy she exuded was quite soothing, like a cup of steamed milk seasoned with cardamom and honey.

More as a means to open conversation than to pry, Michael asked what had so upset her the day they had met.

"Some guy," she blithely quipped. "What was it with that woman? From the woods. Something was wrong with her."

"A bit of a lost soul," Michael clucked. "My uncle's ex of sorts."

A bemused huffing sound came out of Bella. She was quietly smiling in the manner of one contemplating a mean irony. Then she asked Michael what his business was in the area. "What do you do for a living? Are you with the United Bank of Switzerland or Stamford's idea of the stock exchange? Or maybe you're an aristocrat or something that you shouldn't be pissing off your uncle by talking to a 'commoner' like me?"

Michael wasn't sure whether the fairy was speaking in code or metaphor. Had she just referred to herself as a "Commons"? He stuttered a bit before just telling her that he was a toxicologist . . . a neurotoxicologist, he specified. "I travel between Yale and some university laboratories in New York City and other places," he told her.

"Really," she grinned.

"Mmm," Michael affirmed. He told her that he was very much involved in the study of conotoxin venoms produced by certain marine cone snails that inhabited coral reefs of the South Pacific.

The fairy's eyes lit up in recognition as he explained the research: some marine snails of the Conus genus produced highly specific and complex venoms that targeted specific receptors and pathways within the nervous systems of their prey. Some "cone snails," as they were familiarly called, preyed on fish, some on other snails or other shellfish, or on whatever came along.

The snails would lie in wait and dart out a needle-like appendage into whatever they decided would be their meal. They would sting the catch with a neurotoxin that would anesthetize and paralyze it. Immobilized, the prey could be consumed by the snail.

Because the venoms had specific effects on the nervous system, scientists began to play with them to learn more about how neurochemistry worked and about how the neurotoxins — which were found throughout Nature and not exclusive to cone snails — could be used in medicine.

Potent last-ditch-effort pain killers were being developed from cone snail venoms. Researchers also were trying to figure out how to manipulate the compounds of these venoms to find treatments for such diseases as Parkinson's, epilepsy, and schizophrenia. Then, of course, there were governments interested in the development of biochemical weapons, but Michael didn't mention this.

"Aren't the people working on this stuff mostly out on the west coast and in Australia?" Bella asked.

"Well, there's at least one on the east coast." Michael smiled as if to imply that he was very special. Then he acted as if he were flattered and also surprised that Bella was knowledgeable about cone snails.

The fairy told Michael that she was a speech therapist who worked with stroke patients and that she also was a medical science writer. She was mostly familiar with neurology, cardiology, and pain medicine. She had become familiar with the topic of conotoxin research after stumbling upon an article about a snail species called Conus magus—"magician's cone." She said that she simply liked the name and found herself reading about the critters and their kin: Conus victoriae, Conus textile, Conus omaria, Conus geographicus, Conus vexillum. Bella rattled off names that were of particular interest to scientists and stated that their shells were prized collectors' items.

Michael was pleased that she had mentioned this. He confided that he knew a young man who, in fact, collected marine cone snail shells. Unfortunately, he could not name-drop and tell her that the fellow was none other than the young mage Leonard de Lux Junior, the driving strategic force behind a formidable revolutionary movement that was overtaking a territory within the Inner Plane—the North Atlantic Sovereignty—that more or less corresponded with the north east coast of the United States.

Michael had the honor of being called in from time to time as a consultant to de Lux Junior and his father in regard to the uses and nuances of the Conus magus charm.

The charm, in fact, was a very rare talent.

Michael, de Lux senior, and de Lux junior all had the rare power of the Conus magus charm. They had the power of absorbing the vital energy—and indeed the whole being—of a foe. It could be modified, though, and even like some snail toxins, it could be engineered for benevolent use. This fact was elementary to Michael, but apparently no one had realized this before Michael's epiphany as a magical scholar and practitioner, even though the Conus magus charm—although quite rare—had been known about since antiquity.

de Lux Senior, whose familiars addressed as "Leo," had used the Conus magus charm on another human being at least once. It took place during his youth when his family was under attack by a political and corporate rival. Leo de Lux Sortiar ambushed the villain and absorbed him totally. It made de Lux's eyes turn from deep blue to white so that, after that, Inner Plane folk practitioners, in particular, greatly feared him, believing he had "the evil eye."

His son, on the other hand, had likely used the charm several times in self-defense. In so doing, the young man stumbled upon some nuances that heretofore only Michael had a mind to know.

de Lux Junior had been the target of assassination attempts because of his close association—specifically, an apprenticeship—with a notorious maga. The maga herself was marked for death because her magical expertise was deemed too flashy and powerful for a person who held populist and anti-establishment views in Terra Novit.

But the maga managed to become de Lux Senior's consort—his "wife." That's when things went out of kilter, with Leo de Lux switching allegiances and becoming the king-pin of a political rebellion: the Lions of Light.

If Michael had mentioned his association with the de Luxes to a woman from the Inner Plane, chances were that she would be wildly impressed and especially want to cozy-up to him. Michael's alliance with the de Luxes would be meaningless to Bella Drago. No matter. It was clear to Michael that the woman was much taken with him. She carried a tense and elated sensation in her chest that was intensifying—a love feeling. Michael felt self-satisfied about that.

They were walking along the avenue, approaching a Mediterranean-style sidewalk café where they could have a "pannini" and a "birra" perhaps or a frothy cup of cappuccino.

Bella exclaimed, "Oh hi, Bobby," to a dark and rakish fellow with a halting gait who was crossing her and Michael's path.

Michael recognized the man. He fixated on him as they passed each other. He was the slacker expatriate from Terra Novit to the Terra Principalis. Lundragon had adopted him as his "Renfield." Michael kept the villainous devil in his eye all the way until the fellow was behind him. At that point, the gawky imp mocked Michael with distorted facial expressions. Then the guy translocated away—right there on a crowded avenue in the Outer Plane!

Michael regretted hollering at Anderson earlier that day then. He couldn't have the mage over in Lundragon's court—what with the gratuitous intrusion Lundragon had decided to inflict on Michael . . . sending that creepy cripple around to stir things up . . . .

5
[The Hierophant]
The Prodigal Son

When Anderson left Michael after the sorcerer lost his patience with the mage, he translocated directly from the condominium complex to the campus of the Royal Dominion of Principalis Academy of Magical Arts and Sciences. He ascended the great staircase spryly, as if he got from bottom to top in a single leap. He then bristled through the cavernous hallways.

His footsteps made music against the marble floors. The ornate walls were embellished with gold-leaf covered molding and were spotted with tableaus about Pythagoras, Plotinus, Maria Prophetissa, Zosimos of Panopolis, Paracelsus, Robert Fludd, Albrecht Durer, and John Dee. The ceilings were coated with frescos of the passion of Giordano Bruno and other martyrs, and the halls lined with busts of Iamblichus, Ibn al Arabi, Marcilio Ficino, Albertus Magnus, Johannes Trithemius von Sponheim, and Cornelius Agrippa von Nettesheim.

In fact, a new but contentious wing was being built to display hagiography about more modern masters of the occult arts, with every committee meeting on it breaking out into a fiery brawl over who was a quack or saboteur and who was truly worthy of hallowed memoriam at the academy. Anderson had to walk through this bare and somewhat eerie, gray corridor to access the staircase that led to Tristan Lundragon's office.

It was on the third floor of an annex to the main building. It overlooked a small terraced garden and was quiet and removed from the rest of the collegiate goings on.

It was a simple wood-paneled room full of light tables and cabinets that held his prized archival documents. He had some electronic machinery in an adjoining, more antiseptic room that—with its plate glass windows, white plaster walls, and high-tech imaging contraptions—resembled an intensive care unit.

When Anderson entered the office, Tristan was seated at a broad wooden desk set before a large bay window that overlooked the terraced garden. He was perusing documents that were neatly stacked on the desk. Anderson supposed the papers were "evidence" of Tristan's cause of action about the newly discovered fairy—Michael's fairy. Anderson knew that Tristan was expectant and unnerved by the mage's arrival. Nevertheless, the sorcerer did not look up, much less stand up, when Anderson entered.

Anderson tolerated Tristan's casual manner; it was an insult but also it was an act. Anderson could tell that, underneath it all, Tristan was giddy about the encounter and that, as cool as he may have seemed, the man very much wanted Anderson's approval.

Tristan finally looked up and smiled cordially. "So kind of you to keep our appointment, Albright Magus," he remarked.

"The events of late are filling me with renewed vigor," Anderson replied.

Tristan's disposition turned from nonchalance to slightly piqued interest, but before he could speak, Anderson launched into an interrogation:

"What is this interference in Solaris Sortiar's affairs?" he questioned. "For some 20 years now, you've been each to his own; you and I estranged, and he and you behaving as distant acquaintances at best. Were either of you not in my company, you would scarcely recognize the other. Before we go forward, I need to know the basis of this mischief."

"Solaris's involvement is a nuisance to me," Tristan grumbled. "He didn't find her; I found her. Let him do what he will and live with it, as will I." In a gentler tone, Tristan invited Anderson to take a seat. He went on to ask, in his sharp and exasperated way, whether Anderson had "taken up drinking yet."

With a subtle movement of the head, Anderson gestured, "No."

Tristan glared at a tray on a counter of a small kitchenette in a dark alcove on the other side of the room. On it was a tea set, which included thin-lipped china cups, individual tea strainers, warmed crème, and chunks of raw sugar. The tray translocated from the counter to Tristan's desk.

The teapot and its accoutrements were accompanied by a plate of butter cookies, candied violets, very large red grapes, a sliced apple, cracker chips of flatbread, and a wedge of piquant blue Stilton cheese. These items were meticulously arranged on the tray as if Tristan had spent the morning obsessing over the presentation. Anderson knew that he had; Tristan knew that Anderson knew, so Tristan smiled faintly in such a way that a safely guarded sentiment of warmth escaped.

"I've been tracking her for a year now," Tristan said quietly as he poured the tea. "She's not like the other one," he added. "I can arrange to get rid of that one seeing that she's not up to doing it of her own volition . . . but then she's neither a siren nor a fairy in my view. If I did arrange something, would you consider such an endeavor despicable?"

Anderson's lack of response suggested that the answer was elementary.

Tristan bristled uneasily for mentioning it. He waved a hand dismissively and continued about the new alleged fairy-like entity. "As an amusement and solace, she's stumbled onto our kind of disciplines and has taken up dabbling in magic—as a solitary practitioner for the most part. She's accessed me in the Work. Well," Tristan blushed, "I'm often accessed by Commons women dabbling in love spells and unwitting thought-form conjurations. As you know, such behavior is often related to deprived sexual release. I've taken advantage," he confessed. "But it was obvious to me that she wasn't a Commons. Have you been up close to her?"

"I'm not sure what she is, but I agree that she is not a Commons and that she may be of a superior caliber than the other one," Anderson conceded.

"My forbear, Lunaris Dracon, often speaks of a muse in his writings. In three tracts, including the forward of The Beauteous Consorte of the Mirour of Luna, he refers to the muse as the 'Beauty of the Moon'—the 'Bellus Lunaris.'" Tristan glared provocatively at Anderson and pulled out a pile of documents, some protected between laminate plates. He pointed out unintelligible word forms in the spread of documents that were supposed to translate as this term.

Placing one tract before Anderson, Tristan noted where Dracon had explained that he and his muse were each other's scribe. "In the preceding stanza, he waxes on about how she emerged from his head like Minerva from the head of Jupiter."

Anderson smiled condescendingly. "Yes, I see your point—but I never took you for a literalist—or a romantic, Tristan." Anderson reminded the younger man of what he already knew too well—the Dracon material was highly intricate code. Every document meant something else and even the transliterated and deciphered codes most likely meant something else. Anderson added that it was pure coincidence that the new fairy-like character was named Bellaluna Drago —or perhaps the scenario was fabricated as an enchantment meant for mean mischief.

A lost expression came over Tristan.

"You're enchanted — and so is Michael Solaris. That's all this is," Anderson declared.

"No," Tristan protested. "Look here." He selected a few choice documents — including the undecipherable document that he had shown Anderson in the woods the day before. Then he produced a folder from which spilled such papers as cashed checks, contracts, credit card receipts, handwritten correspondence, birthday cards, and pages that appeared to be ripped from journals and notebooks — all signature and handwriting samples pilfered from Miss Drago.

Using a high-tech magnifier, electronic and radiographic measuring devices, and other gadgets, Tristan pointed out that, although some of the alphabets in the various archival documents differed, the handwriting was the same. He especially drew Anderson's attention to a script-like scrawl at the end of the undecipherable text. In comparing the letters with those in the other, pilfered documents, it might have read "Bellus Lunaris." Most curious, however, was that the handwriting matched the script signature of Bella Drago.

"Well, you've done your homework, Tristan," Anderson muttered.

"Can't you see why I'm anxious about this?" the sorcerer exclaimed. "She's the crown of my work. She's the key, and who then barrels into my domain but Solaris."

"Alright," Anderson sighed. "What am I in this?"

"I need your professional support when I present my case," Tristan stated. "And I need assistance in approaching and training her. Everything hinges on securing and knowing what's to be done with her." Tristan waved a document in the air. "You're the expert," he told Anderson.

The mage huffed spitefully. "No. I think you're the expert. You, your companion Paleologos Sortiar, and

Solaris Sortiar all seemed to know exactly what to do with 'fairies' when the other one was running amok. Where was all your reverence for me then?"

Tristan pressed himself back in his chair to cower and sulk.

"I should help you 'secure' this one so that you and Paleologos can enslave and exploit her in ways I blush to imagine how?" Albright scoffed. "Although I don't trust what her intentions might be toward you, I can't abide by what your intentions might be toward her either. I'm not in the business of colluding in the harm of other sentient beings. I am a Celestial Magus, after all," Anderson protested.

"I'm not as ignoble as you suspect," Tristan huffed. He shook his head slightly and flashed a "nevermind" kind of glance at the mage. After a pause he said, "She's my own. She's trying to find her way home. I can't leave her to rot and despair among the Commons in the Outer Plane. And I can't have her being discovered by another of our kind who won't be as gallant and enchanted as the peerless Michael Paracelsus Solaris Sortiar. I can't abide that. Please," Tristan pleaded. "Besides, you need to get back in the game, Albright Magus. Consider how your troubles have moved you one step up rather than back. You have the opportunity to test a hard-come albeit jaded perspective in a new way."

Tristan's sentiments impressed Anderson. They even seemed sincere. Nevertheless, the mage continued to bait the sorcerer. "You're smitten with her. You and Michael. Why is that?"

Tristan rolled his eyes.

"Do you think it bright to pull a staff in a threatening manner on an adept of the Conus magus charm as you did the other day? What can you expect to happen when passions flare over your rivalry about this fairy?" Anderson blustered.

"I'm not interested in fucking her," Tristan snarled.

"Really?" Anderson scoffed. He stood up and told Tristan that the statement was even more ludicrous than his insistence that Lunaris Dracon was his ancient relation. "The only point of securing a fairy is to have relations with her to draw on her energy matrix. Did you miss that in Evocation 101, Tristan," Anderson cracked and went on to tell the sorcerer that he saw through him "as clearly as I see through pane glass. You long for and despise me like the child of a neglectful parent, but I am not neglectful, Tristan. Would I be here otherwise were I not aware of the depth of your convictions and your heart?"

Tristan Lundragon remained silent as if biding his time against the mage's barbs. He smiled faintly and nodded gently. With sharply pointed gaze, he said, "Most everything I've learned and the abilities I've attained — very many things I have no right to know or be able to do — I've acquired on my own because you rejected me, Albright Magus. I came to you wanting something great and sublime. You humored and mocked me without pity. You were a kind of great teacher in that way — a perverse way. It's made me great. But save for my reputation and my extraordinary work, I have lived a banal existence when I otherwise could have been uplifted. You owe me, Sir."

"That is true," Anderson conceded, so utterly impressed by the sorcerer's self-awareness that it threw into doubt the host of unsavory things he had heard about Tristan. "You are a great wonder, and I indeed failed you," he said. "So, this is what we're going to do." And he outlined how they were going to proceed..

6
[The Lovers]
The Sun and the Moon

Michael had managed to secure the love and allegiance of the new-found fairy. The endeavor was relatively easy and seamless, actually. Lundragon had faded into the shadows after he and Albright had their chat. Michael held his tongue, never inquiring about the details of the meeting between Anderson and Lundragon. The subduing of that particular sorcerer was a testament to Anderson's quiet greatness. That was Michael's impression, and it instilled in him a renewed reverence for his mentor.

Aisa, a nuisance at first, had faded into the woodwork as well. This did not mean that intrigues were not brewing; Michael was well aware and on his guard, but time and ease were dangerously softening him.

He was enthralled with the fairy's light, and he cherished her ignorance about it. How to unfold her to the truth of her beauteous self? Michael conscientiously stressed over how he interacted with her. For one, she slept restlessly, which was unnerving. It was not that the fairy tossed and turned; she too often whimpered and startled awake. Then she would huff as if angry, grumble, and nuzzle up against Michael, thinking he was asleep. He would caress her or else persist in playing the sleeping man, but he would be aware of an unsettling energy.

He worried that he might be hurting her in their love-making . . . unintentionally, or more as if he couldn't help himself. He worried that he was sapping her . . . like a so-called "energy vampire." She was full of fire—as if she were no fairy but a seraphim, a fiery, serpentine angel descended from God's highest heaven. Michael took it in. He was ravenous for it, fearing the day the intensity would ebb and the experience would become placid because he had burned through those things that felt thrilling to be released from.

"I have ecstasies when I finish with her," he told Anderson. A giddy, electrical sensation would pulse up his spine. It would open out to a sensation in which Michael would be momentarily lost in an experience of expansion and light. After it ebbed, he would feel refreshed, invigorated, and exceptionally clear. It was the ignition of the secret fire, which was the goal of sacred sex.

He asked Anderson to advise about what he could do for Bella's sleeping habits. The mage laughed at him.

"But I don't want her to be troubled. It reflects badly on me," Michael pined. "She should be happy. She should have the sweetest dreams and never agitation, especially after intimacy with me."

After having a laugh, Anderson shrugged and told Michael to ask the fairy why her sleep was disturbed. "Ask her whether she feels 'alright,'" he quipped as if exasperated with Michael's stupidity. "Really, Michael; I thought you prided yourself on being a hero and a charmer with the ladies. You've become confounded by a very simple thing. Something Commonsly simple. Have you met your match that you're so flustered? Are you the class misfit asking a pretty girl to a school dance?"

Michael glared at the mage, but he didn't mind his mentor's derision. Then he said, "Yes; that's the point. I've met my match. I want her to be in perfect peace. If she is my power, I want to be her savior as spirit enlivens soul and the sun illuminates the moon."

Anderson was caught speechless by the quaint poesy. He flashed a brief smile and a subtle nod in the way he would when satisfied with something he had heard.

"I'm sure that you are not 'hurting' or even 'sapping' her," Anderson reassured Michael. "I'm sure that you are 'saving' her. Find out from what."

Michael not only kept Bella as a lover; he had made her a student — an apprentice in the magical arts. He had done it at Anderson's suggestion and gave her teaching according to the mage's cues: what should be taught and in what order. He began with having her visualize a three-dimensional mandala with herself at the core. She was to contemplate archetypal symbols related to the directions, the seasons, the stations of the day, the phases of the moon, and various other associations and metaphors. It was a launching pad for the study of Cabala, astral magic, angel lore, the secret fire, and the path of descent and ascent. It was a metaphorical anathor — an alchemical furnace — in which the Philosopher's Stone, which was the renewed human psyche hidden in the body, crystallized into the reflective surface on which heaven appeared on earth.

Michael had three other apprentices — teenagers — John, Christian, and Leela. The two boys vied for the girl who was a distant relation of Michael's. She was some niece or cousin a few times removed who was the biologically questionable daughter of some polygamous sorcerer within Michael's clan. She was conspicuously enamored of Michael. He found it annoying.

Technically, what Michael was supposed to do with two beguiled boys and an infatuated girl was to use their teenaged libidinous convolutions to train them in a particularly difficult way. It entailed using their puling and eroticized sentiments against them — to humble and humiliate them. Wisdom would be born through the inspiration of frustration and disappointment, disillusionment, and the dissolution of ego as they wrangled with "unrequited love."

Michael did not have the energy or desire to go there with these apprentices, which made him a mediocre teacher perhaps. Frankly, he couldn't be bothered; he had been through enough wars, melodramas, and altercations. He merely wanted to impart a few sorcerous tricks and some magian-type meditations and alchemical projects to these kids; make sure they knew their Hebrew and Angelic alphabets; the proper way to summon spirits; and how, when, and why to heal or hinder, and then be done with it.

He knew that they imagined — romantically — that they were in it for the long-haul. The great ambition, of course, was that one of them would grow up to be Michael's favorite, his magical child to whom all his knowledge and abilities would be transferred.

The situation with Leela was exceptionally obnoxious, with her thinking she could entice him with love charms. Michael often considered sending her off to another teacher. Whether he kept her or passed her off, he would ultimately be the girl's villainous heartbreaker, and he had enough troubles with fatal attractions with Aisa Morae still at large.

The "Eel" had been stalking Bellaluna early on according to the nasty being's usual habit of interfering whenever Michael took on a new lover. In response, Michael gave the fairy a small mirror with instructions about how to use it to avoid and repel the Eel. He was unsure about how much traction he could expect from the maneuver. But whatever Bella did, whether through Michael's magical abilities or her own wiles, Aisa went away. It, of course, reinforced Michael's contention that Bella would be his greatest love, his soul mate.

Of course a day came, with the growing presence of Bella in his life, when Leela found reason to linger with Michael after a session with the apprentices had concluded. She was brazenly wearing a scarf, a bangle, and a belt stolen from the fairy. A little pouch dangled from the belt that Michael suspected held detritus also stolen from Bella: strands of hair, nail clippings, a blood-soaked tampon perhaps. It was a hotchpot of a charm to confuse Leela's own energy with that of Bellaluna's. Repulsively conspicuous, yet the girl proudly flaunted the items as if the pilfer was a testament to her magical prowess.

"You know why?" she lilted and pressed her body tight up against Michael's. She wheedled her fingers over his neck and abdomen so that he relished a little flush of libidinous urgency. She smelled of cocoa, vanilla, oranges, and Bella's menstruation. Michael did indeed want to nuzzle into the aroma and the luxurious heat Leela was exuding.

"What is this thing with you and Commons, anyway," she whispered. "My father totally does not want me to be taking magical instruction in the same room as a Deeple, if that's what she is,'" she said. "I haven't told him yet because he'll probably stop letting me come here."

"She's not a Commons or a Deeple; she is an incarnate fairy and you would do well to keep your place because if she turns on you, it will be a profoundly humbling experience," he calmly replied.

A Deeple, or "Dimidium Pleb," was a person who was transitioning from the Outer to Inner Plane. These folks were sometimes also referred to as a "half-Commons." Deeples were one of the lowest social classes in the pecking order in Inner-Plane societies, although Leo de Lux had scandalized his peers by adopting a grown one as his daughter.

Leela's brow wrinkled and she sputtered out a scoffing laugh. "That woman?"

Michael merely glared at the girl. He drew the scarf from her neck and brushed it against his face to take in the scent clinging to it. Then he kissed Leela hard and long for a while until the languorous osculation turned into bites and Leela's body went lax and twitchy from the orgasmic tide of Michael's embrace. When she began to paw at the buttons of his shirt and his belt buckle, he peeled her away from his body and disengaged his mouth to hiss, "Savor the taste of it, because I'm fucking a fairy, not you."

After the astonishment faded from her face, it reddened in rage. "It's either/or? That's mage shit, Michael."

More than the jibe, however, it was the familiar address that enraged him.

"What's my name to you?" he questioned.

"Cousin," she brazenly announced. "You just made face-time with me anyway," she griped. "I want you and I think you want me."

"I can give you some options," he said and put more space between them. "We can acknowledge that a conflict of interest has surfaced in our student-teacher arrangement and, parting amicably, you will take up your studies with another mentor. Or else, we can rewind this episode and get back to the regularly scheduled program," Michael said. "I can hone your skills in the art of beguilement to use for your own wiles, and the degree to which you win my endearment will be commensurate with the quality and quantity of expertise you achieve in your art. But our intimacy will not and cannot be of a carnal nature. I can be your favorite 'uncle' instead of mere cousin; and you can be the 'niece' to whom I may bequeath my inheritance. Think on it a while," he said, although his sincerity about possibly making the girl his lineage-holder, as implied, was anything but genuine.

The girl was itching to kiss him again despite his diatribe. Michael hastened her out the door, hoping that it would be the last time he ever saw her even if she was a relative. Her composure was rather sour, hateful, and humiliated when the elevator doors closed between them. He hoped he wouldn't have to deal with scorned-woman shenanigans from her now too.

When evening came, Michael had his way with his fairy, swearing his undying love, with his hands poised on her head as if in blessing while she knelt to stimulate him with her mouth. He scanned the windows to note whether the ascending moon could be spied.

"'Thou art the moon and moonlight and joy,'" he recited in his mind. It was a line from a hymn to a Hindu goddess.

Hauling her up, he girdled Bella's legs around his pelvis and went to stand where the moon would soon peak through a skylight. While penetrating her, he babbled poetics about the alchemical marriage of the sun and moon. He gave her empowerments; he gave her light, and he fed back off her rapture in it.

Then again, later, when she startled awake in the depth of night, Michael felt that he had failed her.

"Tell me what it is. It happens too much," he complained.

"I haven't had that dream for a long time," Bella griped. "I always have it when I'm with you. Can't let myself just be happy."

The dream was about being a bird. In the dream, Bella felt lightness and flittering but she was not free. She was like a song-bird in a cage that took pride in entertaining her captor.

"That's the good part. I don't mind that part," she said. "It has a happy feeling about it. It's like I'm doing something special and having fun. But when I get too caught up in the dream, it becomes very lucid, like I'm awake. Then another part kicks in where the guy I belong to kind of kills me."

In the dream, as man Bella loved who regretted her

existence was burning to death. He was trying to speed the process even though he was going to Hell.

"He sucks me into his head; the smothering sensation starts, and I force myself to wake up," she said matter-of-factly, as if the episode had occurred so often that it had lost its punch.

"That's what you dreamed just now?" Michael asked.

"Yep," Bella replied.

Michael huffed and failed to listen while Bella bantered about what a psychologist's had said about her nightmares. "Or maybe I'm putting pressure on the vagus nerve or the wrong side of my hypothalamus when I'm sleeping. That can make you feel paranoid and anxious," she said.

Michael traced the sigil of his namesake, the Archangel Michael, on Bella's forehead. He gave no explanation about what he was doing. He only kissed the spot and lay quietly to think over what she had told him.

The gravity of her situation was lost on her. Michael hoped it would remain so, as it did for the overwhelming majority of persons who were ignorant about the history and trajectory of their karmic momentum.

The "Law of Karma" posited three lines of force: sanchita karma, prarabdha karma, and agami karma. Sanchita karma was the momentum that had originated in some mysterious and distant past. It had built up over eons like a snowflake becomes an avalanche as it accumulates compacted snow, ice, rocks, twigs, shrubs, small animals, then big ones, all kinds of crap in the path of its ferocious trajectory. Wherever the exponentially building mass was as it fell was the present. That was prarabdha karma—fate, destiny—where the past caught up with a person, dictated the present, and set the direction for the future.

Then there was agami karma, which was where the avalanche might be headed and how its structure might change because of it. It was the potential future, predicated on both where it had been (sanchita karma) and where it was (prarabdha karma). Even though the residual effects of the past were relentlessly barreling from the present to the future, the present still could modify the future's course.

Bellaluna Drago was a fallen fairy because having had the ill-fortune of becoming some sinister Renaissance necromancer's pet (and Michael knew who that fiendish bastard now was), she had haplessly done something despicable that led to the necromancer's and her own ruin. She was now clawing through lives and worlds in atonement. Her redemption had come. Michael felt privileged to play a role in it.

"There is a saying in the alchemical texts that goes like this," Michael murmured. "The dragon only dies when he is killed by his brother and sister at once; not by one alone, but by both at once. That is, by the sun and moon.' You and me," he said.

"We're compelled to create stories for the whys and wherefores of things in an attempt to trump a wild card, which is existence itself. Existence happens despite us and also is a product of our own making. It's a bit of a paradox," Michael continued. "You dream of being attacked by a man who would pull you down to Hell with him. This is all the fluff of the mind — a subterfuge for some other vexation that is limiting you, but even that is a mere projection of mental noise. We torture ourselves with it for no good reason."

Michael told Bella this to console her, even though it was and wasn't what was going on. Nevertheless, he continued.

"In creation mythology, we talk about the world forming from chaos and void by the will of a conscious entity — God. But the chaos — the so-called prima materia — is not matter, nature, or the world; it is the human psyche full of convoluted impressions, habituations, and the conditioning of nature and nurture. This is the seven-headed dragon that must be slain by the hero who is none other than the divine spirit within asserting itself. It rescues the damsel, which is the soul."

The path of inner alchemy and of mysticism in all the great traditions founded in gnosis, Michael said, was to transform the human creature, who was nothing more than a helpless gear of the world machine, into a real person with real will, intention, and creative abilities.

"Some persons call this enlightenment; some call it 'being like unto God'; some call it the Great Work, which is magic," he said.

Michael had decided on it then. No bratty, grasping kid would grow up to be his lineage holder. No. It would all be secretly buried in the fairy like a treasure.

Bella's past, haplessly foisted upon her, would be cut as would Michael's. They would guide each other across the seven philosophical spheres: the limitations of Saturn, the indulgence of Jupiter, the fury of Mars, the sweetness of Venus, the genius of Mercury, the insight of Luna, and the redemption of Sol. In so doing, they would be released from the seven demons that itched in Arrogance, Melancholy, Carnality Wrath, Excess, Malice, and Avarice and would aspire to virtue: Selflessness, Enthusiasm, Graciousness, Patience, Mindfulness, Compassion, and Generosity. They would be the high father and the deep mother, the sun and the moon, and the king and the queen.

7
[The Chariot]
A Giant Pink Dragon

Michael was a great man, and the guy was into alchemy. He knew all about Cabala, angelology, and ceremonial magic—much more than Bella did—even if he was a biochemical engineer.

He called alchemy the father of laboratory science and explained that some of the greatest scientific minds of the Renaissance—Sir Isaac Newton, the founder of physics; Robert Boyle, the father of modern chemistry; and Paracelsus, the grandsire of pharmacy—hit upon truths that propelled modern technology while holding fast to what is now regarded as quaint and crazy mumbo-jumbo.

Michael also spoke about his interests in psychological terms. He said the intrinsic human fondness for magical and mystical experiences arose from puzzles about personhood and mortality. "We think that to know and to control will save us from the inevitable. We use both science and spirituality to achieve this, only to create a buffer zone in which to live sanely in the face of the inevitable."

Michael said that most persons use the banner of science, religious belief, or some sort of ideology to lessen the terror and groundlessness of being. "We need to make it into something, but we make it into a mess," he said.

He was a teacher—a guru of sorts. That's why he was in the habit of speaking this way. In fact, three bright, perky young people—two boys and a girl—who were too bratty and glib for their own good and not particularly polite or friendly toward Bella would visit him often. They did not visit to be mentored in biochemistry or a related science; they visited for instruction in such subjects as alchemy, Cabala, and occultism — and the girl was trying very hard to get into Michael's pants.

Bella didn't like being around the kids, especially the girl — and wasn't sure Michael liked their company either, but he took his role seriously. He insisted that Bella participate. The *Sorcerer's Apprentice,* Bella would joke. But she rather imagined herself as Mary Magdalene in communion with the Gnostic Christ. She received privileged teaching, kissed her mentor on the mouth, and shared his bed, just as the Magdalene is said to have done with Jesus, by some accounts.

Michael was a sun-king. He was otherworldly. He was painfully beautiful in appearance, and he felt like a heavy quilt and a hot toddy on a very cold day. He had a graceful, strong, and happy manner of being and love-making. His body emitted a peculiar and delectable electrical sensation. For Bella, physical intimacy with Michael was not so much the friction of bodies but the suspension in this electrical aura.

Bella gave him her eyes, her ears, her intellect, her admiration, her devotion, her libidinous passion, and her gratitude. He took it and appeared to reciprocate. It was unprecedented and almost unnatural, although it was the way things were supposed to be between men and women — in the happily ever after part of fairy tales, maybe.

Michael was godlike. Oftentimes Bella imaged that he wasn't real so, come summertime when he unexpectedly disappeared, she was devastated but not too surprised.

She could not find the extra set of keys to the penthouse that Michael had given her. She began to suspect that he had taken them back. The thought was a bitter jab. It implied planning on Michael's part. She did not know what she had done to alienate herself from him, but he would not respond to phone calls or emails and, in effect, he was nowhere to be found.

A week would go by and then another . . . and his car was missing from the lot. Dismay and paranoia not only overtook Bella but everyone who Michael knew. It caused uproar in the academic settings in which he worked, and then the government would get involved. The FBI said that Michael Solaris was someone else, but they didn't know who. This opened up more than the usual can of worms that a missing person presents.

Bella found herself in trouble for knowing him intimately. He was a highly specialized neurotoxicologist, after all, and now he was missing, anonymous, and alien.

Bella had to get a lawyer, and she had to pay the condominium board $350 because she admitted having a set of keys to the penthouse that had gone missing. The locks, including ones within the elevators, had to be replaced. The Board wanted to fine Bella more, but the diplomacies of litigation precluded this.

Then there was the problem of gaining access to the penthouse anyway. A lot of Bella's stuff was in it, held in stasis as forensic evidence at what was being treated as a crime scene. That and a lot of arcane and magical artifacts had the Feds in a tizzy. Word was getting out about it. Bella suspected it was why her hours were cut at one of the clinics she worked at and why another had removed her from the schedule.

Then one afternoon in late July about 2 weeks after the authorities started fussing, Bella was visited by two paunch agents. They escorted her along with her lawyer to the penthouse. Smiling wryly and perhaps with disdain, these two guys, who smelled of sweat, told Bella that they wanted to show her something. "Perhaps you can give us some insight," they taunted.

"More magical stuff?" she tepidly asked.

They rolled their eyes and, snickering, boasted that no; they had seen much weirder things in their travels. Again, they asked about Michael's uncle, Anderson, who could not be found or identified either — neither he nor any of those teenagers who Bella insisted had come around. With pointed expressions, the agents opened the door to the penthouse and asked Bella if she knew "how this happened."

Nothing was there. It was empty white space. Every room. Cleared out, pristine. Bella felt an aching pierce her cheekbones and a prickly sensation on her skin.

"Just like in the movies," one of the men quipped to Bella's lawyer. "If it didn't happen all the time in the movies, I'd think it was pretty bizarre," he said.

Bella stepped in as if approaching blinding white light and sunk to the floor to cry. The lawyer, agog, stood in the doorway while the agents lingered in the vestibule and smoked. They let Bella have her tantrum until she started to choke and wheeze. Then they carried her out and were nicer to her. They opted not to bring her in again for questioning.

Days later, Bella scaled the stairwell and made her way through jimmied locks to get to the vestibule between the elevator and penthouse door. She fussed with pins, wires, and plastic cards, thinking she would need to crack the lock, but the door opened freely to the perfectly bright and white-washed room.

An expanse of windows were to the east and west, with a bleached wood floor in between. Toward the south east side was the kitchen with a little, closed-in deck where Bella and Michael kept a garden of herbs and flowers, vegetables in pots, and a fig tree. The garden was now dried out from neglect and looked like the remnants of a sacking.

On the north side of the apartment was the bedroom. It

had a smaller balcony that the sunset illuminated. It was where Michael and Bella would have chats in the evening before or after love making and where Michael would usually go over meditations and also give Bella teaching.

Bella's heart ached in reminiscing on it. It ached literally. She felt her breath catch in her throat and make her wheeze and choke. When a prickly feeling crawled up her neck, Bella was more disappointed than alarmed. It was only gastric bile, not her heart shutting down.

She couldn't imagine that Michael had gone away in an act of malice or disregard. Some heavy sacrifice had to be in it, or perhaps he had been harmed. Bella didn't want to think of that. Better he was playing the prince and the pauper. Better that he was called back on emergency to his regular life in a palatial estate with a queen and royal heirs. Better that Bella was the crown jewel of a flirtation with an alternate life than that Michael had been harmed. Better that he would go on, leaving Bella tormented with neurotic vigilance and false hope about his return.

A breeze swept over her and a light source flashed. It made Bella startle. She turned to see who had come upon her, but no one was there.

She closed her eyes and envisioned the sky as if jettisoned into the vault of night: the myriad of stars spied when the evening was clear and the moon was new. The scintillation before her eyelids was merely the effect of over-breathing from stress and sobbing. Still, with wet eyes and bitter endearment, she held the image of Michael in her mind and while uttering the name envisioned his angelic namesake. Micha-el, "Who is like God": a towering archangel, shining white and made of fiery light who subdues chaos and guides and protects souls as they traverse the spheres. He was the crown of the secret fire and guardian of the interspaces between the end and beginning.

Bella let it embrace her. She imagined it being virile and great, like Michael had been. She let it pity her tenderly and gently command the cessation of tears. Its potency grazed her face. Her sinuses, impacted with bitter tears, cleared. Then she could breathe. A calm feeling overcame her.

So she rested with that feeling of communion with that presence (whether it came from within or without) until dusk descended and then night. Then Bella went home. That would be the end of visits to Michael's apartment.

What was there to do but get on with her life, but things would never be the same. It was a cold summer — not that it was actually, but that it was for Bella, metaphorically speaking. She spent an overwhelming time alone and in a fog until she let that weird kid from the neighborhood, Bobby Fludd, befriend her.

She couldn't decide if the guy was attractive — being a randy 20-something-year-old who would be good for few nights and then move on. Bella wondered whether seduction was a worthwhile ruse to be rid of him or whether it would double her troubles. She didn't fool around with him, though; she just ran into him often until she began to seek him out on purpose. She grew fond of him, and her friendship was something he seemed bent on.

He was a townie — one of those mid-to-late 20-somethings who meandered between the art house theater, the neighborhood pubs, the places that dispensed caffeine. He was the champ at chess and pool and poker, and many girls liked him even though or because he was bright and strange.

He had shown Bella a spot in the woods that he cleverly referred to as a *"Misty Mountain Hop,"* after a Led Zeppelin song. Bella had apprehensively followed him there at a time before she knew he was harmless. It was that pivotal event that turned the tide between them, though.

They were inseparable friends thereafter.

The "hop" was to the top of a hill got to from a barely trod path up a steep and narrow incline splintering off a beaten path. Mountain laurel, pin cherry, beech, and all types of oak sheltered the trail. Wild blueberry shrubs were the ground cover. The narrow path led to a clearing hidden behind brush. Lichen-shrouded granite rock was embedded in the ground there, and an aged pine tree loomed as the pinnacle of that outcrop.

"You can piss or whack off or whatever here, because no one will ever see you except the tree," Bobby said. He insisted that the tree was "real." "More alive and conscious than we'll ever be," he declared.

He tenderly placed his hand on it. Then he pressed his forehead against it in all reverence despite that its gouged out based housed a massive ant colony.

They had a long talk that day about all kinds of things, including Michael. When Bella mentioned alchemy, Bobby rolled his eyes and said, "Yeah, yeah," and told her an interesting story about frogs. Eighteenth and nineteenth century mages used to torture them to death and use their secretions in charms, he said.

"They thought frogs were naturally 'hateful' — but it was the other way around really," Bobby said. "Magicians — sorcerers and mages. They would glare and poke at the frogs to intensify the frog's 'hatred' and then hang the frogs upside down to make them just, you know, torturously die," Bobby said. "They'd put a chunk of wax underneath the things to catch the crap and rot that dripped while they were struggling and slowly dying." He said the mage extraordinaire would knead the rotting frog crap and wax into stinking pellets that the mage would then carry around. The frog-hate that the mage had "magically" collected in the pellet would repel any hate and abuse directed toward the pellet's bearer. "That was the idea," Bobby smirked.

"Pigeons, roosters, cats, and lizards," Bobby listed animals that were eviscerated for their magical parts for use in spells and conjurations. "In the name of Almighty God— they were very God-fearing, those Renaissance and Early Modern magicians. At least they weren't torturing and killing people; that was the domain of Church and State."

Then Bobby distracted Bella with serious talk that got boring and heady about every intellectual who was ever executed from the Middle Ages onward. To regain her interest, with hypnotism or sleight of hand, Bobby released a bunch of butterflies from his fists. They were small, yellow flittering things that emerged like fairies. Then he juggled a bunch of rocks and somehow ended up with a bright, fuzzy green chunk of malachite in his hand. He displayed it as if he were showing a door prize to Bella. Then he lobbed it into the air and it didn't come down—or if it did, it didn't make a sound; or else, it was hidden in his hand. Bella just laughed and made an effort to act wildly entertained.

Bobby liked Bella. It was obvious, but he stewed in it rather than touch her. That was okay. Bella needed a quirky friend; she did not need a lover, much less one who was 10 years her junior. No; that would ruin things. Bobby was her good friend.

She was the girl on the back of his Ducati Biposto, his hiking and drinking pal, and fellow philosopher. He called her "Moon dragon," of course, and the White Rock Girl, Tinkerbelle, Sleeping Beauty, and his fairy godmother. In his bawdier, more drunken moments, he referred to Bella as the *hierodule,* which was okay because no one, aside from himself, knew what that meant. His barfly cohorts and little friends presumed it was one of his made-up words but it meant "holy consort." It was a reference to a temple priestess (that is, a glorified prostitute) in ancient Babylon who, in personifying the goddess Ishtar, had ritual sex with the king at certain times of the year. It was Bobby's way of saying he thought Bella was hot but was afraid to touch her — that's what Bella thought.

He claimed his leg injury was the curse of a wicked sorcerer and that the day Bella "kissed his dick," the spell would be broken. He would turn into a "handsomer" prince and carry her off on his giant pink dragon to Always All-the-Time Land, which was the opposite of Never-Never Land.

"And when is that going to happen?" Bella taunted.

"I'll figure it out," Bobby replied, but for whatever reason, he kept his place, which was fine.

He called himself the cross-eyed pirate, the Jack of Hearts, the Ace of Spades, the alchemist, the juggler, the black knight, the midnight special, James Bond, and the avenging angel. He was an impressive prestidigitator and eerily clairvoyant, flippant and bawdy, mostly disheveled, and beguilingly mysterious: a courier of sorts.

Yes. He was a man of mystery. Internationally perhaps — and even illicitly, but Bella didn't care. She already was under surveillance in light of Michael's disappearance, and she never caught Bobby in drug dealing behavior. No incessant pages or phone calls, no pass-offs to folks he met in the street or in alcoves or johns in bars. But he clearly was a runner for someone about something.

He would disappear for days once in a while, saying he was on a "mission." He also was being watched. It was kind of obvious to Bella — but then she wasn't sure whether it was she who was being watched by folks other than the Feds and that Bobby was protecting her.

Not the townies or beer-bellied students from the local University, not the day-laborers, divorced suburban dads, not the preppy area hoity-toity, but dapper, lean, robust-looking men who seemed to be from somewhere else. They were shadowing Bella. They eyed and spoke to her in passing, and two had stood her up on dates. The only way to avoid them was to stay home and out of sight or else stick close to Bobby.

"Yeah, well, you are a terrorist. You and your mad-scientist boyfriend," Bobby quipped while at bar side one night.

"NOT funny, Bobby. Don't talk about him," Bella scolded. Then she, more gently, told her friend that the loss still stung, but the fellow was unrepentant. He rolled his eyes disdainfully and had the bartender line up three shots of whiskey.

"Men stare at you because you're fuckable. That's what men do," Bobby said sourly. He downed the first shot in a biting gulp and pointed to a crowd at the far end of the bar. "The next guy who turns around—he wants to fuck you really badly."

"You're a retard," Bella swiped "And you shouldn't go off your meds like that."

Bobby swilled another shot and chanted that Bella be attentive lest she miss his portended sighting. His little finger, poised on a glass, gestured to where he had pointed before.

Sure enough, a man turned around. It was one of the men who had been in the woods that first time Bella had ever seen Bobby. He was the lankier one with the light brown hair, not the darker one with broad shoulders. He had a heavy brow and piercing eyes that despite the dim lighting Bella could guess were like an unusual blue-green gem. His nose was a perfectly streamlined protrusion and his beauty was more masculine and brooding than Michael's. He seemed a little age-worn, too.

He directed a cold and biting glance at Bobby that drifted to pierce Bella's gaze and soften. The gesture made Bella sting with fright and a thrill because . . . she didn't know why. He was a nice-looking man. Then he turned away.

"Should we send him over a drink?" Bella asked.

"No," Bobby tersely replied.

He was a "vampire"—he and the other man, Bobby said. The Dukes of Hazard, Tweedle Dum and Tweedle Dee, the darkness before dawn, his uncles, his uncle and his uncle's "fuck friend," international spies, fallen angels, and solar deities from another dimension. That's who Bobby said they were.

Bella had an image in her mind that she couldn't decide was a memory or one of her bad dreams in which she saw those two men clobbering a disabled fellow in the old graveyard that was behind an antique church a few yards from Bella's condominium. She remembered seeing the lankier man lunge with the rabid grace of a leopard to whack his target with an object that might have been a ceremonial staff. It resembled the staff that Michael had owned and had deliberately left with Bella. (She had found it after some time, hidden with other rare items, in her bedroom closet.)

The victim in the false memory was one of Bella's creepier stalkers—not lean and smart-looking but a short man with the grotesquely coarse facial features and distorted limbs and digits. She felt sickened about the brutality inflicted on him but could not remember how the event proceeded. She would've remembered calling the police, and there was no talk among the neighbors or the news about a bludgeoning in the church graveyard. The event had to be the imprint of a dream, although her mind would not tag it as such, so the memory of it was laced with a kind of itchy eeriness.

When October came around again, the world—as if in a tempest to match Bella's mood—brought with it a rash of Nor'easters. Driving rain and gale-force winds, flooding, downed trees and power lines in voluminous masses were the spoils of the storms as were the accompanying blackouts. So one night, at about an hour after a Friday became a Saturday, metal folding chairs that were propped against the balcony railing flopped over and shattered the sliding glass door of Bella's apartment.

The burst of noise awakened Bella with such a jolt that she thought her heart might pop. She didn't get up, though. She knew what had happened. The storm had invaded her home. She dug in deeper under the sheets and went back to sleep.

In the morning, the whir of generators woke her. The power was out. The innards of Bella's refrigerator were melting, and her living room was a windblown mess of wetness and glass. She showered in tepid water and put on winter clothes before pouring out espresso from the previous day's pot. Then she grasped her phone, which began to ring. Bella knew it was Bobby. No sooner was he at her door.

It took about three hours to clean up the glass and seal the breach with plastic sheeting. Bella hugged and kissed her friend in thanks for his assistance. Little kisses and groping followed. They would toy with it now and then as if perennially on a first date. She liked holding Bobby. He was warm and his energy buzzed electrical. He was good to kiss, with a mouth that was sweet and skin that ever so faintly smelled of aloes and spicebush however unwashed he usually seemed.

She fed him cheese, olives, ruby-colored grapes, tepid chinotto, and anything else that she could salvage from the fridge. She opened up jars and cans of things and tried to make him a feast. She wiped her hand over Bobby's face in a motherly way when she brought the food to where he had flopped on the sofa. Then she sat beside him.

They were quiet. Bella thought they were being restful like intimates who were so in synch that they needn't talk, only think things between them. They could simply stay like that forever, she thought. It would be alright. She felt as if she loved Bobby; she was very grateful for his friendship.

Bobby lunged at her then. He braced Bella's head within his grasp and took ravenous kisses. He drew off his sweatshirt and undressed his friend while she fumbled with his belt and fly. Then she saw this boy's most beautiful penis: turgid with mass and length. She gripped it, studied it reverently, and told him that he had a beautiful body. "Every inch of it I'm giving to you," he declared and said that he wanted to be her slave, not like "everyone else" who wanted to "enslave" her (whatever that meant).

It went in like a sword in its sheath: smooth, well-fit, long missed, and rare. Meanwhile Bobby's cell phone rang relentlessly. He got through a few thrusts before the damned phone ringing got to him. He smashed the device on an end table and flung it across the room. It didn't die, though, but continued to sound at a voluminous pitch.

Bella glared at it dumbly. Bobby kept bucking into her, although hos majestic erection was going limp. Then one of his seizures kicked in. *Pain.* Bella had seen it before. Bobby would tense and wince and make breathy pining sounds.

He cursed and collapsed, writhed, and cursed louder. He whimpered in agony and even tears while Bella tried to console him. The bashed-in cell phone would not stop ringing and seemed to be getting louder.

"*What is that,*" Bella screeched. "That's not normal."

Bobby squirmed off her and stumbled across the floor to retrieve the crunched-up thing.

"*What?*" he shouted. "I'm helping a friend. . . . I'm *helping* her," he cried in reply to some testy entity.

Bella watched Bobby's face blanch with anger and then more pain as he vehemently cursed whoever he was speaking with. He froze and composed himself, bristled and harrumphed before acquiescing to whoever was his master.

"What's happening?" Bella exclaimed.

"Duty," Bobby griped. He cried and dressed while Bella, nonplussed, watched him, and then she dressed as well.

"Does someone know what we're doing?" she asked, but Bobby only dragged her along with him as he made his way toward the door. He pressed Bella against the wall and kissed her hotly, saying that he loved her "more really" and that he was her "slave" before hobbling out to a waiting elevator.

Crazy, tortured Bobby Fludd. Bella should've kissed his dick before he stuck it in. He would've been turned into a "handsomer" prince and transported to Always All-the-Time Land but a dark sorcerer got to him first and gave his leash a good yank.

8
[Justice]
Hieros Gamos

Bella wasn't sure how glass doors got repaired. She called a few glass and window replacement companies in hopes of getting into a cue for service, but she was mostly met with impatient remarks and indefinite waits on "hold." After crying for a while between that and the incident with Bobby, she stepped into her rubber boots and drove to the woods.

It was late in the day. The sun had burnt through gaps between billowy purple storm clouds, making everything look that much more scintillating and bright in the wavering contrast of light and gloom. The trees yet standing swayed gently as if breathing a sigh of relief, but the terrain had changed. Downed pines of massive proportion spotted the environs, either blocking or creating dodgy archways over the trails.

The rivulet was high and gushing with the force of a rapids. The winds had nearly defoliated the trees of their golden and ruddy autumn leaves. The muddy, leaf-laden ground leeched out the sweet and pungent odor of rot. Mosquitoes and gnats abounded in the humidity.

Bella tramped through muddy mulch, slipping more than once. She scraped her hands on rocks and soiled her jeans at the knees. The small scrapes felt good — as if they were war wounds.

When she got to the blond boulder where the stream flooded around small islands of rocks and bramble, Bella paused because something in the disheveled reeds and vines had caught her eye. She needed to make out what it was. Her eyes teared and her mood turned mournful when she did.

"'Tis a duck," a sonorous man's voice said.

A small male duck was strangled in the reeds. It bobbed and tossed in the current without tone or resistance.

Bella turned to face the man who had spoken to her. It was one of Bobby's uncles: the slender, light-haired man from the bar.

"Your tears are unfounded. The creature hasn't a care in the world right now. Still the ability to express tenderness is a laudable trait," the man said smartly with an accent that was also slightly foreign, just like Michael and that other man she has one met, Jason.

Bobby's uncle smiled in the way he had the day he and Bella had first seen each other in these very same woods a year before. With a pinched brow, he uttered, "Are you the woman who consorts with my nephew? The 'older' woman? I've seen you before."

Bella smirked and diverted her gaze, wondering whether this guy was being coy or what. Her mind flashed through the episodes in which she had seen him: the gorge, the cave, the wink in the woods, and that look he gave her in the bar. And she remembered how he had lunged like a rabid swordsman and struck another man across the head with a staff in a false memory.

She jostled to maintain a certain distance from the man as if she might need to dart off like a deer. "'Consort,'" she said, and turned nervously glib. "'What? Dost thou make us minstrels?'" It was a line from Romeo and Juliet. (Romeo's friend Mercutio had said it to Juliet's cousin, Tybalt, before the fatal sword fight scene.)

"Nay. Far be it from me to instigate discord," the man replied in step. He was smiling with a deeply bemused expression. He held up a hand as if to calm Bella's flighty posture. She slipped, taking hold of a sapling.

"I'm not sure Bobby and I are 'consorting,'" she said breathlessly. "But I think he's my closest friend. In fact, he was helping me this morning." She made a light gasp and after and "ah" and an "um" asked the man about Bobby's disability.

The man bristled as if perplexed.

"The leg . . . and the seizures," Bella stuttered.

"Mmm," the man muttered pensively and curled a corner of his mouth. After a pause, he winced and proceeded to tell Bella that an accident involving Bobby's family had occurred when the young man was 14. "Political intrigues in a foreign land. I don't know if you can imagine it," he said.

"What? Like a suicide bombing?" Bella remarked, but she was being facetious.

"In that vein," the man replied.

Bella cringed and shook her head. "I think he would've told me something like that," she said. "I work with disabled people, you know. So, you can tell me."

"He was assaulted and orphaned in a particularly traumatic way," the man said tersely. "He's not quite 'right,' but he's not dangerous."

Bella assumed a mournful cast and apologized for being forward.

The man flashed a smile and waved it off, saying, "We try to be supportive."

"Does he live with you?" Bella asked.

"Oh, no. Not with me," the man said wryly. "But I see him often enough. I'm an encryption expert. Robert assists me. You can imagine that he's quite the 'hacker.' Well, more of a spy. That's all I can say about my work. And you?"

With a dry mouth and mesmerized gaze, Bella stuttered through the patent narrative about what she did for a living and why she enjoyed coming to the woods.

Then she found herself blabbing about her interests in magic and mysticism and how fascinating Bobby was with his intellectual trivia about that stuff.

"I had a boyfriend who was into alchemy, Western esotericism, that sort of thing, but anyway," Bella's voice trailed off. "He ended up disappearing on me. It was an interesting trip while it lasted."

The man nodded and acted as if that was way too much information. He introduced himself as Tristan Lundragon and smiled condescendingly upon learning that Bella's surname was Drago. "'That means 'Dragon,' you know," he uttered, and he told her that his own surname was a corruption of the Latin phrase lunaris dracon: "dragon of the moon." So Bella was compelled to tell him that her full name was Bellaluna Drago, an anecdote that made the man's eyes spark. Then he smiled as if impressed and endeared.

"I wager that you did not know that 'moon dragon' was the name of an obscure magician living during the turn of the 16th century—Tomas Ladon. He called himself Lunaris Dracon. He was a mage," Tristan explained. "You know about magi? The three wise men following a star?"

"Bobby told me that magi tortured frogs," Bella quipped.

The gentleman snickered slightly. "Yes, I believe they did that, too," he said.

Bella proceeded to be drawn into an engrossing conversation about unusual historical trivia that only scholars, Bobby, and marginalized modern-day Western occultists knew. Then Tristan inquired on how Bella was faring with the storms. She bemoaned what had happened to the sliding glass door and recounted how Bobby had come to her rescue. "But I couldn't get through to a glass replacement company. I mostly just got grief," she said.

"You'll give me your contact information, and we'll

take care of it," Tristan lilted. Bella's mind itched about who "we" meant. Bobby's aunt, his Uncle Tristan's wife? Or that other man, Jason. Nevertheless, Bella spent hours in the woods with the uncle, who was too charming to be too married and too genteel to be clocking a man over the head with a magical staff, but who knew. He was an encryption expert—and a "vampire."

They wandered, chatted, forgot about time, and generated a false and thrilling familiarity. Indeed, they didn't emerge from the woods until night had fallen. Their walk became rushed when they realized the gloaming, but on noticing the ruddy October moon, they slowed their pace.

"There you are," Tristan said. "My darling beauteous moon." It was an extraordinary moment. It made Bella— and seemingly this man—feel too familiar. Bella knew her behavior wasn't right but the episode was intoxicating. She was feeling dissociated—as if watching herself from above or in a dream. Still, she too intenselywanted to feel what she was feeling and oddly cared little about consequences or safety.

She went home to find still no power and took another cold shower in the dim flicker of candlelight before running out again to dine with Tristan, drink with him, kiss him, and neck and grope in the release of the building tension of their encounter.

Bella, still feeling driven and outside of herself, followed Tristan by car to a curiously picturesque chalet-like house built on an incline on a scenic and high-end residential road in what Bella thought was probably an exclusive enclave in upscale Greenwich, Connecticut. No floodlights were activated when either of them entered the driveway but a chorus of dogs bayed. Against the cacophony, there was only the moon against an expanse of lawn and landscaping. Fruit trees marked the terrain, and

Bella could make out something of a pond in the distance.

In fiery ardor, Tristan grasped Bella brusquely. He tugged at her tresses and laughed and played like a precocious child engorged with joy. Maybe what Bobby had said was true: the man really wanted to fuck her.

"I do know about you," he confessed. "All of it in between Bobby's wild tales about his and your escapades."

"Does he have one about the 'bioterrorist' who disappeared on me just when I thought we were going to get married?" Bella remarked. "I told him to shut up about it under pain of castration."

"Michael Solaris. I knew him . . . vaguely," Tristan said, and then things got quiet. A pain jabbed into Bella's chest as if Cupid's arrow, which was broken, had to be yanked out before sepsis set in. She felt even more separated from herself and dreamlike.

"Bobby said that he drove off a cliff," Tristan muttered, sounding more jaunty than mournful.

"Yeah, well, that's what I tell people sometimes," Bella sighed. That he had a fatal car accident on the Pacific Coastal Highway near Big Sur, California, and that he was with a woman who turned out to be his wife. That's what Bella had told her mother when she asked about whatever happened to that nice man. Bella told that story to a few people when she was going through a time of being very angry at Michael for what he had done.

"And the real story is?" Tristan asked.

"He disappeared," Bella listened to herself say. "The FBI can't find him, and their pissed because they can't find any real record of him, so they think he's a terrorist, and they're following me around. How do you know him?"

The man snickered wryly and with blustery disdain said that he and Michael had belonged to the same lodge many years ago. "Secret societies and men of means. An age-old European thing. Not the 'Elk's Club,'" he glowered.

"I thought he was odd then," Tristan remarked. "Then Bobby—who as you've noticed speaks in code or is possibly autistic or I don't know what—begins chattering about a beautiful beleaguered woman he's befriended. That woman from the woods, he says, and I don't know what he's talking about, but my associate, Jason, says he's spoken with you. 'Alright,' I say, and then Bobby points you out from afar. 'Ah, yes; I remember,' I tell him. 'The beautiful damselfly with the tiger mosquito in the cave in the woods.' In Bobby's carrying on from day to day, the name Michael Solaris came up, who drove off a cliff. It was very strange," Tristan concluded.

"And that tiger mosquito. You shouldn't have been with her," he went on. "Her presence should've been the tipoff to me that Solaris was around. She follows him like his shadow. If you want to find him, look for her. A bit of a fatal attraction."

"Can we not talk about Michael anymore," Bella requested. (It was wrecking the mood and turning the dissociated feeling into panic.)

"Certainly," Tristan smirked. He embraced her in a possibly vampiric maneuver. A blood-red light burst before her eyelids and her body crumbled in an orgasmic rush.

He was imploring her to be giddy again. He was going to make love to her, and they were going to have a grand time of it, he promised. "Be happy. It's a stolen moment in time," he said, and walked her toward the house.

They entered through a solarium and continued through airy and rustic high-ceilinged rooms one after another, doffing apparel along the way while reveling in lusty cheer. Then they were on the floor of a den overlooking the grounds and the moon through a large bay window.

Tristan paused, holding Bella as if desperately. Bella listened to his halting breath. She smelled the curiously intoxicating aromas of sandal and galangal in his skin. She could feel his pulse, his heartbeat, and a distinctly scintillating electrical current pulsing from his chest. She tried not to weep as she held onto the man. He fatefully assured her that everything was "alright" and that she had "come home." He said he would give her "refuge."

He sat on his knees and yanked Bella's thighs to his pelvis. "Look at me now. In the eye," he instructed. His fingers stroked her clit and gently slid into her vagina to prep her as he spoke about aligning the eyes, the point of the forehead, the tip of the tongue, the heart, the hands, the solar plexus, the bud of an igniting spark in the pith of the pelvis. Bella knew about all this from her time with Michael. The energy within all these stations were to be engaged, consolidated, aligned, and transmuted as earth strives toward heaven, form toward spirit, dark toward light, and lead toward gold.

"Have you done this with Bobby?" Tristan asked.

"Does he know how?" Bella replied.

"Have you been with him," Tristan smoldered.

"Almost," Bella tepidly told him, and it was strange to think that it was just that morning, which felt like ages ago.

The man did not speak but Bella could tell that he did not like her answer.

"Alright," he said as if in finality and told her for the 100th time that she was "magical" and also "divine." Then he snickered as if Bella were in for something exceptional. His penis was bullet-shaped and thick for someone of a slender build. It spliced into her to hit a rapturous spot in her viscera in a single thrust. The sensation shot from her cervix to her brain such that the world vanished momentarily in a swoon of white fire. She basked in ticklish, spacious release that surged, wavelike and left her, momentarily, in the pristine joy of dissolution.

Tristan remained, poised, however, breathlessly

thanking her and uttering endearments. Bella wondered whether he had come and was done considering the extravagant build-up. It would be anticlimactic but business as usual.

Tristan uttered something like "fairy queen" before placing another thrust as remarkable as the first. Again and again until the sharp light that the man's maneuvers wrenched from Bella's pineal gland became molten gold and merged into the most extraordinarily luminous and thoughtless orgasmic reverie.

The man was in a kind of ecstasy, too. He merrily told Bella that he "loved" her, but Bella was content to assume that he meant that he was having a good time. Bella definitely could love Tristan. She was overwhelmed with infatuation with what he was doing to her. All so insidiously deceptive. She knew there would be hell to pay when she came back to her senses. The guy would be using her going forward because he obviously was a player and she was a girl who was too fast. What's more, Bobby would have his feelings badly hurt, but this momentous and likely ill-fated interlude would surely wipe away the tragedy of Michael and herald a new one.

Tristan finally asked Bella to say something, but the only words Bella could eke out were "My God."

He must've found humor in that. He snickered and remarked, "Yes. I am."

9
[The Hermit]
Solve et Coagula

Anderson Albright Magus had dropped everything after Solaris Sortiar's demise. He ran away to a retreatant's cottage in a site so wooded, misty, and remote that it could have been Hyperborea. He was living as an anchorite in a small stone cottage near a water source that tumbled down rock face and pooled into a deep and glassine reservoir. In the morning, mists surrounded him such that he had to take care in his walk among the crags and rolling hills; the vistas were only clouds and misty pinkish morning light. It was as if he were on a little platform way up in a heavenly place where he might risk stepping off the edge to free fall into void.

He ate grains, fish, and foraged foods sparingly, kept silent, and conserved energy to solely spend on meditations and especially on the performance of purification rites and rituals for his own merit, for the good of all, and especially for Michael's soul.

Anderson insisted that Michael was transmigrating from one dimension to another. His associates had humored him before he left for the hermitage. They thought he was pathetic. Expert opinion was that obliteration had been Michael's fate—complete and total annihilation.

"That view is flawed and presumes an advantage of darkness over light. It cannot be," Anderson argued. But the rumored circumstance suggested that little, if anything, could have been left of Michael Solaris Sortiar in light of the volume of death charms that were lodged against him on the fateful day that he was ambushed.

Still, it was Anderson's view that despite fancying so, no magical person—at least none in the Inner Plane in which the drama occurred—could totally wrest existence from another being—even through a Conus magus assault. That was the option of the Divine Source alone and not the prerogative of any type of being however powerful he, she, or it might be.

As stated in one of Michael's favorite scriptures, the Bhagavad Gita: "What is not can never come into existence and what is can never cease to be."

In that text, too, it is noted, Anderson had said, that extinction is the fate of only the most basest of entities who, somehow managing to avoid making amends from one life to the next, sink down to the realm of demons. From there, if still unhindered by saving grace, they go to further degradation until their ultimate end is disintegration and nothingness.

That could not be Michael's fate. It was impossible. No. Michael Solaris had passed into another plane in full consciousness. Perhaps he had aportated to another realm even before the assassins had hit their mark.

Michael had his faults, failings, quirks, and unique appetites no different from any magical person, but he was a good soul at the core. Had he lived to mature and mellow, he might've further approached the likeness of whom he had been named, the archangel Micha'el, "Who is Like God."

The entity was the solar agency, sun rising to its highpoint. He was the summer, the secret fire, the upward thrust, and everything virile and heroic about the male gender. He was the lion tamer and dragon slayer, the champion of the cause of right, and the faculty that beat back chaos and unbridled energies and transmuted them into sheer, focused conscious efficacy.

This splendorous archangel was the light of

consciousness subduing wild, undifferentiated force. For this reason the angel stood in armor, wielding a flaming sword and thrusting a spear into a dragon that lay crushed beneath his feet.

The magical staffs wielded by adepts in the Inner Plane and used as stately weapons harkened to Michael's spear. That staff, too, represented the axis of the esoteric body. Through it, a secret fire ignited from the combustible energy. It burned through the limiting habituations of life in the flesh toward heaven and its promise of liberation.

It was a shame that Michael's staff was missing. It was not among the possessions cleared out from his lodging in the Commons' realm. Its shaft was made of rowan that was thoroughly masked in gold plating on which tongues of fire were embossed. The signature image at the top of the staff was the archangel Micha'el — God's champion and warrior. The figurine was winged, armored, and thrusting a spear into a seven-headed dragon. It was fashioned from chunks of topaz, citrine, and other gems associated with the sun.

Michael either had taken the staff with him when he crossed over . . . or the fairy had it if his assassins did not.

The fairy . . . It seemed she had been what she was supposed to be . . . what Michael had hoped for. She was the moon embracing the sun in an eclipse. Poor thing. With Michael gone, she would be at the mercy of Tristan Lundragon and his special friend, that devilish Paleologos fellow.

Anderson wanted nothing to do with it when he upped and left after the tragedy of Michael's death. Let it all go to chaos, he thought. Let these characters persevere in their meaningless dramas and momentum that had no goal but would turn in on themselves like ouroboroi in acts of perverse self-consumption.

The more he thought of it while in retreat, however, the more Anderson felt redeemed. It was an alchemical journey truly. Michael was an ingredient in a catalytic process. Anderson was merely at a midpoint now. A new distillation arising from putrefaction and fermentation was forming. As Tristan had remarked: although seeming otherwise, Anderson's troubles had moved him forward. They provided an opportunity to realize certain new views about himself and about other people, ideas, and things.

Solve et coagula, "separate and recombine" was the famous alchemical adage. Separate and recombine the vital teachings from the twists and turns of fate until the essence is realized and one becomes fixed and radiant like a diamond.

After a time in his woodland retreat, Anderson left off with meditations for Michael and turned his attention to Tristan. He wasn't sure which one to champion: Tristan or the fairy. Anderson would have to . . . lightly, keeping his own suspicions and prejudices in check . . . command agents of light to descend upon them, monitor and guide them, and amplify whatever good was in their beings. After all, in this pathetic turn of events, Tristan Lundragon himself might, by perverse circumstance, become Michael Solaris' lineage holder. It could happen through his sexual exploitation of that fairy. What a turn of events it would be if Tristan got hold of the Conus magus charm through energies extracted from Michael's fairy lover.

The more he thought of it, the more intercession seemed imperative. Still Anderson thought that he had time. He was incubating, he told himself. Fermenting.

Anderson sat with it and schemed. How could he save the world, he thought. He mused that he would have to test Tristan's claims concerning his sentiments for the fairy: Tristan's tender desires to bring her "home" and not leave her to "rot and despair" in the Outer Plane or open to vulnerability or exploitation by persons even more self-serving and notorious than himself.

It rather sounded as if Tristan were chattering about a distressed damsel that would make a good consort. Indeed, it sounded as if Tristan was preparing himself to fall in love. Yes. Why couldn't Tristan find himself in love with that fairy, Anderson snickered. Tristan wanted to be redeemed, did he not?

As much as the entity was Michael's special student, power receptacle, and treasure trove, she was Anderson's student as well. He, after all, was the teacher of her teacher. Thus considering it, Anderson decided to devote himself to influencing her and her covetous sorcerer, Tristan Lundragon, through magical means while remaining in seclusion. This, in the Eastern disciplines that inspired Michael, was called tapas, "burning." Tapas denoted unwavering and obsessive zeal, faith, and perseverance in an endeavor. It was the cornerstone of accomplishment in self-actualization, prayer, and magic.

Nearly two years would pass by before Anderson would learn that his work had come to fruition. He would learn that, after much surveillance and procrastination, Tristan had taken the fairy. He would also learn that the sorcerer was quite doting, like a witch fattening up a child destined to be cooked and eaten like a lamb. But, no, Anderson told himself; Tristan Lundragon, like Michael Solaris, had become enthralled with Bellaluna Drago. Tristan was in love, desperately and ruthlessly. It was Anderson's Art that he should be so and that the fairy would challenge and perhaps even heal him.

10
[The Wheel of Fortune]
Revelations

The bed in which the fairy now slept was warm and exceptionally downy — like a heavenly cloud. Many mornings had come and gone in the past twor months that were just like this. Bliss and warmth and love. Bella was hunkered down in the sheer magnificence of it.

Tristan Lundragon was a magnificently magical and doting man and utterly on fire for a guy in his early forties. His whole manner differed from Michael's, which worked well. Bella did not want to compare them.

Tristan lived in a home marked by eccentricity and rustic comfort, like a king in his lodge. It was a chalet-gingerbready kind of building set on an incline among well-placed shrubs. The abode probably looked particularly picturesque coated in snow or perhaps in the spring when the dogwood, azaleas, and rhododendrons were blooming.

Inside the home were ruddy wood floors and exposed ceiling beams. Three tiers of airy chock-a-block rooms were furnished with inset bookshelves and ornately carved cabinets, fireplaces, pot-bellied stoves, and showcase windows.

Tiffany table lamps and torchiers abounded as did sensuously carved statuettes of dragons and other mythical beasts. Indeed, Tristan's baroque bedstead looked like the personal barge of an ancient queen. The headboard was a massive block of dark wood on which was carved an ornate terrain of roses, mythical creatures, and sigils. At top center, like a crown, was a horizontally bisected oval. It was the letter theta θ, which had something mystical to do with the planet Jupiter. Beneath the theta was the largest creature within the carved panel. It protruded nearly fully formed from it. The creature had the winged body of a pot-bellied lizard and the head of a hawk. In short, it was a moon dragon.

It loomed out of the headboard as if to communicate with a serpentine figure of a winged mermaid — or maybe it was a siren — that formed the prow-like foot of the bedstead. "You and me," Tristan would simper pointing out the figures to Bella. "Beauty and the beast." They would joke about which was which.

Bella, caught up in a morning sleep, smiled at the faint recollection of it.

"Tristan tells me you're a thrill to be in," a man's voice said in her head. Then she heard Tristan say, "Isn't she lovely."

"Mmm," affirmed the other voice. "So when can I have her?"

Bella's eyes flashed open to recognize the other man — the very handsome dark-haired man she had run into when she first met Bobby. He was crouched at eye-level and gaping at her.

"I'm not sharing her," Tristan scoffed.

Bella watched the other man grimace before rising. She listened to Tristan insist in a low, strident tone, "I'm not sharing her, Jason. It's not feasible, and I don't want to."

"I knew you were going to do this," the other man hissed, "and with all the insufferable time-wasting besides!"

Tristan stammered in a jeering manner that included a sore note about someone named Regina, but he was caught short. "She's awake," the other man hushed sharply.

Bella heard Tristan sigh hard. A conspicuous aura of antagonism saturated the sudden silence. Tristan's hand pressed on her head. It felt more like a shield than a caress.

The haste with which the other man left the room suggested that he had been slighted. Bella didn't speak or move.

She listened to Tristan's windy respiration. He knotted his fingers in Bella's hair so that the tension on the strands made her scalp sting. Then he started away with the same heated pace as the other man.

"Tristan, please don't crap out on me yet," Bella whined.

"Don't mind him," Tristan said in an impatient tone that he mostly used for others, but Bella became tearful. "He's randy but harmless. Just making a very stupid joke. A unique sense of humor," Tristan stuttered and apologized for what was an impertinent intrusion to begin with — bringing that man into the room to show her off . . . What was he thinking. "Get put together and linger please. I'll be in the loft. Working. He's not so bad really — my closest friend and colleague," he added. "You've met him before."

Tristan indeed was an encryption expert: a steganographer and cryptographer. He had some military contracts but preferred archival academic work. He had an obsession about that medieval occultist, Lunaris Dracon, who wrote tracts on magic in code.

No sooner had Tristan left Bella than she could hear the men angrily bickering. The words were unclear but the tone grew fiercer until pounding and thrashing resounded. The men were apparently scuffling.

Bella heard them yell Bobby's name several times. . . . Bobby who had dropped off the face of the earth and wasn't returning Bella's phone calls. She also heard the name "Regina" shouted back and forth and some banter about a guy named Albright Maygus, who Tristan must've not liked because in between some intense pounding, he was roaring something about "that fucking closet Maygus."

But Bella also thought she heard the word "Solaris" a few times, too, which was very curious. And the men also were carrying on about "the Terrible Prince Ippallus."

Bella wasn't frightened, though. "Good," she thought. Let Tristan beat him up and send him away. She wandered over to a small desk in Tristan's bedroom on which he kept a calendar mat and nothing else. Notes were written in almost all the little squares, but they were written in a different alphabet—a secret-code. There were lots of little documents around the house like that in addition to what the loft was full of. Bella had begun copying down some of the glyphs and trying to decipher them.

She looked at the coded entry penciled in for that day. It was in large and emphatic letters just like his notes on days corresponding with important moon phases and astrological transits. She finally could recognize, among the jottings on the mat, her own name, "Bella," and she realized that another set might've read "Jason." Bella took an excited breath and grinned. She had eight letters of Tristan's alphabet, which would be more than enough to decode it.

She wandered into the master bathroom, the wood-paneled walls of which were covered with small blooming orchids. The room contained a porcelain sink with old-fashioned spigots, a toilet with a pull chain, and a bathtub that had lion's feet. But the most curious artifact in that room was a large, revolving looking glass in an antique oval frame made of oxidized copper. The glass was a little greenish and reflected back a somewhat faded image of whatever was fixed in it.

Bella dallied in the shower and realized that a whole section of shelving adjacent to the sink already housed her stuff: a tooth- and hair brush, deodorant, moisturizing massage bars, and cosmetics. Pretty soon tampons and panty liners, and hair removal and wrinkle creams would be there, she thought.

She expected that if she dawdled enough, Tristan's lewd colleague would be gone by the time she ascended to the loft, which was a large attic with a high, sloping ceiling. As she ascended stairs leading to it, she was surprised to hear cordial banter. She wondered whether Tristan was on speaker phone or if another associate was visiting. She heard computer keys tapping, scanners intoning, and a phone ringing. Maybe Bobby was upstairs.

Bookcases, file cabinets, light tables, and computer work stations abounded in the attic. They were clustered at the western end of the mostly open space. On the eastern side was a sitting area near a fireplace and also an alcove that contained a kitchenette. Beyond that was an outdoor deck, constructed directly above the master bedroom.

On the other side of the staircase, more toward the southern part of the floor plan, was an open space that was marked by a large multicolored circle stenciled on the floor. A cupola that had a skylight in it was directly overhead. Tristan had performed rituals and meditations there similar to what Bella had seen Michael do when they were having their time together. Tristan had even made love to Bella in the center of that circle when the moon was full and shot straight down through the cupola.

Having climbed all of the wood plank steps to the loft, the first thing that caught Bella's eye was an overturned desk and two chairs. A bunch of crystal rods (two cracked) and some small gadgets were strewn on the floor, and a painting was not only askew but dented. Even though the scene portrayed the remains of a robust scuffle, Tristan was calmly sitting at his wooden desk, which was set before a large, square window.

Two of his three English retrievers were moping on an area rug beside the desk. Tristan was having a telephone conversation that sounded very cool, technical, and business-like even though it was Sunday. To Bella's dismay, his audacious friend, Jason, was sitting amid a mass of papers on a loveseat beside a coffee table near the fireplace. He was gripping a parchment and an old-fashioned jeweler's eyepiece. He glanced up at Bella and smiled brightly.

"Beautiful Dragon!" he exclaimed.

"It's Beautiful Moon Dragon," Tristan corrected tersely.

"Is it 'beautiful' or 'beauteous'?" Jason snipped.

Tristan shrugged and flexed his eyebrows. He was dismissive and appeared preoccupied with his work. He eyed Bella fondly and quipped, "Have breakfast." He flecked his hand toward where his friend was sitting.

A tray was on the coffee table that Bella hadn't noticed before. A tea set with a dragonfly motif was on it as was rye toast, marmalade, and eggs.

"They're soft boiled and still warm," Jason told her, but Bella wouldn't look at him.

She tepidly pulled a chair toward the little table and poured a cup of ruddy, aromatic tea. She grasped an egg, which indeed was warm, and cracked it to spoon its innards into a small white bowl. Jason handed her a slice of toast, which was unnaturally crisp and warm. Bella held it and tried to fight off a budding sensation of alarm. She watched the tea tremble in the dainty white cup that she held in the other hand.

"Michael Solaris is dead, you know," Jason said.

The tea cup slipped and sloshed onto the tray. The dogs howled and skittered as Tristan slammed his hand on his desk and shot up.

"Bastard!" he hollered. "Don't tell her like that."

Jason merely glowered at Tristan. "How do you suppose I should say it?" he uttered in a defiant tone.

Tristan bristled.

"This interminable tip-toeing about is maddening," Jason said to Bella. "Not that it's any of my concern anymore." He sunk back into the loveseat, swept a lanky arm over his head, and suggestively splayed his jean-clad legs.

It was way too comical for Bella to be annoyed, but panic overcame Tristan. His eyes flashed between Bella and his nasty friend. He caught his breath and warbled, "You've met Jason previously; yes? He's going to tell you something now. Go on. Proceed," he ordered. He had the flushed demeanor of a terrified toddler who had lost sight of his mother in a crowd. Then he flung himself back into his chair.

"Bobby already told me," Bella interjected.

"Bobby?" The men looked at each other in dismay.

"About Michael," Bella asserted. "Bobby Fludd." She said this only because she wanted to steal the satisfaction from Jason for his mean mischief.

Jason wrinkled his nose and looked suspicious. Tristan, in turn, studied Bella before nodding his head and uttering, "Your wit is impressive, my love." He tapped his brow and then pointed to Bella to communicate that he knew she was lying and why.

But with the knowledge that the disclosure about Michael was true and that Tristan, Jason, and Bobby had known all along, Bella's heart sunk to her feet and through the floor. Down it plummeted into the Netherworld where the organ stood skipping beats and waiting for a relatively wise and sympathetic entity to put it out of its misery.

Tristan looked as if he might cry about it—not that he cared a whit about Michael. That was too obvious. But Bella knew that he could feel her pain. And he was threatened by her feelings for Michael anyway.

He glared at Jason who, in a soft and coddling tone, went on to confess that he and Tristan knew Michael Solaris well—not that they associated with him, but nevertheless, they had long-established ties. They knew that Michael had found a woman who had inspired him—Bella—but that he also had strange allegiances in his work as a neurotoxicologist. Jason claimed that Michael didn't depart on his own accord but had been disappeared.

"Biochemical weapons," Tristan announced.

"That's crazy," Bella shot back.

"It's crazy certainly," Tristan replied, "but so many true things are."

"Certain governments had an interest in his work and he was caught in the crossfire," Jason explained.

"I don't want you to think on it," Tristan declared. "It's said. Alright? No more of it. I wouldn't wish his fate on anyone, but frankly, he was annoying. I also wanted what he got to first. Do you think Robert Fludd befriended and took care of you for months out of sheer nobility? And never touched you—or hardly," he grumbled. Tristan poked a middle finger into his breastbone. "Me," he said. "Me."

"Tristan is a very high sorcerer," Jason interjected.

"Sorcerer," Bella muttered wryly and glanced at the ceiling as if it might come down along with the moon and planets. In a burst of quirky insight, she exclaimed, "You're the guys who make Bobby have seizures. He's like your slave." Then she pointed at Tristan and indignantly accused him of stealing Bobby's "giant pink dragon."

"Now he's disappeared and won't call me back!" she announced indignantly. "So I have two people who I love who disappeared on me."

Tristan's jaw dropped after which he shot up and hollered "No!" (somewhat plaintively) before bellowing that Bobby was to keep his place or his "giant, pink dragon" would be cut off!

Bella faked not being alarmed by the outburst. "I know

who you guys are," she said. (The vampire evil sorcerer fuck friends from outer space!) With a hand braced against her brow, Bella sighed wearily. Her nose prickled and her eyes sulked.

Tristan and Jason winced at each other perplexedly before Tristan dryly clucked, "Well, now you know," and vowed to wring Bobby Fludd's neck if he ever showed up for work again. Then he kicked Jason out of the way to nearly fall on his knees to confess that he loved Bella madly and had her in his heart long before Michael did.

"That's really, freaking crazy,'" Bella cried. "I don't know what to make of you today — you two guys. What the hell are you telling me?"

"We are trying to tell you what happened. What is happening as well," Tristan said stiffly. "Would you prefer ignorance, pretty lies, and riddles? As for Bobby, he's off sulking and very much alive, still . . . but that could change on the turn of a dime . . . Michael Solaris, however, is dead. Assassinated, if you will. Executed. I did not want to bring it up, but someone twisted my arm about it," he grumbled and glared at Jason who shrugged.

Bella merely blinked and eyed them both. What could be said?

"We're not to talk about it again," Tristan announced. "Just know it. I can't go into detail."

So Bella was left to sulk, causing Tristan to resort to panic once again when a massive tear rolled off her face and splattered in her tea cup. After announcing that he hated Jason and that he should keep his "trap shut," Tristan declared that Bella was a magical, special creature. "You're displaced, and I want to bring you home," he pined. "Michael knew it and so do I, but I am not Michael Solaris. I'm not up to his wiles and intrigues. Still, I will pick up where he left off, and I will protect you ferociously."

"If you've been hurting Bobby, I don't like that. I really

don't," Bella sobbed.

Tristan winced and looked puzzled that the subject of Bobby had to come up again. Jason, unmoved by Tristan's comment about being hated, sputtered that Bella's thoughts were unfounded; Bobby was their nephew, he protested. But considering that neither Tristan nor Jason was apparently married or looked at all related to Bobby much less each other, Bella told them that they were lying.

"So what if we are," Tristan exclaimed. "We're not 'hurting' him. He's damaged already."

"He's an apprentice. He's being trained in invaluable skills," Jason added. "Thankless bloody prick to fill her with insinuations about persecution and abuse. Good riddance with him, Tristan," Jason exclaimed.

Tristan grunted in agreement.

Then, assuming a cordial tone, Tristan explained that his colleague, Jason, was an historian and a high sorcerer as well—as was Michael Solaris. Jason and Tristan collaborated with each other and had made many discoveries about occult medieval and Renaissance texts.

Jason went on to say that Tomas Ladon, aka Lunaris Dracon, like the theologian and philosopher Giordano Bruno and others of his kind, had been burned at the stake. Whereas Bruno, after having been imprisoned for 10 years, was executed because he refused to take back certain philosophical positions about the nature of God, Ladon was executed under the suspicion that he had done away with his wife and also had been dabbling in black arts, which included cavorting with demonic entities.

"So very many great minds were censored and brutally persecuted during the Middle Ages," Jason mused. "One wonders what perversity in the human spirit manages to transform a simple teaching about compassion, generosity, and enlightenment into a rationale for censure, torture, and genocide." He ceremoniously formed the sign of the cross with an index and middle finger.

"Can you imagine being bound to a post and roasted alive because you were brilliant?" Tristan added.

"Did Michael ever work with you?" Bella asked.

The men glanced at each other and smirked before cackling and sputtering as if the thought were ridiculous. They called Michael a "bloody closet-magus" between themselves, at which point Bella realized that the guys had been saying nasty things about Michael — not somebody named Albright Maygus — earlier that day.

The men abruptly sobered upon noticing the look on her face. Tristan cleared his throat and gently said, no; he and Jason worked separately from Michael but that they were all esteemed academicians. Michael actually was a doctor of sorts — a healer despite his experimental laboratory work with toxins and defense systems, according to Tristan. "He was very well respected," Tristan conceded, "and is considered a hero and martyr by some. It seems important that you should know this."

Bella endured Tristan and Jason's nutty banter until midafternoon. Then, with a head spinning and slightly aching, she announced that it was time to go.

Before she departed, Tristan gave her a parchment on which something in an encrypted alphabet was written. "This is a facsimile of an actual very early 16th century document that belonged to Lunaris Dracon," he murmured. "When you have a moment now and then, look at the words carefully and tell me what impressions arise from doing so," he said. "You have a talent for this. I want to teach you."

Bella asked Tristan what the document meant, but Tristan told Bella that he wanted her to tell him. "Play with it; it's like a word puzzle," he told her.

While their goodbye became drawn out on the doorstep of Tristan's fairy-tale-like house, Bella asked him whether what was said about Michael was true. When Tristan nodded yes, Bella's eyes flooded over in tears once more, which caused Tristan to fidget and pine.

"It's what it is," he finally said. "You needn't have known, but then it was decided . . . that . . . perhaps . . . you should," he faltered.

They shared a cloying embrace. Bella made Tristan promise to have Bobby call her. She also made Tristan promise not to do anything hurtful to him when he came around again. Then she got into her car with the intention of going home.

11

[Strength]
More Revelations

After the fairy had gone, Tristan considered doing some Work to solace her, but he was too exhausted. His pact with Albright Magus concerning her, made long ago when they had met at the Royal Dominion of Principalis Academy of Magical Arts and Sciences, was that the mage would mentor her by proxy through Michael Paracelsus Solaris, poor unwitting bastard. Now that Solaris was dead and Albright supposedly cloistered at some secret locale, Tristan had to pick up the ball. Jason was wholly exasperated by the months of hesitancy and procrastination—and now he was threatening him with sabotage. "If you won't let me have a go with her, you have to let me tell her about Solaris then," he said.

"What kind of juvenile nonsense is that?" Tristan replied after he had already screamed and threw furniture around for what Jason had said in front of the fairy in the bedroom that morning.

It was just that Tristan felt tender about the creature. He truly did. But then, he had to give in to Jason in some way or risk having him do something far more spiteful. So, when the sorcerers' spat was over, Tristan agreed to let Jason tell the fairy a somewhat "true" story about Solaris' demise. Tristan insisted that it would make no difference whatsoever in his relationship with the fairy; she was enthralled with him, he said. But, beneath the bravado, Tristan knew that the woman would now think he was a freak; this would make her antsy, faithless, and difficult to manage. This would be Jason's revenge until the bastard felt the need to up the ante again.

At least Michael Solaris had delicate intentions toward the fairy—but Jason; he only wanted to ravage her. Certainly, Tristan had led Jason to have certain expectations about what would happen when they got hold of the fairy, but his intentions had changed—and they had done so early on. Tristan did not want the fairy to be exploited. It was why he was dragging things out. He was protecting her from himself.

In retrospect, it seemed sinful and stupid of Tristan to have agreed to let Solaris become intimate with his fairy. Tristan had reasoned that he would figure out how to claim her for himself later, after Solaris had tamed and trained her and, ideally, had passed on some choice empowerments that Tristan and perhaps Jason could then pick off.

What could be said about Michael Solaris? He had lived and died by the sword. Tristan figured that his own demise would be the cloak and dagger. At least Solaris had gone out as a hero and martyr—a "Lion of Light." Tristan was more of a voyeur in that intrigue. He was a silent witness, an unseen puppeteer—godlike in a way. His interface in the Lions of Light movement was far more subtle than Solaris's had been and far more secret than Sandalphon Magus' intrigues and quaint encryption tactics. If not for Tristan and Bobby Fludd's secret intervention into her goings-on, Sandalphon Magus would have long ago found herself in the same straits as Solaris: tripped up by the enemy and quite gone from this world and any other.

Yes. Tristan Lundragon was a Lion of Light in a way. He was a secret admirer of the Cause.

Although he was glad Solaris was out of the way, he took no pleasure in how it came to pass. It was said that Solaris was ambushed by five assassins, all experts in death charms. It bespoke how formidable Solaris was. Tristan was impressed, so he reasoned that it was okay that Michael enjoyed the fairy before he met his end.

When Jason came down from the loft and joined Tristan in the den, Tristan finally leveled with him about how he felt about the fairy. He related his feelings about her relationship with Michael Solaris. He also confessed that he had transmitted an empowerment to the fairy in a provocative way on the first night that they were intimate.

"That was . . . not good," Jason muttered.

"I like her too much," Tristan protested.

Jason harrumphed and shook his head. "She's completely unremarkable," he said.

"You're a bloody liar," Tristan shot back.

"Giving fairies empowerments through the vaginal canal," Jason mocked. "Your polarities really do run in reverse, don't they?"

"Yes, you're the expert on how that works," Tristan griped.

"I want to suck her off your cock," Jason announced.

"Shut up! You utterly annoyed me today!" Tristan yelped.

"I want to play with her—with you—and you're cutting me out of it now after all this," Jason pined. "She's an elemental, for God's sake. You're reclaiming property, Tristan. She's a tool, not a person."

"She is a person," Tristan countered. "We all come from the same place in the same way. She's simply closer to her origin, which is why her potency is coveted and why it's greater than ours."

"Don't turn into a mage on me, Tristan. Please," Jason whined in ridicule.

"We bring each other to life," Tristan announced just to rile his friend. "Lunaris Dracon brought her to life. He adored her, and she served him because of it. I intend to continue that."

Jason snorted derisively. "She was the death of him," he said and recapitulated the tragic anecdote about Lunaris Dracon aka Tomas Ladon: he was tortured and burned at the stake, having been accused of heresy, sorcery, disposing of his wife, and deviant behavior related to consorting with demonic entities.

Tristan smirked. "Well, this is an improvement over that life, isn't it? Fucking around with you."

Jason grasped Tristan's shoulders and placed his forehead against the man's brow. The two were very close, after all. Their affection was genuine, intimate, and long-standing. In any case, each was attempting to settle down and establish a marital-like partnership with at least one person of the complementary gender. They might have trouble progressing as magical persons otherwise. Further, they had yet to procreate, each being repelled by the burden of fathering offspring. Who would carry on for them, though?

Besides achieving union with potent and alluring-enough female consorts, they had two other options. One was to be unfairly labeled as "dark sorcerers" because of the energy of their suspected homoerotic intimacy. The other option was to go celibate like some radical, turbaned "white-coat" magus. Neither choice was a desirable option.

The truth was that Tristan and Jason wanted to love—and screw—each other as needs saw fit and each also wanted a perfectly powerful magical woman or two or three to fascinate as well as serve, service, and adore him. Indeed, they had been riotously indulging themselves on womenfolk for years with the off-handed idea that, eventually, one of the party girls they ran with would turn into the queen of their dreams. They had a few trial runs and shared consorts and polyfamilies, but it was never lasting.

Just as it seemed that the men, now approaching

middle-age, were kidding themselves about acquiring worthy-enough female partners, Regina Poinciana Magus showed up. She was an exceptionally elegant, lithe, and angelically near-albino maga with porcelain skin, platinum tresses, and eyes that resembled small blue-violet flowers. She also was sexually hopped-up.

Jason wooed her to the point where their compulsive and languorous interludes interrupted his and Tristan's daily workflow. Even though Tristan had had go-rounds with her at the outset, Jason became adamant about keeping her all to himself.

News about the existence of Dracon's fairy came shortly thereafter. Tristan took more than a year to claim the creature. He didn't expect to fall in love with her, but he did.

She was not conspicuously stunning or glamorous as magical women go, but looking at her, no one could deny that she was not a Commons. The tell-tale magical-ness of her was the wildness: the unkempt, shimmery, and voluminous tresses; the airy physique; the piercing eyes the glint of which leaked dissipated force; the musical gestures of her limbs; and the whole appearance of sylph and indeed . . . of a fairy in need of wings.

She was pretty in the way deer, small pets, and very young children naturally are, which made her endearing. She was quick-witted, and most importantly, she was full of a mysterious force that Tristan was sure neither Regina nor any regular magical woman could come close to expressing.

Tristan thought his fairy was very special. She was otherworldly, and their partnership was fated, after all. (The gall of Jason to expect to get into her—Lunaris Dracon's fairy—Tristan's long-lost fairy from history— especially now considering how Tristan felt.)

"Make sure she's yours and not the other way

around," Jason cautioned. "You'll end up shell-shocked, like Albright—or obliterated like Tomas Ladon—or Michael Solaris for that matter."

"My fairy is not like that," Tristan sulked. "She was protecting Dracon. She was protecting him from his bitch-wife. She didn't understand that there would be consequences. I'm sure she's paid for her crime in her sojourn through dimensions and lifetimes these many centuries—and Tomas Ladon as well. I'm sure he's paid."

"Still paying perhaps," Jason added.

"No doubt," Tristan grumbled. "And Albright is incommunicado now in some hermitage who knows where, flailing himself for not getting rid of that Eel bitch—Aisa Morae—who sold out Solaris to his killers. But we almost did her in, huh," Tristan said proudly. "Bleeding heart magi," he scowled.

Tristan had been one of the early suspects in Solaris' assassination, actually—because of this fairy-business—until it became known that Aisa Morae had betrayed Solaris to the authorities in Terra Novit. She set him up to be taken out, volunteering all she knew about his talents, habits, and weaknesses.

"Five adepts in death charms. Five," Tristan reiterated. He always mentioned this when the subject of Solaris' assassination came up.

It was kind of stupid for Aisa to do-in Solaris. She had effectively ruined her fun. She would have to find someone else to become impassioned about and bent on ruining, and she wasn't getting any younger. She was aging—deteriorating—wearing away or transforming into the ugly creature she really was. Once she aged into a gorgon, no one would waver about her disposal. In any case, her days were numbered whether or not someone saw fit to put a lid on her. Those to whom she sold out Solaris might even do it; she was trouble and had no allegiances, after all.

Tristan and Jason persisted in an embrace. It was conciliatory, consoling, and quietly impassioned. Jason was the "nicer sort" between the two of them despite his behavior that day. Tristan mused on this. Jason was more alluring, more libertine, more good-humored, more contented, and gave the appearance of being kinder than Tristan, although this was just pretense.

He had a soft, cajoling manner yet was not one to shirk from exerting coercive or punitive force when required. Age had not marred the perfection of his body or his facial features. But then it was natural for Tristan to feel this way about someone he loved. Jason presumably persisted in seeing adorable and enviable qualities in Tristan as well, and Tristan did pride himself on maintaining a youthful yet distinguished appearance.

He and Jason were pressing their erections against each other and gnawing on each other's necks, but the endeavor wasn't going anywhere anyway regardless because Robert Fludd had just pulled up to the house.

"Bobby Fludd," Tristan growled.

Jason huffed as if contemplating an irony.

They watched the vintage green camouflage jeep, which Bobby — in his quirky humor — thought was stylish, linger in the driveway . . . motor running.

"He's none too happy about the turn of events," Jason remarked.

"He's going to be none too happy when I crack his head open," Tristan replied.

They watched the young man alight from the vehicle and make for the side entrance of the house, but he didn't enter the den. He let the door slam hard and tried his best despite his bad leg to briskly scale two flights of stairs to the loft. It left more time for Tristan and Jason to neck and dry hump but Tristan ultimately pulled away. He lurched up the stairs to the top of the house.

When he entered the room, Bobby was dutifully sitting at a computer station. He was matching and breaking apart glyphs within an archival document on one screen and blowing up pixels in search of microscopic-sized encrypted messages in an intercepted jpg file that may have originated from Terra Novit's Central Intelligence Network on another.

Tristan wanted to throw him against a wall but he patted Bobby's shoulder gently and welcomed him back. He quietly told Bobby that the fairy was very upset that he was avoiding her and suggested that Bobby resume the friendship but refrain from touching the fairy in sexually provocative ways. Then Tristan sat at his long, wooden desk. He resumed sifting through some work he had been decoding as well as correspondence from persons wanting to buy or sell manuscripts or have them authenticated.

When Jason entered the loft, he pulled up a chair to sit near Bobby. In a smooth tone, he beckoned the young man to not "fuck with the fairy." He patted Bobby's back and returned to the work he had been engaged in earlier that day.

They were quietly absorbed in their projects. Evening was crawling into night, and they were about to wrap it up for the day when Bobby's cell phone rang. He opted not to answer it. It stopped ringing but shortly began again.

Tristan glared at Bobby. "Answer her," he growled. "And remember what I said."

With a long, huffing sigh that squelched curse words, Bobby answered his phone.

"No, I'm at work," he told the fairy sullenly. "Yeah, well I needed space. You're killing me here, fucking my uncle. . . . Yeah, well, I didn't feel that way; I felt another way all that time. I just . . . there was a reason for it," he stuttered and then argued that he couldn't go further into it. The fairy then related what she had been told by Tristan and Jason earlier that day.

"They told you that?" he startled. "Today?" He uttered "fuuuck" in a giggle. "Yeah. It's true," he said. "It's the reason I've been so 'kind' and 'CUM-passionate' all this time, you being 'widowed' and all. Some thanks I get for it."

Tristan wagged his head disapprovingly, and Jason also looked askance.

"I wanted you to get over him without knowing that part. . . . Yeah, well, Jason's an asshole for bringing it up. You didn't have to know," Bobby declared.

The fairy then said something that caused Bobby to startle to standing stillness. He blanched and hastily strode to the far southern quarter of the loft, back where he could hide in an alcove beyond the ceremonial circle to continue the conversation.

Tristan tried to focus on his paperwork and not appear overly anxious. Meanwhile, Jason had sidled beside Tristan and was whispering that they should dismiss Bobby so that the two of them could be alone.

Tristan was pushing Jason away when Bobby stormed back into their presence. "Uh, excuse me for interrupting the 'buggery,' but you'll be happy to know that Tinkerbelle just informed me that she met Lizard Boy this afternoon while she was trying to drive her way out of the Inner Plane. I don't know how you're getting her in and out of here, but she couldn't get back," Bobby yelled, "and he stepped right in, that slimy bastard."

"What did he do to her?" Tristan asked uneasily, knowing exactly who Bobby was referring to.

"He gave her 'directions' home, and they apparently worked," Bobby remarked. "He tried to chat her up about me. And he had it all worked out, too, because the fairy said she was trying to call us while she was freakin' driving around lost, but the calls weren't going through."

"What is he talking about?" Jason snipped.

"Raimondo Tyrano-Sauros Sortiar," Tristan snarled (even though the "Lizard Boy's" middle name actually was "Tyrone"). He was a prodigy of about Bobby's age—perhaps more approaching 30. He had been the attaché of a character named Hipparchus Gorgon Sortiar—a high sorcerer and corporatist who basically ruled Terra Novit despite its having a government. The story was that Gorgon was killed in a showdown with the teenage son of the leader of the Lions of Light. After Gorgon met his end, Sauros took over his operations.

"Now I'm really fucked, thank you," Bobby whined. "I have a death warrant out of me in Terra Novit, in case you've forgotten. Now I got Lizard Boy playing Bounty Hunter." He pouted and flailed his arms before blurting, "You could've left me alone with her that day. I spent all this time with her—working her up for you! And I get shit for it. I get fucking tortured for it."

Jason simpered and wagged his head as he hurriedly left the loft. Bobby's eyes flashed with lividness or terror as if he were braced for more pain.

Tristan stood up and approached Bobby. He caught the younger man's head in his hand and flung Bobby into one of the wooden pillars that spotted the loft space. Bobby's body cracked against it and slumped down.

"Don't fuck with fairy. Number one!" Tristan shouted, "And this unmanly whining is despicable. Two! If anyone saw an apprentice of mine in such straits, my reputation would be shot!"

After brutally yanking at Bobby's hair and jostling him against the post until he was concussed, Tristan hollered that the idea that Bobby had been intimate with the fairy was abominable. "Pollution!" he yelped and caught his breath. "There's a reason why Commons men can't do it!"

He left Bobby to stew for a while and stormed out to

the deck to cool down in the late autumn chill. He had promised the fairy that he would not hurt Bobby. It was an oath he had broken. In time, if he continued to adore and train the fairy rather than sap her, she would know his mind and deeds. Then she would be revolted and would scorn him. She might even take revenge. But Tristan did not want to be a vicious wretch; he wanted to be Albright Magus.

He returned to the loft. Crouching beside Bobby, Tristan softly told his apprentice that he had done exceptionally well in his work with the fairy over the past few months. Tristan said that he sympathized with the young man's frustration and that what he had said earlier about their intimacy was wrong. The fairy was greatly endeared to Bobby, Tristan said. He added that envy got away with him about it sometimes.

He told Bobby that he was free to go if the training and work became too harsh but that Tristan hoped Bobby would explore his experiences in a different way. He requested that Bobby examine how his experiences and trials had changed him, how they provided an opportunity for insight about himself and other persons and an opportunity to generate both compassion and ultimately power over others.

Tristan placed himself very close to Bobby. The young man flinched when Tristan hugged him. "It's taking you too long to 'get it,' Robert," Tristan whispered and continued in a lulled voice and pointed gaze: "You're brilliant, devious, and valiant. You are the wounded hero. Prove my suspicion right, and you will win the battle. Surpass me. Do it."

Tristan was aware that Bobby was weeping. He pressed his forehead against that of his apprentice and basked in the tenderness of the young man's wrenched heart. "Clean it up," he said quietly. "It's time already — and don't cross me. You'll manage your way around this Lizard character — as will she. I'm sure of it. Be content to be her angel rather than her lover. The bond will last much longer. And don't underestimate your refuge in me or your own wiles."

Bobby sniffled and gave Tristan a robust nod of compliance. Tristan in turn planted a wet kiss on Bobby's forehead. He maintained a warm and consoling manner while he gave Bobby time to compose himself. Then Tristan told Bobby that his next assignment was to locate Albright Magus and bring him back.

12

[The Hanged Man]
The Fragment of a Dream

Early in the morning when dreams tend to be particularly strange, vivid, and recallable, Bella found herself caught in a familiar narrative in which she was a bird. A tall man made husky by aging was her keeper. In the dream, Bella was fond of the man but also a bit stressed. Having had the dream for years and years, she maintained vigilance. There were parts in the dream in which the man didn't like her so much—parts in which he turned gruesome and proceeded to hurt her.

This time, she dreamed that the man was supposed to be Tristan Lundragon even though he wasn't. It wasn't that the gentleman was supposed to be Tristan but looked like someone else, as often occurs in dreams. Rather, an uncertainty persisted about who the man actually was, Tristan or another fellow.

The man had outgrown salt and pepper hair and a broad, kindly face that bespoke a quiet demeanor. He had smoky eyes that were somewhat squinted and a furrowed brow as if he were very pensive.

Despite his gender, he was supposed to be Bella's mother even though Bella was much older than him. In the dream world, Bella could pop in and out of the man's head. She loved him—not romantically exactly, considering she was a bird. She loved him in the way pack animals are ardently devoted to their masters.

The man had an assistant who was very nice-looking. If anyone, Bella had a crush on him. He was fair, spry, and beguiling in appearance and sly and intense in manner. He also was much younger than his master and generally avoided the master's wife. The wife did not like the assistant or the master's bird, which the assistant cherished. Indeed, the wife evolved into a hag-like shrew as the years went on in which Bella lived with this dream.

In the dream, Bella, the assistant, and sometimes the master would go through giddy intrigues to avoid the wife. When the wife did show up, she would threaten to rat out her husband, his assistant, and Bella-the-bird to the authorities. With that, in the way dreams go, the scene would flash to a foreboding dignitary—a bishop or some such person—smartly clad in black and garlanded with crucifix bling. Sometimes the appearance of the wife or the cleric was enough to startle Bella awake. If those two characters could just go away, the dream would be alright, she thought, and it might never go into the bad parts.

That very thought crept into Bella's consciousness during that morning's dream. It caused her to build a part that was like a missing link in the story.

She dreamed that she wrote a letter to the wife. The letter was the document that Tristan had given her a few days before when she was at his house and he and Jason told her about Michael. The letter resembled an intricate seal full of interlocking geometric shapes, sigils, glyphs, and words in—not Hebrew or Latin—but a cryptic alphabet. It was supposed to describe what was to be known through which all things are known. In the dream, Bella composed the "letter" for the wife not because she intended to be helpful or instructive. She did it because she wanted to blow the lady's mind. Get rid of her, that is.

The dream bird that Bella was smiled wickedly and felt mean and guilty when she gave the document to the wife. The lady eyed it, wrinkled her brow, smiled, and then placidly fizzled into an iridescent mist.

In the next part of the dream, which was not

completely new, the man who was Bella-the-bird's keeper was howling in agony. Armed with a club-like cane, he swatted at Bella as she flew around the room. Meanwhile, the assistant was weeping bitterly and taking blows from his master's weapon. He was trying to restrain the older man from harming the bird that Bella was. Then Bella woke up.

She felt agitated, shaky from the adrenaline jolt that the dream set off. She also was pleased with herself; she had finally gotten some closure on the dream. She knew why the nice man in it was always freaking out and attacking his magical pet bird. The creature had killed his wife. Bella had the whole story now. She could write it down.

But the dream was an effect of the strange and heavy mind-state that Bella had lapsed into after her last visit with Tristan several days before. From that time forward, her thoughts had been on Michael Solaris. She couldn't believe he was gone from this world. She also felt that she was betraying him in her dalliance with Tristan Lundragon. The more she thought about it, the more she thought that Tristan and his friend, Jason, were evil and strange.

A week-long string of events had caused her to wallow in misery and stress. Among them was a nutty phone call she had had with Bobby right after she left Tristan's house on that crazy day that he and his friend weirded-out on her. She had gotten lost while driving home.

Bella was supposed to make a turn at a peculiar five-way intersection marked by a flashing red light. Tristan always reminded her to make full stop there because it was very easy to take a wrong turn. Bella, her mind utterly distracted after plowing through Tristan and his provocative friend's banter, didn't remember coming to the light. She found herself lost along narrow winding roads among exclusive estates in the woods. She did not know where she was: Greenwich, Armonk, north Stamford, or perhaps way off course in Pound Ridge or Bedford. No path was running into a familiar road.

She drove around for 40 minutes, completely at a loss about where she was. Neither Tristan nor Bobby — or anyone — could be reached. Then her cell phone died. Bella took to orienting herself in relation to the sunset in hopes that a large-enough road would lead to the parkway or some landmark, but she was going in circles. Finally, she pulled to the side of the road to think things through.

A sharp-looking young man of about Bobby's age tapped on the car window. He was clad in an elegant, black cashmere coat and had the bone structure of a model. His hair was dark and cropped, and he had intense and hedonistic eyes that were sapphire blue.

"You need directions?" he shouted.

Bella regarded him as if he were an angel.

"Where you wanna go?" the guy yelled through the car's window glass.

Rolling down the window, Bella abashedly told the man that she was looking for a main road that would get her back to Stamford.

"Stamford? Why do you want to go back there for?" he quipped.

Bella was stuck for a reply.

"Where's Bobby? Is he making you do a run for him?" the guy said. "Bobby Fludd. You're his girl, right?"

Bella yet still did not know what to say to this fellow. She was flustered. She merely wanted to go home.

"Alright," he grumbled, as if Bella had rebuked him. "Just click your heels three times and follow the road up that way to a flashing red light." The man pointed in the direction opposite the one in which Bella was headed.

"I know about the flashing red light, but I've been up and down this road, and I didn't see any light," Bella snapped.

"Listen, I'm telling you that you're going to go that way," the man said in an edgy tone. "You're gonna' see a flashing red light. Make a right and an immediate left and you'll come to the parkway . . . eventually."

Bella argued that the light didn't sound like the one at the five-way intersection.

The man shook his head as if he didn't know what Bella was talking about. He insisted that she follow his directions. "You'll be alright," he said.

She calmed down. She thanked the man. She apologized for being agitated and short-tempered. "I got some bad news and my head's messed up. Sorry," she said.

The man snorted and shrugged. "Things come and go," he replied. He passed a business card to Bella. It had an iridescent purple-green stencil of a Grecian mask that resembled Medusa on it. The name on the card was Raimondo T. Sauros, SE, Chief Executive Officer, Gorgon Enterprises, LLC.

"I'm a big shot. You should go out with me instead of Fludd," he said.

"I'm not dating Bobby," Bella simpered.

"No?" the man smirked incredulously. "Well, that's good to know. But when you see Bobby, tell him Ray was asking for him. Where's he staying now?"

"I don't know where he lives," Bella laughed.

The man huffed and shook his head. "Alright," he concluded—again peeved as if he thought Bella were lying. "You can call me when you get home. To thank me," he said.

Bella agreed, but she didn't call even though his directions proved efficient. She tried reaching Bobby instead—and miraculously got through. He was at Tristan's house. He and Bella had just missed each other's comings and goings.

The conversation was very weird, but that wasn't unusual, of course. Bella didn't mention that she knew Tristan and Jason were the evil sorcerers who were mysteriously subjecting Bobby to their sinister wills, but she told him what they had said about Michael. And she told Bobby about Ray Sauros.

Bobby told Bella that she should've run over Ray and then backed up and run over him again a few times. He exhorted her to take out a restraining order on the guy. Bobby said he was a dangerous freak and on no account should Bella say or even think anything about Bobby if the "Lizard Boy" should ever approach her again.

"Move in with Tristan and live happily ever after," he sulked. Then he hung up the phone.

That was how last Sunday ended. The whole week was a miserable bitch thereafter. Tristan had taken her to dinner that Wednesday but parted angry because Bella kept questioning him about Michael or Bobby. Their subsequent phone conversations continued to be testy, and he kept bugging her about looking at the parchment he gave her.

"Do you want it back?" she asked.

"No. I want you to study it," Tristan growled.

Bella did not like the tone of his voice, so she hung up on him. She was thinking it best to break things off with the guy and go back to acting like a mourning widow.

On the morning that Bella had woken from her definitive dream, she retrieved the business card that Raimondo T. Sauros had given her. She was sitting at a small dining table placed at the far end of the living room near the sliding glass door to the small balcony that overlooked the parking lot. She was consuming a buttered and jam-smeared piece of rye toast and a cup of milky espresso while keeping Tristan's document in her view. She felt an eerie excitement, because the damned thing had figured into her dream.

Rather than focus on the document just yet, Bella rubbed a thumb over the shimmery embossed line art of the Medusa image decorating Ray's business card. She thought the waxy feel of it was interesting. Nevertheless, she crunched it up and avowed to dispose of the card by fire in a little, improvised magical ritual that would be meant to keep the guy away from her and keep lovelorn Bobby safe and free and to help him find his bliss.

Having finished her breakfast, Bella finally grasped Tristan's document. The letters in its cryptic alphabet resembled the hatch marks of bird's feet, but Bella also had a very staccato way of forming letters. Indeed, whenever the document caught Bella's eye as it languished on her dining table, she would do a double-take because, from a distance, the document looked like something she had written. Even a phrase at the bottom of the document looked like her own signature. She wondered whether this was what Tristan wanted her to recognize.

She pondered how looking at the word-forms and the other parts of the document made her feel. She wondered whether, if she looked intensely at them enough, she would be stricken by such an unbearable ecstasy that her being — body and soul — would transform into a rainbow and flash out of the present dimension and into another — like what had happened to Mrs. Lundragon in Bella's dream.

Φ

It was early evening on a Friday night that smelled of imminent snowfall and fireplaces. The Commons Christmas season was approaching. The air was charged with stress and festivity.

Bella had just returned home from her usual late afternoon repast at a café. There she had had a light snack and worked via laptop computer. Tristan had tracked her movements through his antique looking glass, which he used as a scrying device.

Besides entertainment and solace, the tracking via scrying was important. Tristan did not want other men to approach the fairy, especially not men from the Inner Plane. They were indeed abounding. Bella seemed to not notice, but they had been lurking about since Michael Solaris's death. Bobby had impressively warded off these interlopers. Tristan gave him credit for that, but Bobby was no longer in the picture. The kid had disappeared after Tristan beat him up and told him to go find Albright Magus.

Regardless of Bobby, Tristan had intervened in the fairy's welfare more than once. Indeed, about two weeks into his liaison with her, he had to interrupt an indulgent sexual interlude with one of his regular magical lady-friends to rescue Bella from assault in a dimly lit parking lot. The perpetrators were two audacious mid-level sorcerers who had approached the fairy in a bar that she had been lured to by a friend who never arrived.

Tristan had his sorceress-friend rigorously mounted upon him when his gaze passively turned toward a wall mirror that held the reflection of her riding him. But, however luscious the site — what with the corseted get-up she was wearing — it was not what his vision fixated upon. He was so accustomed to remote viewing through the agency of mirrors that he saw and heard the fairy instead.

She was being asked about Bobby. She told the fellows addressing her that she hadn't heard from Bobby for weeks and that they were not romantically involved, just good friends.

The men began to insult Bobby for his timidity. They flirted with the fairy and then drunkenly asked if she would like to be alone with them — either one or both.

"Emergency call," Tristan announced as he frantically

pried himself out from beneath his playmate. He lurched from the bed and made haste to dress and translocate to the scene all the while listening to his sorceress-friend curse and berate him.

"Jason said you should bind that stupid Commons fallen fairy already instead of getting all sappy and p-whipped," she bitingly drawled.

Tristan's rushed and parting words to her were to go find Jason if she needed to get finished off; he had to run. The fairy was in trouble.

By the time Tristan appeared at the club, the two sorcerers masquerading as Commons were tailing the now panicked fairy as she fled to her car. Tristan broke between them. "Mine," is all he said in a reverberating growl. He looked oddly dashing and rabid standing there in the winter chill without a jacket. His shirt tails and buttons all askew for having dressed in haste from his interrupted sex romp.

He poked an index and middle finger into the temple of one of the two offenders and gave him a zap. The man faltered backward. Stunned, his eyes jostled in their sockets. He rasped to catch his breath. His buddy bolted into the shadows.

That episode was the worst of it so far (except for the time Tristan and Jason chased a gremlin off the balcony of Bella's apartment and beat the crap out of it in an old graveyard next to where Bella lived). It was an annoyance, but useful ultimately. It assured the fairy of Tristan's attachment to her. It also demonstrated that his inscrutable powers were at her service.

When Tristan called Bella that Friday evening, he also was watching her in his scrying mirror. From it, he could see that she was still in a moody disposition. She fidgeted with the refrigerator and kitchen shelves as if discontented about what they stored.

On the other side of the room on a small, exceptionally cluttered dining table was a bowl of withering grapes; an ensemble of pine cones, pebbles, and crystals; a crumbled shard of paper; a pile of books that included reference material, notebooks, and probably a grimoire or two; and the document Tristan had given her as well as encrypted memos that Tristan was very pleased that Bella was stealing from him. Also amid the disarray were three photographs of Bella and Bobby Fludd and one photograph of her and Michael Solaris.

A container resembling a decanter that was half-filled with an exceptionally brackish liquid and a candle were on the table as well. The decanter was probably being used as an alchemical vessel called a retort. Its presence suggested that the fairy was revisiting the alchemical potion-making that Solaris had started her on. There also was the sense that she may have been using the container of the mysterious liquid as a scrying device.

She sat down at that table, phone in hand, and shook the decanter. She peered at the tiny fragments suspended in its effluvium against the backdrop of the candlelight. Then in a tone that sounded facetious, she asked Tristan whether he stilled "loved" her.

"Unrelentingly," he responded. "Is it not the same for you?"

Bella cringed and fingered her photographs. She asked Tristan whether he had done anything torturous to Bobby since their last conversation.

"This is the last time I am going to say this, my darling," Tristan spit. "I've been very kind and patient with Bobby for all the time I've dealt with him." A feverish panic flushed over him, though, as he watched Bella give her decanter a shake. He was sure that she knew he was lying. "Have you heard from him yet?" he haltingly asked.

"No. I told you; he hung up on me last Sunday, and I

haven't heard from him since. He won't respond to me anymore." Tristan watched Bella's eyes well up. "I feel very bad about it," she whimpered. "Bobby's very special to me."

"Undoubtedly," Tristan muttered and confessed that Bobby was on one of his missions. "Frankly, he needs distance. He's upset about us. But do you need the pent up and passing affections of boys to feel validated as a woman?"

"That's not the point," Bella replied and became weepier.

"Enough with Bobby," Tristan pleaded. "He has women lying themselves down like train tracks before him. He's just being petulant. What is this pain in you? What have I done? How do I turn back time about what happened last Sunday?"

"How are you related to Bobby exactly?" Bella questioned. "And where's Mrs. Lundragon?"

A long, perplexed silence ensued. "Does it at all seem as if a 'Mrs. Lundragon' lives in my house?" Tristan snapped.

"Maybe she lives in the big condo in Paris or Manhattan or something," Bella said.

Tristan answered with more silence. This time, it was of a fuming and exasperated sort. Then he said in a controlled but gruff voice, "Bobby and I are not related. I'm more of a guardian—was a guardian . . . friend of the family. Did he tell you I was married? What did he tell you about me?"

"He said you were 'a very nice man,'" Bella replied.

Tristan was certain this could not be true. He was quiet, nonplussed. "He didn't bend your ear about what a rake and a player and how very cruel I am?" he asked.

"No. He said you were a vampire, but that was a long time ago," she cracked.

"I'm a sorcerer; not a 'vampire,'" Tristan replied. "A wizard, as in a 'wise man.' An adept. You know what that is, Bella."

"One of the three magi following a star," she yawned, and went on. "That crazy lady in the woods said you guys were vampires, too," Bella said. "'Energy vampires.'"

A rasping gasp came out of Tristan. He raised his voice, sharply admonishing Bella to maintain her distance from that woman. "You haven't been associating with her?" he scolded.

"No, I haven't seen her since," Bella placidly responded.

"She's extremely unstable," Tristan insisted. He said that Solaris had had a go with her and if not for that, he might still be alive.

"Now, what are you telling me?" Bella questioned, but Tristan caught himself:

"Nothing. Nothing. No more talk about Michael or Bobby. We are not talking about it," he insisted. "I want to hear kind and delightful things; to hear your sonorous voice utter reassuring and stimulating words, but you are wounding me now with this sour disposition. For what? Nothing bad is happening. Tell me something beautiful and interesting about you and me."

Bella huffed. She went back to shaking up sludge in the decanter and announced, "I dreamed you had a bitch for a wife and a slew of kids."

"Did you now," Tristan said remarkably. Now that was something. Finally.

"Yes," she replied brazenly.

"And who were you in the dream," he asked. "Not the bitch-wife?"

"I was a bird. Right before I woke up, you were trying to kill me. It's a recurring dream I have, but this time, you were the person who was trying to smash me. I was protecting you, though" she stressed, "but you didn't appreciate it."

"And are you in a pique with me tonight because of this bad dream about me and 'Mrs. Lundragon'?" he murmured.

"I'm just trying to figure things out," she replied. "They're a little weird, Tristan."

"Much more than a little, I hope," he exclaimed. "What's the alternative? Limp, Common, and boring." He then announced that he had an extraordinarily "weird" place to take her. He would be coming for her in an hour. "Be put together and alluring," he instructed.

13
[Death]
An Exquisitely Beautiful Dragon

When Tristan came for Bella, he held and kissed her as if they had been bitterly separated for a long time and were now in the ecstatic throes of reunion. He told her that he was very proud of her, but she didn't know why and feared to ask.

He was driving a silver-gray Aston Martin that Bella had not seen before, and he was driving it as if intending to be air-borne. Bella had hardly boarded the vehicle when Tristan asked whether she had found anything in the document he had given her. Bella lied and said that she had become obsessed with it. She said that she was sure her mind had spun out the just-mentioned dream because of it. She also said that the handwriting in the document, from a distance, resembled her own.

"Is it an optical illusion?" she asked.

Tristan grinned and shrugged.

"When you look at it, do you feel as if you're looking at your own handwriting? "she questioned.

"No. Not particularly, but it's interesting that you do," he replied.

"I dreamed that the paper explained the secret meaning of everything. The person who deciphered it would become so instantly enlightened that she couldn't stay in the ordinary world," Bella said.

Tristan didn't respond. His grip on the steering wheel seemed frozen. He also was holding his breath.

"Tristan?" Bella coaxed.

"Yes, my sweetest love," Tristan drawled but hardly

moved.

"Are you alright?"

"Very quite," Tristan replied.

He reached out to stroke her hand. Bella told him that if he intended to drive so fast, he ought to concentrate on maneuvering the car. She wasn't sure whether it was a good idea to chat, but she went on:

"I was thinking, especially after I had the dream, that it's not about what it 'means,' but about how it feels," she explained. "You have to know how it feels to know what it means. It's like a piece of abstract art or a very groovy polyphonic musical composition. You don't ask what it means; you're transfixed in the mystery of it. You come out of time and space and come into a way of knowing something that's different from the ordinary way."

Tristan had come to a full stop and lingered by a flashing red light on a very dark, snow-dusted road while Bella talked this out. He seemed oddly awestruck about what she was saying — or perhaps he was preoccupied or disoriented.

He kissed Bella robustly. "When we get to the club, you'll explain this dream of yours and how it spurred these thoughts. I think Jason and some other colleagues would find your musings entertaining. Are you ready?" he asked.

"For what?" Bella shrugged.

With a jarring screech, Tristan swerved the tony car into a sharp turn and sped at break-neck speed so that the velocity pinned Bella to her seat. With a lurch, the car slowed and abruptly turned onto a long driveway lined with lights and topiary. It led to the parking lot of a compound that was obviously a country club.

"So, where are we?" Bella asked.

"Somewhere over the rainbow," Tristan quipped. "It's called the Orion Club. Very high-end, saucy, and sorcer-y."

"But what town are we in?" she asked. "Are we in

Connecticut or New York?"

Tristan didn't reply; he only squeezed her hand as they scurried inside the main building.

It was a sprawling, dimly lit space that was made to look like a tropical get-away. Ponds with aromatic exotic flora spotted the area along with cozy sitting areas and tiki-type bar stations. If you looked at the ceiling, tiny lights formed constellations, the most prominent of which was Orion, with its signature belt of three stars.

"There's another establishment down the road called The Phoenix and Harp, but it's—" Tristan wrinkled his nose. He said it was full of "pompous magi and low-life folk practitioners." Bella had no idea what that meant.

Smartly groomed and good-humored men approached Tristan and told him that they were glad to see him after such a long absence. They mostly gave Bella a pan-faced once-over. The women did so, too, after pawing at Tristan and sometimes uttering provocative words. If and when Tristan introduced Bella to one of these persons, he or she would smile strangely and ask a question in a tone used to speak to young children.

Bella spotted Jason. He was sitting in a lounge area with a woman who would've looked like Cinderella at the ball if she were clad in a glistening hoop skirt—or maybe she looked like "Princess Barbie," but no; she was much more unusual and elegant. She was very white, very blond, and very perfect and ethereal-looking, like a fairy queen. She and Jason were holding hands. She was engrossed in chatting with him but he was glaring at Bella without much expression. Finally, he gestured for Bella to approach.

Bella squeezed Tristan's bicep despite that a woman with too much cleavage was hanging onto him. She motioned toward his friend and the gorgeous platinum blond.

"Beautiful Dragon!" Jason exclaimed enthusiastically,

according to what was becoming his custom.

When Tristan caught up to them, he introduced Jason to Bella again, this time announcing that Jason's surname was "Paleologos." His elegant girlfriend's name was Regina Poinciana. The woman smiled kindly and reached out with the daintiest, airy hand to touch Bella's.

Tristan swatted his friend's thigh as he took his seat and snickered that Bella had dreamed that he had a bitchy wife. "And Bella was a bird in the dream," he said. He then asked Bella why he was trying to kill her in it.

"You were upset because I killed the wife," Bella said blithely. "I made her disappear because she was nasty, like some of your lady-friends here are but in a different way."

Tristan was unfazed by the swipe. Rather, he and Jason glared at each other and guffawed gleefully.

"Jackpot," Jason muttered.

"And Albright's missing this," Tristan replied.

Bella looked at Jason's girlfriend to try to get a handle on the inside joke, but the woman abruptly stood up without expression and walked away. That annoyed Bella, but Jason seemed wholly unaffected.

"How did you kill her, Beautiful?" he asked. "The wife."

"I wrote her a letter—a special letter that was for her eyes only—like what you were talking about the other day. I guess that's why I had the dream, because I've been looking at that parchment that Tristan gave me," she told Jason. "So I had this weird dream about it. It filled in parts of a regular dream I have."

Jason cast a quizzical look toward Tristan. Tristan shrugged and let out a laugh.

"I often dream that I'm a bird that belongs to a man who has a nasty wife," Bella explained. "The dream is fun until the wife shows up and then, if it keeps on going, or if it starts out with the part where she's in it, there's another part where the man is killing me. Then it becomes a nightmare and sleep paralysis . . . but Michael made that part go away," Bella said. "So last night, after years and years of having this story in my head, I dreamed that the man was killing me because I killed his wife," she glibly quipped. "Except that, last night, the man was Tristan over here." Bella motioned her head toward him.

"So what did the wife do with the letter?" Jason asked as if he truly were interested in her silly nightmare.

"She read it and turned into a rainbow," Bella replied.

"Because she couldn't deal with what the letter said and stay in her ordinary body," Tristan interjected and anxiously asked Bella whether she had insight into the specific parts of the document he had given her.

"Just what I told you in the car," Bella said in a tone edged with impatience. "What if it's not about the readability of the parts but something else? Some mood that is supposed to be communicated or instigated," she shrugged. "You tell me; you're the experts."

The men merely gloated. Tristan stood and robustly patted Jason's shoulder before announcing that he was going to get drinks and order some small plates. Then he pointed a finger at Jason and commanded him not to touch Bella, and he said it in a tone that did not at all sound cordial or cajoling considering the festive mood the two men were in. Bella watched Jason glower at Tristan as he wandered away.

No sooner was Tristan up and about than women were swarming around him. Jason quietly smirked and played with Bella's feet. He pressed his own into hers and trapped one foot or another between his two. His hands were turned palms up on the top of his thighs as if inviting Bella to hold them. The sight of them made Bella feel hot and faint. She wryly reminisced that Jason was a vampire and a sorcerer, after all—"a very high" one, like Tristan.

In Tristan's absence, Jason chatted about how obnoxious people in the club were. He said that Tristan liked to network, so Jason had to humor him and "haunt" the "wretched" place "with all the other ghosts." Then he said that if Bella showed him her palms he would tell her fortune. She was afraid she might burn up—or even orgasm—if she made physical contact with the man. Nevertheless, she exposed her hands and endured a fiery adrenalin rush when he took them into his own. He held them very gently and told her in a soft and compassionate tone that Michael Solaris had been extremely fond of her.

"Bobby says you guys are vampires," Bella muttered.

"Oh, we are. We are," Jason laughed. "And we're going to make you one, too."

"Fabulous. I can't wait," Bella simpered.

Tristan returned with a fragrant goblet of red wine for Bella. He held it poised by her hands, which were now in Jason's despite Tristan's parting directive. Jason threw a wanton look at Bella as Tristan's pelvis grazed by at eye level when he forced his way between them.

The friends sourly glared at each other before Tristan composed himself to motion toward two men who had accompanied him back from his jaunt to the bar. He introduced them as Professors Phoenix Dionysus and Roger Tau. Professor Dionysus was a sinewy man who may have been in his mid-thirties. His hair was long, red, and stringy, his eyes were an eerie aqua, and his face was bony, as if the skin were taut over his skull. He was wearing a mauve leisure suit accented by an olive green shirt.

His fellow academician, Professor Tau, was a more normal-looking, dark-skinned man with plump cheeks and bright black eyes. He was wearing something like a man's frock: a long, satiny white night shirt over which he wore an ornately embroidered sapphire blue poncho-of-sorts. The ensemble resembled a dalmatic and chasuble worn by

Catholic priests during high mass. Some other persons in the place—men and women both—were attired similarly, as if in ceremonial dress.

So the professors, being informed that Bella had some background in neurology as well as spiritual philosophy, engaged her in chatter about consciousness, cognition, memory, and personhood. Who were you when something happened in your brain so that you forgot who you were or forgot who you lived among? Or who were you when your personality abruptly changed or when by some tragedy, your intelligence degraded or became deviant or psychotic. Was there a ghost in the machine, they asked each other.

When the professors questioned Bella about what she "believed," Bella said that she had entertained the idea—in a religious way perhaps—that there was an underlying reality to existence that was consciousness and energy—an Eastern idea actually. She said that this ground reality had coughed her up as well as everything else as a reflex action, and that mind, ego, personality, and even one's sense of self were mechanistic, impermanent, and illusory. Only the ground consciousness was real; everything else was its thought-form—or a dream.

"'God is real; the world is illusory,'" Professor Dionysus muttered. It was an adage of certain Eastern mystics who imagined the world was a dream-like projection that obscured a transcendental reality.

"So why are you cavorting with these rogues here and not meditating in a cave?" Professor Tau teased.

"Real or not, a person has to live in her body and mind and endure her life," Bella said.

"Very few can do otherwise," Professor Tau declared. "Do you feel yourself to be 'unreal'?" he questioned. "Or else, is it that you feel a distinction between yourself as a personality and ego-entity and as another, larger and impersonal self?"

"I sometimes get a feeling that we're all made of circumstance—things happening, but circumstance isn't a real person, it is a result," Bella said.

"But do you feel like this or is this merely an intellectualization?" Professor Tau questioned.

Bella shrugged.

"Because if you truly felt this way, you should be sitting on a proverbial cloud somewhere," he scoffed.

"Oh, but I am," Bella countered with a sweet grin. "I'm sitting here talking with you."

The professors simpered bashfully.

"Alright then. Get on with it now," Tristan cut in.

Bella was asked to recount her dream in minute detail as if being interrogated. She had to admit to her audience, that in the dream, she knew what the letter said but could not explain it to them now. "Who knows; you might become rainbows and disappear," she nervously cracked.

The men paused. They jotted down notes and glared at each other. Finally, Professor Tau smiled in a kind and condescending way. He commented that Tristan had mentioned that Bella was a "sound healer."

Before Bella could reply that, no; she was speech therapist, Tristan exclaimed that she had "a beautiful voice. Sonorous and polyphonic, like the call of an undine."

"Or a siren," Professor Dionysus muttered.

"You think so?" Tristan said and grimaced at Jason.

"Feminine creatures from the deep that lull human beings to the Netherworld through the 'sweetness of their song,'" Professor Dionysus said, quoting Homer's tract about sirens in the Odyssey.

"They were psychopomps," Bella interjected. "They guided souls from their deathbeds through the Netherworld. They calmed the dying and the dead and helped them navigate their journey. They told them certain truths that they weren't meant to hear until they were passing into the next world. That might have been what they were before the Greeks and Romans took over. You know, because the Greeks and then the Romans demonized all those feminine wisdom-beings from other mythologies and turned them into scary man-eaters."

"Well, there you have it," Professor Tau announced.

The academicians smiled cordially. Rising, they asked Bella whether they could take Tristan and Jason away for a moment. The two friends were smiling intently, seemingly having become best buddies again. Bella shrugged, being perplexed by this whole episode.

Before walking off, Tristan handed Bella a staff-like object that he hadn't had a moment before. She hesitated to grasp it. It was like Michael's staff. What's more, she had seen this staff before—in her mind in a memory that might have been a dream . . . or not. This was the implement that Tristan had bludgeoned another man with in the old graveyard near where Bella lived.

It was a long, impressive rod of wood that was completely embossed with exquisitely finely worked metal filigree. Chains with jangling amulets dangled from the top end of it, and it was crowned with a large figurine of a creature that Bella knew was a moon dragon. The figurine was made of a deep, green crystalline stone that resembled an emerald.

"Keep hold of it," Tristan stressed. "I'll explain later."

It wasn't as if Tristan and Jason were back in a jiffy or as if Regina ever showed up again or as if anyone acted normal and cordial toward Bella while she sat there gripping a giant, conspicuously priceless, "magical" staff. Bella knew people were staring at her, though. Then she heard someone say it: "Lundragon's fairy. She used to work with Solaris Sortiar."

The White Rock Girl. Tinkerbelle.

Tristan and Jason were elated when they returned to

her.

"You've had more than enough of all this, my darling," Tristan quipped. With doting and concerned glances, he and Jason nodded at Bella as well as each other and readied to depart.

A woman or two intercepted the men as they briskly made their way from the cavernous club, but both fellows were dismissive—even brusque—about the attention. Tristan jerked Bella closer to him at which she realized that he didn't have his staff.

Bella swerved back. "Where's your thing. Your staff is—" she pointed in the direction from which they had come and startled. Ray Sauros was in the crowd. His eyes lit up, and he smiled as if thrilled to see Bella. He stepped forward with open arms. Tristan lunged at him with his staff miraculously in hand!

"I don't think so," Tristan growled.

Jason gently pulled Bella back against himself and guarded her behind a similarly spontaneously produced and even more exquisite staff. Its wood was embossed in jewel-studded gold and silver, and it was topped with a translucent milky blue figure of an arching winged man.

Uproar and scuffling ensued.

"This is a PRIVATE club!" Ray bellowed. "What's with the foreigners in here pulling staffs on the patronage?"

Husky men bearing their own staffs were placating Ray and telling Tristan and Jason to back off and leave.

"This is the guy?" Ray shouted at Bella and huffed. "You'll be running in circles, Sweetheart. Try something new and move up in the world for a change," he yelped.

Tristan and Jason stormed off with Bella in tow.

"The 'Princies' got themselves a pet fairy," Ray hollered after them. "You'z better mind yourselves. You don't know who you're dealing with!"

"This should be interesting," Tristan muttered once

they got outside.

"Shall we go to my place?" Jason asked.

Tristan flecked his hand at Jason and pulled Bella away. Jason called after him plaintively.

"It's not for you," Tristan insisted. "It's dangerous besides."

Jason appeared dumbstruck at that.

"Get off! You're an interloper," Tristan hollered.

Jason's mouth dropped open. He looked as if he might cry. He sank down to squat. An agonized hand pressed against his brow. Bella heard him sob. She felt badly for him — whatever it was. Her nose prickled and her eyes welled with tears. Tristan was tugging her away but she resisted; she didn't want to leave the other man strangely weeping in the parking lot of that freakish place.

Tristan finally harrumphed and bolted toward Jason. "Not here," he hushed and hauled him out of earshot.

Bella watched Tristan hug Jason. He appeared to whisper apologetic and consoling words to his friend before uttering something pointed and menacing. Jason seemed to protest and offer assurances in response. Tristan seemed assuaged; then he kissed Jason. Really kissed him. Jason melted into it, cleaving onto Tristan in the embrace.

With an equivocal expression, Tristan stepped back and gestured that it was okay for Bella to come forward and do she-wasn't-sure-what. When she got within arms' length, Jason drew her to him and held her, puling something incoherent about "not hurting each other."

She hugged him sympathetically and felt a pulsing electrical heat radiate from his chest into hers. Then he kissed her longingly with his face all damp with lust and emotion. Bella felt confused about kissing him back. She couldn't help herself. Her legs collapsed from the overload that the sensation was jamming into her genitals from his embrace.

Tristan nuzzled his head against theirs. "Alright, leave it for now," he muttered. "Let her sort it out."

Bella drew back to cower and rue while the men nodded at each other, apologized, and patted each other's backs. After passing a desperate glance at Bella, Jason walked off among the parked vehicles while Tristan walked Bella toward his car.

"It's been about 20 years for him and me," Tristan confessed after he and Bella boarded the vehicle. "And he's developed a tenaciously strong interest in you."

Bella merely grit her teeth and tried to wrap her head around what Tristan was saying. She felt wholly unreal and trapped.

"I'd rather he take you along with me than take you away from me," Tristan said, but Bella could not respond. His hand was weaving itself into her hair and stroking her cheek, but Bella brushed it away, which only made Tristan sink his head against hers in a weepy way.

She said a prayer in her head to Michael asking whether it would be okay to die to be with him instead of these people. Then she asked Tristan what being a "fairy" meant. "I mean, me being a fairy," she said.

Tristan shook his head. He continued to cleave to her but she continued to pull away. Nevertheless, he uttered: "You're not a fairy, Love. We all thought you were; but they decided that you're the something quite else. A siren: an exquisitely beautiful dragon.

14

[Temperance]
A Perfect and Committed
Arrangement

I t was more than a week after Bellaluna's "big adventure" with the sorcerer-people at the country club when she was sitting in a café that she frequented in a neighboring town, liking it not because the coffee was so great but because, among other things, it served a green, loose-leaf Chinese tea called Ti Kuan Yin: "Iron Goddess of Mercy." It wasn't that Bella liked the tea so much; she liked its name, imaging that any libation called Iron Goddess of Mercy had to be an especially auspicious elixir. She especially drank it when she was feeling miserable.

The café was the kind where the lighting is dim, cushioned furniture taken from attics and curbs was the décor, and nerdy caffeine-head 20-somethings, like Bobby Fludd, congregated to play chess and pick up Internet access. Once every two weeks, the café would host an open-mike poetry night and, in the summer, local acoustic musicians would play for a sparse crowd.

Bella was nestled in her usual spot by the front window with her laptop computer, her stack of articles from research journals, a pot of the goddess tea, and a pannini. It was late in the afternoon of a sparkling bright and crisp winter's day — a day Bella should've been putting off work to walk in the woods.

She was weaving anecdotes from the professional literature about dopaminergic dysfunction and Tourette's syndrome with passages from a transcript of a presentation that a doctor had given at a big medical conference in

Chicago. Bella had attended the conference within days of the sorcerer country-club incident.

It was not easy being alert and personable during her stint at the conference. The night before she had left for it, Tristan had proposed that Bella quit the job or two she had managed to hold onto and move into his house. He had done this by phone. Bella didn't want to answer the call. She was packing for her business trip and was drinking (too much) wine.

Her mind was swimming in compulsively livid thoughts about what Tristan and Jason did together and how, exactly, they "shared" each other's girlfriends. This, in turn, led Bella to rue that there was no freaking way she could compete with Regina-Poinciana-Snow-Queen-Christmas-Shrub. And no way was she doing a four-way much less a three-way with men who stuck it in each other. Besides, why would these fellows deign to heap such smoldering attention on Bella with the likes of the Regina-babe around? It didn't make sense.

Tristan and his friend had to be playing Bella for the most amazingly dense imbecile in the cosmos, she thought. But for what? Michael probably wasn't even dead — or maybe these guys killed him. Maybe Bobby Fludd knew too much about them and fled to save his skin. Maybe he had been protecting Bella from them all summer and then gave up.

Bella had developed a consuming and bitter love for Tristan nevertheless. The neurochemistry of too-good sex; it made a person into an addict for another, compromised and blinded to all the prickly things that could go on between two people when they weren't at it in the sack. When she and Tristan were alone, he acted as if he loved her more than life. He protected her and doted on her, but whenever someone else of his kind was around, all this weird, freaked-out stuff happened.

There was no denying that Bella was attracted to Tristan's (fuck) friend, Jason. He had an odd and coercive charisma. This was a problem, but it wasn't after all, was it? Tristan had dictated the course of action. He wanted her so much that he wanted his buddy to have her too. The whole thing made Bella furiously angry at Michael all over again for dying and disappearing or whatever-the-fuck had happened. Whatever it was, he left her to be subsumed into very dodgy circumstance.

Bella let the telephone call go into voice mail, but Tristan was adamant that she respond. She let him plead and scold for nearly eight minutes of voicemail recording. She hollered curses at the answering machine, angered that Tristan simply could not believe that she wasn't present. It wasn't until Bella realized that Tristan was talking even though the recording time had long run out and that he was reporting what she was doing that, panicked, she cautiously picked up the phone. She let him ramble about the incidents at the Orion Club until he got around to his little proposal. He wanted to be with Bella always. He wanted to "keep" her.

Bella told him that it would be problematic—what with all those "beauteous sorceresses" honed in on him like bees to honey—or was it flies on shit. And the men, especially that friend of Tristan's who was "adamantly" bent on being her special "fuck friend," too. She announced that for nothing else, gay men were "germy."

"I have to go get tested now!" she screamed. And would she also be expected to cavort with Little Miss Snow Queen, she asked. "You know, Reg-I-na Vag-I-na Christmas Shrub." She balked, took a swig of her drink, and finished off the last square of the half pound of chocolate she had consumed that evening. Bella cracked that she would only "do" Jason's girlfriend if the woman showed up with a strap-on.

She was sure she heard Tristan growl Jason's name then. It was as if Jason were with Tristan. In fact, Bella heard Tristan threaten to kill Jason right before he hung up the phone on her.

She had to go off and be a professional press representative at a super-big medical convention with that bobbing up and down in her consciousness.

But a week later, she was sitting in the café writing about how docs always wondered why kids with Tourette's syndrome were so much bigger and gawkier than normal kids until they realized that the big kiddies were big because they were on meds and that the kids who had yet to go on meds were actually smaller than normal.

Bella was applying herself to the assignment, but she also was fantasizing about letting it all go and agreeing to being kept by Tristan Lundragon—if he hadn't killed Michael or his best (fuck) friend, of course. In his cajoling that last night that they had spoken, he claimed that he wanted to mentor Bella in decryption—the decryption of the Dracon documents. She would work in his office, live in his house, sleep in his bed, presumably screw his handsome boyfriend on occasion, and figure out, first-hand, how at least three people "did it" at the same time. The idea had become oddly attractive; but mostly, after being distant from Tristan, Bella felt at a loss. She didn't care about the implications of the liaison; she only cared about resolving a desperate feeling.

Bella assumed she would be entering strange and sinister terrain. Still, it would be a new and luxurious experience. When Tristan got bored and threw her out, she might still be one of his best friend's lovers or else, she would probably be the special friend of some other character from that milieu—Ray Sauros perhaps.

More likely, she would simply be left with some nice jewelry and a high-end car or other effects to sell. She would take her earnings and move far, far away with only a picture of Michael Solaris in her pocket.

So she was sitting in the café, immersed in editorial work, and also thinking about what she was going to say to Tristan if she decided to answer the phone when he eventually called again. Then she noticed Ray Sauros standing outside the café looking in. He smiled at Bella in a warm and reassuring manner. She, in turn, felt very wanting of the attention. She watched him step toward the entrance of the building, but he never crossed the threshold. Instead, he could be heard arguing with someone.

Bella pressed her head closer to the café's showcase window. She looked sideways to view what was happening near the door. There was Jason Paleologos having it out with the guy. Ray backed off, shooting a livid glance at Bella before storming away.

When Jason entered the café, his brow was a little pinched. He seemed slightly peeved until he exclaimed "Beautiful Dragon," and took a seat beside Bella. He quietly asked about what testiness was going on between her and Tristan and questioned why she had spoken to Tristan in a crude manner the week before. She told Jason that what was happening was very difficult, but Jason said that, no; it was very special.

He had a little heart-to-heart with her. He seemed to have a way of making every explanation, however odd, seem reasonable. On the one hand, it seemed as if they were speaking very candidly about the sorcerer-people; about the mechanics, logistics, and importance of Tristan and Jason's agendas; about the men's friendship and sexuality; and about how Bella fit in. On the other hand, it was clear to Bella that Jason was doing some vampiric magical thing to her because she could feel an odd heat and electrical sensation streaming from his chest and pulling at her.

As Jason spoke, he physically closed in on her until his head was very near hers. His skin and breath smelled of vetiver, aloes, sandal, and all kinds of heady aromatic woods and resins. Their conversing assumed the timbre of a whisper. Bella was feeling as one might on an opiate and wondering whether Jason had drugged her. She was enrapt in ecstatically amorous sensations and no will to repress them. Jason kissed her. She brought him home. They made love until long after night had fallen.

At least he was joyful about it, as if part of his own ecstasy was the sharing of it. He had an intense and magnetic solidity about him. He rode and glided over Bella at a pace that did not weary but matched and heightened her rhythms and made her feel almost like Michael had — as if her whole body was a plucked chord and that the resonance of it was her soul unbound so long as the chord maintained its sustain. So even though the event was marked by the violent friction of bodies trying to make a prickly dragon full of scales and spikes roar and breathe fire in a furnace down below, Bella's mind felt like a dove launched into spaciousness and celestial light.

Rather than carrying on she was a "special" creature, as was Tristan's habit, Jason told Bella that she was a "potent" one. In the giddiness of passion, he avowed to magnify that potency and to himself become unparalleled in magical prowess through her.

In the morning, Bella felt strangely peaceful. Her mind was unusually blank. Things looked brighter and seemed new. They seemed unfamiliar in a way, in fact, just as they had the morning after she had first been with Tristan.

When the phone rang, Bella did not answer it. When Jason did and spoke with the caller (Tristan), it was as if this was the natural way things worked. The conversation was remarkably happy and cordial and, at a certain point,

Jason wasn't talking into the phone but to space as if Tristan were "out there" as an invisible overseer, just as Bella had insanely suspected.

When Jason put the phone to Bella's ear, Tristan requested that Bella not feel confounded or compromised by the turn of events. He said it was important for his and Jason's work and for their convenience—and also for her protection—that they be three.

"Can you do this with an even heart?" he asked.

In weepy fit of tenderness, Bella agreed.

He assured her that it would be a perfect and committed arrangement and that the three of them would achieve great love, great magic, and great power.

15

[The Devil]
Riding the Dragon

For the spring equinox, both sorcerers ceremoniously made love to the fairy (who they continued to refer to as the fairy even though they knew she was something else) in the magic circle in Tristan's loft. The episode was more ceremonial and sober than it should have been. After some months of their special arrangement, something dire had occurred. It had thoroughly shaken things up, turned them upside down, and established a new precedent.

In any case, Tristan had assured Jason—in anticipation of the ceremony—that the fairy knew how to manage it; the sex-energy work, that is. He acted as if he were appalled when Jason claimed that he was unconvinced of the fairy's expertise in the matter. Jason only said this to bait him, though.

It was not as if Jason and Bella had been together that often. Although Bella could not resist him, she did not trust him much although she did seem to like talking to him. If only for that, Jason found himself being soothing and tranquilizing on purpose, like an emasculated sap. But he liked being kind to her. He thought the fairy made him feel this way through her inscrutable power. Jason had indeed climbed the alchemical ladder of the planets with the fairy. He had been remarkably and graciously invigorated. Like Tristan, he was inspired to give back light and even empowerments through intimate acts. He was endeared to her, but he lied about it to protect Tristan's feelings, which the fairy had ripped apart recently anyway . . . deservedly.

In any case, Jason had told Tristan during their

discussion before the solstice that he wasn't ready to use the fairy for heavy duty magical rituals; he wanted to have some fun with her, not only for himself, but for her. He wanted her to experience some joy and levity and draw a distinction between what went on in their intimacies and whatever went on between her and Tristan. He told Tristan that his desire was to provide some refuge for the creature, considering the strange terrain she had been drawn into.

"I'm the refuge," Tristan growled. "You're the add-on." He berated Jason for twisting Tristan's arm to get hold of and then not know what to do with the fairy . . . "and for screwing over the whole operation by dredging up the ghost of Michael Solaris. Just to get your way," he scolded.

Riled, Jason countered that he did indeed knew what to do with the fairy and claimed that he had been doing it rambunctiously for weeks.

"Well, she's not been any worse for the wear," Tristan quipped. "At least she has a place to go to finish it off after you get through with her."

Jason then reminded Tristan about his dire fuck up. Yes. Tristan was the one who almost blew it with the way he had been abusing Bellaluna, parading her around the Orion Club and like places almost daily for months. He was bent on proving to everyone straight-away that he had found the bloody infamous entity conjured by Lunaris Dracon a half millennium ago. And he had to keep up the public pretense that she was a bound and subjugated thing, not a precious love object. Her existence proved Dracon's existence and proved Tristan's special worth as a sorcerer and academician. Because, according to lore, she was a dangerous and volatile thing, Tristan had to maintain an air of detachment and control, as if he were imposing a bondage and domination trip on her.

Too many of their peers scoffed. They said that Bellaluna was completely unremarkable and Commons.

They spoke to her as if she were a 3-year-old or an imbecile. Then she would be encouraged to explain some text or ideology so that Tristan could gloat when her insights, tedious banter, or exasperated humor silenced her audience.

She knew what Tristan was doing and played along like a good sport, but after a while, she came to feel abused. She knew she was on exhibit, like a freak. Jason knew things had gone too far when her response to "How are you?" was "Unreal." He warned Tristan about it, but Tristan went on pushing her. Then an evening came—a week before the solstice—when he hauled her into a seaside dining club called the Trattoria Centauri, which was modeled to be like the deck of a tall ship. One felt as if moving on a billowy tide while within it. Illusory sails rustled overhead, and the club's ceiling was like that of the Orion Club except that Centaurus was the celebrated constellation.

As too often happened, some casual girlfriend within Tristan's hoard clamped herself onto the new celebrity as soon as he arrived despite that the fairy was in tow.

"Get off him," the fairy told the other woman. When the rival and Tristan both laughed, Bella pushed against the woman—a sorceress, of course—in an attempt to trip her. The sorceress continued to scoff as if Bella were small, silly, and brazen.

Then Bella told the rival, loudly, that if she didn't "get lost," Bella was going to ram the sorceress's staff so far up her ass that she would choke on it. Bella growled and dug her hand into the woman's hairdo, tripped her, and screamed "Fuck off!" at a pitch to shatter glass.

Before Tristan could play the master and put his creature in check, Bella turned toward him and thundered in spitting vehemence, "I hate you." She said it more than once, and she called him a "fucking demon."

She stormed away, escorted by staff-bearing bouncers. Jason observed it all, being there in the company of his soon-to-be-ex consort, the alluring Regina Poinciana Magus. The maga was pulling on him while he was lurching forward to intervene in the fray.

Tristan appeared to be in shock, his mouth speechlessly agape. His cheeks were ruddy as if they had been slapped. He and Jason had to linger coolly for a few minutes. They had to appear to be slightly incensed but cool about what the fairy had done. They would have to act as if they were conferring about her punishment. Then it would be alright to saunter out. By then, though, where would the fairy be?

"It is not as if she can 'go' anywhere," Tristan griped.

"Unless one of her many pursuers accommodates her, of course," Jason remarked.

Simpering and feigning indignation, the sorcerers wheedled their way out of the club, not retrieving their jackets from the coat check room and breaking into airborne sprints once it was safe to do so.

The two split up to scan the marina and the parking lot only to find their darling in the escort of Raimondo Sauros Sortiar. The devil was ushering her into his car. The sorcerers pleaded with Bella in urgent cries that she step away from the fiend. They insisted that he was no friend and intended to harm her.

Sauros quietly muttered to the fairy that it was well known that her two friends were nefarious and homosexual as well as insane.

Jason was cautioning Tristan not to charge at the foe but to reason a bit. It would be the death of them all, he said. He translocated a few yards to be strategically placed so that he and Tristan could see who was at each other's backs. Phoenix Dionysus joined them then, looking regrettable about making the choice. They all had their staffs in hand.

Sauros was telling Bella to get into his car and away from the crazy men.

"He killed your Michael. He's the one!" Tristan bleated. "He is the cause of all your sorrow so much more than me. Please," Tristan pleaded.

"Come away, Bella," Jason commanded. "What Tristan says is true. We are endeared to you. Our love is awkward, but sincere. There is no malice here, but there is your archenemy laying a trap!"

"You screwed yourselves big time with your bullshit, Old Men," Sauros grumbled. He sourly watched Bella retract from him. Scoffing as if the scene were droll and ridiculous, Sauros got into his car and, with a revving, gaseous screech, translocated himself away in it rather than merely drive off.

The fairy did not seem surprised or even fascinated. Her affect was gray and flat. A grid of wispy lines of silvery light could be detected around her. The light swirled up like a ray or a pillar, and there was something bright and white way "up there." It was almost like a portal, the thought of which was fearsome somewhat. Jason reached out to clutch Bella. He felt an electrical sensation as his hand penetrated the light field. It was not smarting but it was prickly and droning as if it had a sound.

"Don't touch me," Bella balked, and shirked from his hand. Her gaze was directed upward. "I'm finished with this," she panted. "Will you just be my friend and take me home to where I live and leave me alone."

"It doesn't work like that, Bella. Especially not now," Jason grimly replied.

The response caused the fairy to tremble and cry. She repeatedly screeched the name of Michael Solaris when her protective light web dissipated. Tristan exacerbated her torment by shouting banishing charms at the thing. He was battling it, as if were, and trying to embrace the fairy. Jason had to watch Tristan and her scuffle, sob, and attempt atonement. Jason also had his maga girlfriend reprimanding him for neglect in one ear and Phoenix reproving him for this turn of events in the other.

As mentioned, Jason and the fairy had worked up to having a good rapport. Jason thought that the entity came to be more comfortable talking with him than with Tristan. She felt more "friendly" toward Jason than Tristan. The relationship was lighter, and it was seemingly unconditional whereas she brought a certain tempestuousness to her interactions with Tristan. The emotions ran too hot and desperately; but not with Jason. After all, he was the "add on."

Jason used her confidence to learn how impish and astute she actually was. He intended to leverage it against her at the outset (after all, he and Tristan were supposed to subjugate her, considering they were sorcerers and she the incarnation of a siren), but then, it was more fun to behave as if he and the fairy were in collusion in some mischief rather than as if he were commanding her to fulfill his wiles.

She could exert a modest level of magic through improvised witchy spells and had a collection of adorably primitive hand-made wands and other magical flotsam. Jason suspected that she had learned how to divine and scry from observing Tristan and how to charge objects — and ultimately materialize things — from hanging around with Jason. She also was quite the amateur alchemist, which Jason had to begrudgingly acknowledge was Michael Solaris's doing. Most impressive, once Tristan launched her, was that she seemed able to decode encrypted documents in a way similar to that of persons who can instantly calculate complex mathematical equations in their heads.

"You've cut your legs out from under you in this sovereignty—perhaps my legs, too. Thank you so much," Phoenix griped into Jason's ear in the lot while they and a host of askance onlookers watched Tristan and Bella woefully sort things out.

"You've made your point about the 'fairy,'" Phoenix said. "Leave her to fate and go home to the Principalis. Do something else with your life—something pleasant, useful, and inconspicuous—while you still have a life."

Jason couldn't do that. He, like his counterpart, Tristan Lundragon, liked the fairy too much. They were beguiled. Jason even wondered whether he should feel in competition with Tristan about the fairy. He found himself reasoning that he could get an upper hand now that she was so angry with and threatened by Tristan.

On the day following the fray at the Trattoria Centaurus, Jason went by Tristan's place to follow up. He was informed that Bella had spent the night there but not in Tristan's company. Tristan added that he might have to let Bella leave and imagine that she was free. He would have to spend his life protecting yet never interacting with her. It was amazingly odd for Jason to see his heretofore brittle and sinister friend . . . cry over it. Piteously.

"I'm not a happy man. I've not been," Tristan confessed.

"It's been quite obvious, Tristan," Jason replied, "but you're trying too hard and not hard enough. She's beguiled us anyway," he remarked.

"Yes, I know," he sighed dismissively and went on to pine, "How do I compete with Michael Solaris? Did you see the light last night?" Tristan pined. "It was him. Dead and still interloping from a Deep Inner Plane."

"Did you hear what I said about our condition? We—especially you—are beguiled, subjugated through an erotic attachment to that entity," Jason stressed.

Tristan flecked his hand. "Yes, I know," he repeated off-handedly again, as if the notion were a bit of trivia.

"And she put her foot down last night," Jason remarked. "You did not manage that little drama well. In fact, that display was worse than Commons. Besides now thanks to your histrionic antics, everyone knows that she is cuckolding us with the good white knight/closet-magus/ascended-to-a-Deep-Inner-Plane, Michael Solaris," Jason peevishly griped. His intent was to rile and shame Tristan and make his anger flare. Jason just felt like doing it—on a whim. If Tristan got mad and shamed enough, maybe he would reject that fairy and then Jason could have her all to himself.

"Solaris did not much like me and vice versa. He could smite me. He wouldn't, though; would he? Who else would protect her as zealously as I? Who else alive, that is," Tristan sulked.

Of course, Jason couldn't admit that he might consider rising to the occasion. The situation was rather demoralizing. Tristan and Jason ended up having a conciliatory rub-down and mouth action in the solarium on account of it. Meanwhile, the fairy had barricaded herself in a wing of the second floor that Tristan had partitioned off to allow her to feel as if she had a private domain in his milieu. There she remained until midafternoon. The sorcerers suspected she was up and about, though. They supposed she might have been lingering in the master bathroom and that she was knowledgeable about how to use the looking glass kept within it. Why else would the water pressure be lost and the fluid turn bitingly cold while the men were in the throes of more hot carrying on in the shower of the downstairs bath? Someone had to have had simultaneously opened the hot water faucets of a sink and a tub and flushed a toilet several times.

They expected Bella to bolt from the premises in a livid

smolder when she emerged from her confinement if she hadn't already snuck out and run. The sorcerers were discussing this while they, after their intimate repast, dolefully nestled on a sofa facing the large bay window in the den. The fairy appeared and told them that they were behaving in a pathetically Commons manner. She presented them with a platter of red and pink peonies before entering the kitchen.

When Tristan asked where she had acquired those nice flowers in the dead of winter, the fairy said in a proud and wondrous voice that she had made them with her hands. "And I made a yellow butterfly."

She cupped her hands together in an attempt to show them how but became too flustered. So the men demonstrated how such things were done and coaxed her into grasping the poise to duplicate what she had apparently spent much of the day doing: materializing things.

Everything seemed to be okay after that. The three of them spent the night together for the first time, ecstatically banging each other in the midst of butterflies on a voluminous mound of flowers that they had spent the afternoon magically making. The fairy never had to go back to the Orion Club or elsewhere, and Tristan never allowed another woman to touch him in a provocative way again.

So the spring equinox came and went. Then for the summer solstice, the sorcerers gave the fairy an ornate ring made of three intertwined bands of gold, silver, and platinum. The face of the ring consisted of a fiery trillion-cut opal set in a vine and grape motif made of tiny clusters of multicolored jewels. Woven into the grape motif was an emerald snake that had three heads. It represented the alchemical trinity of philosophical sulfur, mercury, and salt—that is, spirit or consciousness, soul or energy, and form. The ring was a token of the sorcerers' partnership with Bellaluna. It was a statement about the bond between the sorcerers as well.

It was official and public; although, given the circumstances, Tristan and Jason did not make many appearances in North Atlantic-Sovereignty social haunts. This all vehemently riled Jason's other consort, Regina Poinciana Magus. She took revenge.

Whenever Jason delayed being accessible to the maga, he could expect something to spill or fall on him. Further, he was beset with odd, often violent dreams that made him thrash and bruise whoever he was sharing the bed with. In addition, it seemed that his penis was slowly losing its usual tone, which was the most horrific aspect of the onslaught as far as he was concerned.

He had tried to reason with the maga until it came to warning her that she did not want him as an enemy. As she well knew, he was very well skilled in coercive and avenging magic.

"You have no power here," Regina scoffed just like Glenda the Good Witch in the Wizard of Oz and pulled her fake maga trip of being above it all.

"Then why are you being such a bitch?" Jason protested.

In truth, hevdid not want to do anything too noxious to Regina despite her bullshit. He was a gentleman, after all. Furthermore, he and she had had a nice-enough history irrespective of the fairy. And it wasn't as if Regina didn't know about Tristan and Jason's great ambition about Dracon's fairy all along.

She knew that Tristan, having discovered the fairy's existence, was going to end up with her and that when he did, he had to share her with Jason. That was the deal. That was the laurel crown that Tristan owed Jason for dedicating his life to Tristan's academic, existential, and magical agendas: the legacy of Lunaris Dracon.

Regina argued that the creature was Tristan's thing. Tristan was Lunaris Dracon. He was destined to embroil himself in the legacy of his past and ultimately consort with that hapless, sinister entity in this life to achieve closure. What was Jason in all this? Tristan's lackey. Jason already had a consort. Why did he need to mix with Tristan's dicey little partner, too? What if she got uppity and killed someone again?

Jason conceded that he did not know why he was so closely linked to the work, but damn if he wasn't going to collect on the spoils of it! He was reduced to begging the bitch-maga not to force him to choose between her and Bellaluna.

"Don't you want a share of what I'm getting out of her?" he cajoled, but Regina cringed, saying that she hadn't been getting much of anything—least of all her due share of Jason's time and affection—since he started in with that thing. Besides, she had become a pariah because of her liaison with Jason. He and Tristan were personae-non-grata in the North Atlantic Sovereignty of Terra Novit now because of the contentiousness over the fairy-creature. They had resorted to living as if denizens in the Outer Plane. It was demeaning, Regina said.

When Jason dropped Regina altogether, all hell broke loose. It was bad timing, considering that the fairy seemed to have been getting along okay with her new life.

Although Jason was inconvenienced, the magical warfare was waged mainly against Bella. It took the form of eerie chaos and poltergeist bugaboos. It was Regina's way of insulting the fairy as well as assaulting her. She chose a motif that particularly confabulated Commons: inexplicable things that went bump in the night.

As with Jason but even more so, the fairy was, thus, continually at risk for being clobbered by spontaneously moving objects and attacked by animated things that were supposed to be inanimate. She could hardly sleep or be alone at night. She claimed that phantoms were assailing her: prosaically floating around, poking her, buzzing in her ears, and banging on walls.

Tristan and Jason assured the fairy that it was an auspicious event—something that all novice sorcerers had to face to test their metal. She was riding the dragon. It was an opportunity to prove herself as a magical person. She would have to figure out how to repel the scorned maga. How she handled it, assuming she did so deftly, would send a warning to the magical community about what reckoning with her was about.

As for Jason, he was hoping that if he pushed back enough and went about his business, Regina would tire. It wasn't as if there weren't a grand hoard of magi and sorcerers who were vying to be next in line for her affections. No doubt dozens were spending their Friday nights performing Venusian love charm rituals in hopes of being her new man. Jason could only pride himself on being a hard act to follow.

He tried to neutralize her onslaughts and monitor Bella lest the fairy get too frustrated and end up unwittingly—or perhaps intentionally—perpetrating irreparable damage—like she had 500 years ago.

And there was another reason why Jason was reluctant to go to war with Regina. Jason had picked up a special power from the fairy soon after the spring equinox. It was something volatile and rare. Jason had to get a handle on it so that he wouldn't use it haphazardly. He kept the news secret from Tristan while yet wondering if the fairy had passed the empowerment onto to him as well.

As for Tristan, he took the assault on Jason and Bella as a personal affront. While his loved ones endured Regina's scorn, he spent hours spying on the maga via his antique looking glass. He went about instigating all sorts of embarrassing and peevish trials for the maga, ultimately conjuring the thought-form of a small but repulsively boil-covered ogre.

The little monster tailed Regina, managing to disrupt all manner of her interactions, and was programmed to duplicate itself off the energy she spent trying to make it go away.

Finally, however, the maga performed a very powerful exorcism. It rebounded on Tristan, causing him to have explosive diarrhea for a week. Further, the fairy accused Tristan of secretly being infatuated with Regina, considering all the time he spent barricaded in the bathroom with her reflection in his giant mirror.

"For all I know, you're whacking off up there!" she scolded. Annoyed, she wandered from Tristan's house and out of the Inner Plane. As was customary whenever she felt slighted or unnerved by him, she made her way to an estate in royally countrified north Stamford where the other one—the add-on, Jason—lived.

The fairy found him making deer on his property disappear—not with a gun or bow, but with his mind. He was making the things dissolve, the act of which forced him to gasp in a way that sounded—and felt—equivocally distressed and orgasmic. It was the Conus magus charm—the rarified thing he had gotten from the fairy that he had to keep secret. He was trying to perform the feat seamlessly, without displaying a reaction.

"Aren't there other, nastier creatures you could be doing that to? Like tics and mosquitos?" Bella quipped.

Jason was naturally startled when the fairy came upon him. Her expression was pinched and repulsed. He assured her that he wasn't "killing" the deer, he was translocating them elsewhere. She scowled and wouldn't look at him for a while, but Jason certainly couldn't admit that he was practicing a secret power that he had caught from having sex with her because she had had sex with Michael Solaris.

He asked her whether Tristan was misbehaving. She blithely joked that the man was in love with "the evil snow queen Christmas shrub lady."

If only it were true, Jason thought. It would make life a lot easier. Besides, it wouldn't have been the first time Jason and Tristan had swapped lovers.

They walked back to the house, which was a not-too grandiose stone Tudor with a terraced patio and lots of windows. It stood in the midst of a wide expanse of woodland acreage complete with crests, gullies, marshes, and rivulets. Jason had acquired it on a whim shortly after he and Tristan crossed over into that region of the Outer Plane. He only recently came to inhabit it. In fact, it was a hiking spot to which Bobby Fludd had often taken the fairy in the late summer past. Bobby had led the fairy to believe they were trespassing on the estate of a filthy rich person who was never home even though it was where Bobby had lived in a cottage on the property.

Upon entering the kitchen, which was large and designer rustic with ruddy wooden walls and copper pots hanging from rafters, Jason and Bella decided that they would make tea and chat about their troubles. Jason asked her how she was getting along with Regina's onslaughts. The fairy said that she couldn't be alone at night anymore because of them. She said she had virtually moved from her condominium apartment and had become Tristan's constant bedmate regardless of whether he wanted to be alone or have some variety.

"You know he's not engaged in 'variety' anymore, Bella," Jason reproached.

"I don't know what anyone is actually 'engaged in,' and it's not my business nor mine theirs," she snapped.

Jason rolled his eyes and bristled. "Why don't you spend time here anymore," he asked. "You have a room upstairs with your needful things in it and luxurious spot in my own bed, which has been remarkably empty these days." He went to embrace her, but half a dozen eggs jumped off a counter and pelted the fairy. When the shock wore off, Bella hollered in expletives that Jason had only otherwise heard Bobby Fludd use. She screamed that she had had enough of the "Christmas Shrub Queen bullshit!"

The fairy vowed, on the top of her lungs, "to rip [the shrub-queen] fucking apart!" after which she asked Jason whether life wouldn't be easier if he just went back with the lady mage.

It wasn't as if Bella and he wouldn't see each other, she reasoned in a weary voice. She argued that Regina had been broken down anyway. The fairy said that the maga would probably be happy just to have Jason's attentions again and would tolerate the rest of it at least for a while.

In any case, when the novelty wore thin and the party was over and everyone was bored because they had sucked Bella dry of vital force, they would conclude that she — now a vapid and crazed wraith (like that Aisa Morae) — was just a Commons person after all. Jason would then go back with Regina anyway, Bella wistfully said. "You and Tristan. And then I'll be nowhere in this fucked-up place because I had sex with vampires. I'll be just like the crazy woman who helped kill Michael."

"Don't play me with that talk," Jason chastised.

"What? I can't say what's true?" she countered.

"Has your head fallen off?" he hollered. He gruffly demanded that she go upstairs, wash up, and change her clothes. He found himself trailing and berating her all the way for persisting in throwing around "this vampire tripe."

"I sacrificed my life to help Lundragon Sortiar find you," he scolded. "That ornament on your ring finger is no trinket from a Crackerjacks box! You're not dismissing me. I'm the sorcerer; you're the fairy. I say when we're through!" He reminded Bella that she was supposed to be a deadly and beguiling siren that was full of threatening knowledge and force.

"Avenge me! Why won't you?" he hollered. She had done it for Tristan centuries ago; why not Jason? Why not rip the world to shreds. Get it over with. "Constantly pining over being gypped out of the 'simple life' with that bloody closet-magus, Michael Solaris!" Jason griped. "How does Tristan put up with you? But then, you are his crowning glory, and you well know how tightly you have him bound. So fuck your fake little piteous pique," he spit. "If you turn me out, you'll fight me, too, because you're mine, whatever you are. You're not at leisure to decide!"

Jason had hollered most of this through a bathroom door beyond which Bella was washing and presumably sulking. It was the first time he had ever raised his voice or uttered such brutally high-handed things to her. She waited for him to stay silent for a long while before opening the door to bolt for a room in that house that had been reserved for her. Jason was waiting in it to resume his tirade.

He thundered that Regina called herself a lady mage as a matter of pretense. She was absolutely nothing like a mage. It was all glamour—all trickery and subterfuge. "She's a sorceress! And no damned puppy with a yapping bark, like you! She has a bite—like a springing viper," Jason snapped. "That poison was delectable, but she's utterly banal in comparison to you and your potential. Do you at all understand what I'm saying to you?" he questioned desperately.

A pane glass window shattered then. The fairy was compelled to duck-and-cover. Jason did not flinch although he was standing in the shattered glass. He hated it when Regina broke into his home. That was why the fairy did not visit anymore.

He quietly sent an earthquake over to the "maga's"

place of residence. Then he took a deep breath and told the fairy that he was waiting for her to do something extraordinary and put everyone in their place. "Else, if you intend to dismiss me, sing me a siren song and put me out of my misery," he said.

Bellaluna rolled her eyes sourly and shook her head only to blanch and weep. Jason wasn't sure whether the heart-rending feeling streaming out of her was terror or awe.

"I want you to love me like you do him," Jason finally said. "More."

The fairy seemed dumbstruck, but the moment was interrupted when the glistening shards of the shattered window threatened to congeal into a glass snake. Bella flinched as the fragments jangled and slid toward her. Without an utterance, Jason materialized his brilliant staff and thrust it into the rubble with such force that the weapon penetrated the wooden floor. The glass turned into ice that steamed to melt into a damp spot.

Jason neared the fairy but did not embrace her. He merely stooped to eye level. "You are the very special and rare consort of two high sorcerers. This is what life is now, Beautiful. The idiocy going on with my former consort and the myriad other niggling and freakish things that you have been encountering are the normal business of the day in this sphere. Acclimate to it. Discover how you are to work with it in your own personal inner world. Love me jealously and singularly regardless of your commitments to Lundragon Sortiar, and do not mention Michael Solaris or Aisa Morae again, neither to me nor Tristan," he stressed. He topped it off by saying that he was madly in love with Bella and hated getting the short end of sharing her.

He kept the fairy cloistered on his property for the ensuing three weeks. He made love to her ferociously and taught her a bag of magical tricks about how to be mind-fucking, energy sapping, and truly darkly sorcerous. He nearly went to war with Tristan about it; but he didn't care.

Regina let up. Word was that her hair was falling out and that her skin was turning ruddy and might even have been darkening.

16
[The Tower]
A Fantabulous Spectacle

The boys might have found their bliss finally, if not for the usual mayhem, which was more than "the usual," actually. But they were controversial figures, Roger Tau Magus-Sortiar told them. That was not going to change however much they strove to look better to others. Besides, they bore the brunt of professional jealousy. Tristan and Jason should have been proud rather than vexed, Roger said. Better to be disparaged than dismissed, he told them.
Albertus Magnus Rogerio "Roger" Tau, SE, MC, PhD — a high sorcerer and celestial mage — was not much older than Tristan Lundragon or Jason Paleologos, but he was their senior academically, magically, and spiritually. He did not hold it over them, though. He was their academic associate and their friend.

He felt that the pair was sincere and formidable and that the two were not sorcerers of the dark sort but essentially had good hearts. Having found Lunaris Dracon's fairy, their goodness shone through in newfound poise and placidity and in the renewed work ethic with which they tackled their archival documents.

The fairy-siren had lulled them alright, but seemingly toward the light and the creative rather than the unknowable and void. She was a moon dragon, the starry head of which was Jupiter and tail of which was Venus — the two prime beneficents among the fixed stars. Good for them. But it was a shame that people wouldn't leave them alone.

It wasn't merely the critical debate about their work.

Interpersonal problems plagued them. Jason had recently split from a woman who he had, until then, identified as his consort. She was a stunning sorceress named Regina Poinciana whose "glamour" was to pose as a maga. Roger had her number right away; but everyone else was duped in a kind of complicit self-denial. Jason may have known what she really was. If he did, it may have been why he liked her so much.

The beautiful "maga," having been cast off by Jason, was on a rampage of scorn and vindictiveness. Between that and ills related to academic rivalries and class status, the tension had taken a toll on the sorcerers and their fairy, but they seemed to be rallying of late.

Roger was dismayed that no one questioned Poinciana Magus's behavior, considering how un-mage–like it was. He was equally appalled that her mentor—if she had one at all—hadn't intervened in the noxious and sometimes violent mischief she was directing toward her estranged partner and the innocent and yet unskilled fairy who had come between her and Jason. But then, if she had a mentor, he or she was not a mage but a wily sorcerer/ess whose expertise was in the arts of glamour and duplicity.

There also was talk, which Roger didn't completely understand, about repercussions concerning political intrigues. He knew that Tristan had a fascination with the Lions of Light movement and that he had been involved in some cloak-and-dagger business when his AWOL apprentice, Robert Fludd, was around. He had thrown off that diversion once he got hold of the fairy. Nevertheless, noxious phenomena that could be interpreted as taunts, threats, and warnings that mimicked but were far more violent than the activity of that spiteful "maga" were abounding.

Tristan confided that he and Jason were being muscled by politically antagonistic persons in Terra Novit. It was not merely Tristan's dabbling in Lions of Light issues; it was related to the link that the fairy haplessly forged between him and Jason and the late Michael Solaris Sortiar. Through her, Tristan and Jason had become Solaris' lineage holders. That is, they had acquired at least some of Solaris' talents. "The Powers-that-Be in Terra Novit know this, and are taking action against us," Tristan blithely said.

The first incident was no small matter. Jason had been in a car accident while driving home from New York City. The brakes went out on his fancy sports car, forcing him to translocate from the Audi R8 in a hair-splitting second before it smashed into the foot of a trestle. The impact caused part of the trestle to collapse, resulting in a 16-car pile-up and an ungodly traffic jam that paralyzed all major roads within a 40-mile radius. It also spurred a commuter railroad inconvenience of catastrophic proportion as well as torturously panicked talk and mobilization among the Commons about the perpetration of terrorist mischief, especially considering that no body was found in the wreckage of Jason's high-end vehicle.

The sorcerer had a concussion from the rapidity with which he had to perform the emergency translocation from the car. He was full of contusions from landing in a free fall from six feet up into the murky and shallow pond in Tristan's yard. He insisted that Tristan not tell the fairy about the incident. She was supposed to have been traveling with Jason but had remained behind in the city to muck around and visit friends.

Tristan insisted that a swift and even deadly response was in order. Jason argued that it wasn't an effect of Regina's magic and that, however annoying her work might be, she would not go to such rabid lengths to undo him. She was a lady mage, after all, Jason told Tristan ridiculously. Magi were supposed to be "spiritual."

"I can thoroughly and irrevocably disarm her if you

can't," Tristan said.

"Don't," Jason insisted.

"Go back to her and leave us alone then," Tristan remarked.

At that, in accordance with the nature of the dynamic between this sorcerer duo, Jason one-upped his companion by disclosing that the fairy had passed a very provocative empowerment to him. The point, however, was that he was being marked because of it—marked for death.

In retelling the tale to his wise friend Roger, Tristan wouldn't disclose what the empowerment was, but it was obvious that he was referring to the deadly Conus magus charm. Tristan seemed strained—hurt—that the fairy had passed it to Jason instead of him despite what was happening to Jason as a consequence. Roger had to remind Tristan that he had achieved everything he ever wanted because of that fairy.

"You do a disservice by being soured by Jason's lot rather than grateful for your own," Roger told Tristan. "Invidia—envy—is the deadly sin within the domain of Leviathan, the serpent of chaos."

Tristan scorned Roger for playing up the magus-talk, but Roger was not offended. He was confident that Tristan, regardless of his attitude, had taken the words to heart.

Tristan had become a celebrity, in fact. He had just taken on a visiting professorship appointment at a prestigious school—the Bythos Academy of Magical Sciences—within the capital of the North Atlantic Sovereignty, but he and Jason had become recluses in reaction to everything that was going on. It had been many weeks since either Tristan or Jason had visited the Orion Club or any other hot spot in the Inner Plane.

Rumors buzzed that the fairy had rebuffed Tristan after that incident at the Trattoria Centaurus and was the sole property of Jason Paleologos now. Tristan's aloofness encouraged these rumors. Then a nasty little girl claiming to be the true, official lineage-holder of Michael Solaris Sortiar came forward. She was the 17-year-old fledging sorceress named Leela Solaris, the niece and apprentice of Michael Solaris Sortiar.

Leela said that the fairy was not only thriving and deceptively viral, but was very much still with both of the two dark sorcerers, who she claimed were accessories to Solaris' death. The teenager persistently asserted that far from being the servant or tool of the two controversial foreign sorcerers, the fairy was the sorcerers' shared consort. She also insisted that the sorcerers were bound and beguiled by the entity and that the entity had stolen the girl's promised inheritance.

She said she had it on good word from Robert Fludd (of all people) that the fairy controlled the sorcerers even though their evil plan was to use the fairy to steal what she had stolen from Solaris.

"She has things of my uncle that belong to me," Leela insisted. "If she shows her face in the Inner Plane, my family will totally trash her," the girl avowed.

In truth, however, members of the Solaris clan — primarily those on the Terra Novit-side of the geographical divide — disavowed any association with their assassinated relative. They wanted nothing to do with the retrieval of his "things." Most did not want to jeopardize their standing among their peers. Others presumably did not want to intercept the fairy because it would mean broaching magical warfare with the notorious foreign sorcerers that she belonged to (or who belonged to her). Meanwhile, other kin — Michael Solaris' parents and other close relations over there in the Terra Principalis — were in a race with Tristan Lundragon to find the celestial mage Anderson Albright, who would know the truth about the whole situation.

Roger had asked Tristan if the fairy was indeed in

possession of Solaris Sortiar's staff.

Tristan confirmed that she was.

"Have you seen it?" Roger asked.

"No," Tristan quietly replied.

When Roger pressed him about it, Tristan told Roger that it was a forbidden topic of discussion. "We do not speak on it. I respect her privacy," he said.

"Do you think she understands how to use a staff?" Roger questioned.

"Oh, yes," Tristan replied.

When Roger then told Tristan that he was becoming quite placid now that he had attained his life's goals, Tristan grunted thoughtfully and said "thank you."

Roger encouraged him, Jason, and the fairy to make an appearance at the Orion Club to make a statement about their contentment and perseverance in the face of petty obstructions and adversities. Roger argued that the gesture was important especially that Tristan had become such a big celebrity because of his Dracon work, with stampedes of students from the Bythos Academy begging, pleading, cajoling, and offering to prostitute themselves to be his apprentices.

It was important for Jason to mingle among peers, too, Roger argued. In his seclusion, the sorcerer had resumed interests in artistic endeavors. He was creating very interesting multidimensional conceptual pieces that were not made of paint, wood, stone, polymers, glass, ceramics, metal, computer graphics, video footage, or holographic projections like Commons art was. They were multilayered thought-form experiences that were visually stunning to observe and mysterious and awesome to feel once one was in close-enough proximity to them. They emitted mind-altering vibrational patterns, polyphonic sounds, color frequencies, and phantasms and were in the style of a one-time mentor that Jason, like Tristan's situation with

Anderson Albright, had alienated himself from. That mentor was a mage, too, and a woman. Her name was Dorrie Auriel.

She had a son who, like Tristan, was now a professor at the Bythos Academy even though he also had grown up in the Terra Principalis. He was a strange, nerdy character named Aurelio Zosimo. Tristan and Jason were in the habit of tormenting him back in the day despite that Jason was apprenticing with Dorrie.

Zosimo grew up to be a sorcerer with a mean streak for vengeance and supposedly had some kind of special relationship with a famous magian adept named Sofia La Maga. She was the one and only wife of the head of the Lions of Light, the renegade ex-Consul Leo de Lux Sortiar. Thus, Tristan took special pains to avoid Zosimo while ambling through the corridors of the Bythos Academy. In any event, Jason had it in his mind that, on top of the rest of it, this Zosimo Sortiar was also throwing pot-shots at him for what he and Tristan had done to him when they were kids.

He stoically endured it and also pressed on in his academic work with Tristan: he and Tristan, together with Roger, the fairy, and sometimes their other associate, Phoenix Dionysus. They had either published or were preparing numerous papers — both light and heady — that focused on the Dracon material.

Mediumship, Stenography, and Steganography: Communications between Commons and the Higher Planes in Low Renaissance Europe.

Sirens, Psychopomps, and the Fairy Familiars of Lunaris Dracon.

Thought and Feeling in the Interpretation of The

Beauteous Consort of the Mirour of Luna.

Visceral Excitotoxicity and Dracon Tract-Induced Enlightenment.

Roger wondered whether Tristan had acquired a special understanding of the Dracon work. That is, he wondered whether Tristan had grasped the profundity of it while yet remaining in the body. The hint was in how Tristan had become so less smoldering and crass and so more introspective and placid. It was as if, despite the petty onslaughts and uppitiness of those around him, he had cast off a burden. His behavior was almost like that of someone who had received something called a Pyr Sacra empowerment. He seemed in possession of a graceful self-transformation.

There was talk about enrolling the fairy in Bythos Academy. Roger thought it was a great idea. Tristan was all for putting the fairy through school so that she could acquire a magical degree. Jason, on the other hand, said she would be better left to her own devices, considering that she was being mentored by expert sorcerers of distinction. Besides, who could really teach her anything? She was an otherkin belonging to the Fates—a wisdom being. She was transliterating the Dracon texts and coauthoring papers, after all.

Attending school would be a distraction and probably a nuisance, he said. If her name appeared on enough papers and if she eventually managed to perform some kind of fantabulous spectacle, some institution would award her an honorary degree, Jason argued.

Tristan countered that "fantabulous spectacles" were out of the question. Jason said that it was the only way that they would be able to best their enemies.

"Your enemies," Tristan countered.

Then the bitter bickering that progressed to physical roughness ensued between the two, but that was the way they had carried on for years. If it were not because of the fairy, it would have been because of some other melodrama.

In any case, at Roger Tau's bidding, Tristan, Jason, and the fairy went to the Orion Club to show everyone that they were alive and very much together. Admirers swarmed around them and detractors jeered.

They hadn't been there for 20 minutes when a frantic ado was provoked because the lighting fixture that made the ceiling of the place look like the night sky crashed down within centimeters of Jason's feet.

Giggles and hoots from the periphery of the club went up as Jason shirked away from the mess. Tristan materialized his staff and reached for the fairy. She, however, bolted from him, stomping through the crowd with fiery eyes turned toward those who mocked her. She was mumbling something like, "Enough with this stupid bullshit."

"It's not her, Bella," Tristan yelped because, of course, the fairy was headed for an overdue cat-fight with Regina Poinciana Magus.

Roger watched the fairy scowl and fleck her hand back at Tristan.

Regina was propped against one of the many bar counters and trying her best to maintain the captivation of her companions while mayhem erupted around her. She was ignoring the fray.

When the fairy came upon her, the maga placed her drink on the counter. Turning to face the creature head on, she flared out her milky white arms as if she were an angel spreading wings. She emitted an opalescent glow besides.

"What can I teach you about yourself today, Bella?" the maga said.

"Well," the fairy paused, "I was wondering if you could tell me what this is?" With a showy twist at the wrist, she displayed a beige and white dappled cone snail. A Conus magus. The creature's needle-like legs as well as a stinger flirted from the shell's aperture.

"Some people think I may have a really nasty power named after this little thing. I got it from having sex with a guy named Michael Solaris. You know the story," Bella boasted. "Do you know which one of my new special friends is infected with the Conus magus charm now because of me?"

The maga winced disgustedly and breathily scoffed. She was about to walk away when the fairy flecked the venomous crustacean dead-on at her.

With impressive reflex action, Regina materialized a glistening staff topped with a pale-blue figurine resembling the statuette of a Roman goddess. She used it like a bat to deflect the dangerous sea creature that was hoisted at her.

Roger watched the fairy smile, as if amused by the way the snail was launched through the air. A mad scatter ensued when the thing bounced off Tristan's head. At that, the fairy lunged at Regina, screaming that the maga was a "killer, another EEL!"

A melee of staffs abounded around the fairy and maga then.

Roger was confused. He felt panicked. He watched Tristan bolt toward the ruckus within a now amassed crowd. Jason appeared dumbstruck and held back. Roger couldn't tell whether he was appalled or fascinated.

Aghast screams finally went up, with only the bravest among the club's occupants yet holding the fairy and maga apart. A strange and utterly awesome apparition lay before them.

Regina had fallen and sat, shrinking back, on the floor. Hovering over her, restrained in a web of staffs, was a winged creature on which was draped the torn-out flowery pink dress that Bellaluna had been wearing that evening. The creature's wings were feathered in bright and shimmery opalescent blues, greens, and violets, like those of a tropical bird. A long, piscine tail covered in multi-colored jewel-like scales coiled out from where legs were supposed to be. The tip ended in a trio of tail fins that wagged and slapped the floor, threatening to whack Regina's if they could only inch closer to her.

With a face now whiter than white, the Regina Poinciana was screaming that Jason Paleologos Sortiar was consorting with a monster.

As the fairy's companions edged closer, they could see that the creature she had become had human arms. The right was caught at the wrist by intersecting staffs. It did not end in a hand but bright red talons, like the claw of a large bird. It gripped a fiery golden staff. The staff was topped with a figurine made of gold, citrine, and topaz that depicted an angel spearing a seven-headed dragon. There was no doubt whose staff it had once belonged to.

The left arm, also ending in a talon, gripped Regina's glistening staff. The flesh of that arm was ruddy — blanched in patches, taut and blistering; burned, in fact, by the charge the maga issued through the weapon when the scuffle began.

The creature's wings flapped and the tail bristled when Tristan and Jason approached. The siren — as that is what it appeared to be — ducked and thrashed to keep the two men from seeing her face, but they had to get a glimpse, of course.

From their breathless expressions, Roger could only gather that they were observing something exceptionally sublime. It was almost as if the two sorcerers were compelled to kneel, with the way they hesitated on their feet and got all sappy and red in the eye.

A wondrous creature. A fantabulous spectacle. Approaching, Roger observed that the face of their transfigured damsel had become perfect and idealized. Her eyes had become rounder and birdlike with sultry, purplish lids, and her skin had a shimmery, translucent, blue-violet hue. Her golden ringlets of hair had turned bright orange and flame-like.

While Tristan implored the siren not to speak, Jason and Regina volleyed biting words. The maga swore that she was not behind the attacks on him, and how dare he insinuate such a pathetically insane notion!

"Get it off! Get it off me!" she finally screamed and went back to hollering that Paleologos Sortiar had become unutterably perverse in his magical and sexual tendencies. She claimed that he, Lundragon Sortiar, and their infernal creature had been harassing her for months!

"You're in big trouble, 'friend,'" she yelped at her ex-consort. "I'll SUE you. I'll have you deported and exiled! The whole lot of you! And believe me, someone will send that thing back to the Netherworld!"

The siren's grip on Regina's staff faltered as the transfiguration began to ebb. Jason caught the staff and told the creature to keep hold of it. "It's yours now. You've earned it," he said. The maga screamed in protest, piteously wailing that Jason was abominably cruel. Someone hauled her up and dragged her away.

Meanwhile, persons were handing Jason and Tristan albs, dalmatics, and other pieces of apparel with which to clothe the fairy once she lost her tail, wings, and talons, and became a person again.

A polished gentleman who Roger knew was a foreign diplomat beckoned the sorcerers—Roger and Phoenix included—to follow him into a private salon within the club.

"Gregory Hrasvelg Sortiar," the man said, extending a

hand to Tristan. Hrasvelg was an ambassador from a Nordic sovereignty in the Terra Principalis. "I know your work," the dignitary added. He nodded with a slight wink of the eye and motioned toward the fairy who, although protectively nuzzled between Tristan and Jason, was not quite right. Her breathing was strained. She winced and shuddered now and then.

"Utterly marvelous. An utterly marvelous transfiguration," the ambassador exclaimed. "She worked with Solaris Sortiar?"

"Solaris Sortiar discovered her," Tristan murmured as if it were true and candid rather than galling to admit. "Fallen to the realm of Commons. I retrieved her after Solaris' assassination. We both studied with a high sorcerer named Anderson Albright Magus years ago in our youth. Well, Michael was a few years behind me . . . my junior. Of all of us, he was the closest to Albright," Tristan mused. "I was the throw-away."

"Solaris Sortiar was very close with Leo de Lux Sortiar," Hrasvelg said in a barely audible voice.

Tristan bristled with brows that were pained and perplexed. "Was he?"

"de Lux very much wants to avenge our felled comrade," the ambassador said. His eyes slyly swept toward the fairy.

Tristan harrumphed and gritted his teeth.

Jason's face, in turn, appeared to darken in anger at what the ambassador was suggesting. "We have our own problems," he growled.

"They're the same problems as those of Solaris but they need not end the same way," Hrasvelg countered.

"I'm not interested in your politics," Jason said.

"Yes; but your associate is," Hrasvelg replied. He gestured toward Tristan.

Tristan protested that he worked alone for the sake of

self-interest. "I am not being 'recruited,' and Bella especially not," he said matter-of-factly. When he glanced at her, his eyes flared and his face blackened. "She's injured!" he exclaimed.

Indeed, her pained and wincing disposition was because the burns on her arm, sustained form her magical fray with Regina Poinciana Magus, were no illusion. Transfiguring into dark things to match their indignant fury, Tristan and Jason stormed from the salon and back into the club. A magical rumble ensued that wrecked the place.

17
[The Star]
Three Things

Before returning to the Terra Principalis after a bit of a ramble, Bobby cut his hair and shaved, as suggested long ago by that bastard Tristan Lundragon Sortiar. The make-over revealed the prominence of Bobby's forehead. His nose looked bigger and his eyes were deeper set and darker. Bobby also took to wearing black pants, matching sports jackets, white shirts, and thin black ties, rendering him into a cross between a secret service agent and a maitre'd.

He was working with Alba Sandalphon Magus now. She was a stern and stoic woman who was kind and doting toward Bobby. Bobby reciprocated the tenderness and embellished it with reverence and gratitude.

A day came when the maga paid him a visit at the crack of dawn in the small apartment he lived in on the outskirts of the Royal Dominion of Principalis Academy of Magical Arts and Sciences pavilion. Sandalphon told Bobby that Leo de Lux Sortiar wanted to have an audience with him post-haste. When Bobby got the news, he was shaken.

"The Lion of Light?" Bobby gasped incredulously.

Alba gracefully smiled and nodded. "He's heard good things," she said and winked.

"You are the Sovereign Goddess of the Cosmos," Bobby blurted.

The maga bowed her head, blushed, and told Bobby that it wasn't so much that she had put in a good word with de Lux; Bobby had independently come to the great sorcerer's attention. It had to do with those renegade fairies flitting around the Outer Plane and with "that dreadful Solaris-assassination business more than two years ago. It seems Solaris had close ties with the Lions of Light. He was a confidante of Leo and his son. And he was another adept of the Conus magus charm," Alba hushed.

"No way," Bobby gasped again.

"Yes, quite. Quite quite," Alba stressed. "That's why they killed him."

Bobby winced thinking he had wasted so much time; he should've apprenticed with Solaris, not Lundragon.

"Be friendly and personable in your meeting with de Lux," Alba instructed. "Be genuine; let him ascertain your talents, your curious eccentricities, and your guile. Let him be entertained by the uniqueness of your character. If he takes a liking to you, you'll have your redemption. You'll have won a great prize."

Alba Sandalphon Magus was close to de Lux. The maga had used her judicial influence to save the high sorcerer's consort, Sofia La Maga Magus. La Maga Magus had been under threat of being imprisoned or exiled after being implicated in the death of a diabolical sorceress named Medea Sarin.

The story was as complex as it was convoluted. The sorceress's real killer was not La Maga Magus but a trio of sorcerers to whom La Maga was dear: de Lux; La Maga's mentor Dr. Giordano Bruno, who was the dean of the H. Trismegistus Mystical Arts Academy; and an odd fellow named Aurelio Zosimo, who was a professor at the Bythos Academy. The only person who knew this was Alba, who also suspected that Aurelio Zosimo was related to Sofia La Maga because they looked very much alike. All three sorcerers killed the sorceress Medea Sarin perhaps to share in the responsibility — or the honor — but they made it look as if La Maga did it because the sorceress was on the brink of killing La Maga during a public sports event in which the two women were magically jousting.

The sorceress had overcome the maga and was threatening to impale her with a staff that was hovering overhead like a missile ready to drop. Just when it seemed that the maga was done for, the staff shattered to bits, and the sorceress exploded into flames that festered into a stinky cloud of ruddy smoke.

Medea Sarin Sortiar was not working alone in her violence against Sofia La Maga Magus, though. She was in collusion with the maga's arch-nemesis Hipparchus Gorgon Sortiar. Gorgon was subsequently taken out later, supposedly by La Maga's apprentice, Leonard de Lux Junior.

The stories were like Wild West stuff—the Inner Planes version of it—a double-fisted shoot-em-up free-for-all but packed with magical intrigue. The tales made Bobby feel as if he were part of the action. They also made Bobby feel as if he were a close associate of the de Lux clan. Being close to Alba Sandalphon Magus was almost like being in their inner circle. And it could happen now. "Quite quite."

Bobby did not meet de Lux Sortiar in Terra Novit. That would be too dangerous. The Master once had presided as something of a governor (a so-called "consul") of Terra Novit's North Atlantic Sovereignty, but he was a persona-non-grata now. Like Bobby, he was living in exile in the Outer Plane, but also like Bobby, he had the wiles and balls to come and go as he pleased anyway.

Sandalphon helped Bobby pack lightly and saw him off to New York City. He met de Lux in a posh office in an architecturally historic building on the Upper East Side. It was one of the sites where the sorcerer dealt in high-end art and antiques. The floors and walls were marble, and the high ceilings were encrusted with gilded plaster molding. Tiffany and carnival glassware abounded as did flowering tropical plants despite that the plants could not have had sufficient light or moisture in that cavernous office environment. Colorful butterflies flounced around as did tiny tropical and apparently non-crapping birds, both seemingly kept alive—like the plants—by de Lux's magical will.

Bobby expected de Lux to be in the company of an entourage but the only other person with him was a husky but debonair man named Victor. He was standing amid three tawny, snub-faced boxer hounds when he greeted Bobby. He nodded slightly and smiled faintly. "Robert Fludd," Victor stated and nodded again as if impressed by whatever he had heard. He said the name louder as if announcing it, at which de Lux emerged from an adjacent room.

Bobby trembled when the man appeared. He wasn't much taller or broader than Lundragon Sortiar but he had a big presence—as if he were very large and very bright. Most intimidating were the man's eerie white-blue eyes.

de Lux smiled in a fascinated way at Bobby's reaction to the sight of him. "Robert Fludd! My ace spy-master," he said in a gentrified New York accent.

"Honored. It's an . . . . I'm honored, Sir," Bobby stuttered.

"Sandalphon Magus was worried that you're more of a thrill seeker," de Lux remarked.

"Sandalphon Magus doesn't appreciate how much I appreciate her," Bobby replied. "Not aware of the lengths of it," he stressed.

"Mmm," de Lux mused with icy scrutiny. "You once were an enterprise onto yourself actually," he remarked in a peeved tone. "You and your randy, interloping, foreign, and unofficial mentor, the moon dragon man." He sighed wearily. "I don't begrudge you. It was brilliant, actually, but it's all fallen through, hasn't it?"

de Lux invited Bobby into the room from which he had

emerged. It was a wood-paneled study full of antique European furniture, velvet, more Tiffany and carnival glass, elaborately sculptured blown glass, and abstract multimedia mobiles. Abstract Expressionist paintings hung on walls, and incongruously flowering tropical plants and distracting butterflies abounded. A weepy sonata for cello was quietly pervading the airwaves.

"Your family — parents and a brother — were disappeared, I was told," de Lux said.

Bobby grunted. It was a fact he forced himself not to recall. Sometimes disappeared persons were annihilated — as Solaris Sortiar allegedly had been. This was probably the least horrific fate of the disappeared. Some were rendered frozen in comatose cataleptic states or were otherwise discombobulated and holed up in Outer Plane's psychiatric facilities or prisons — or were brain-fried and on the streets.

"There are mystical methods to redeem persons from damnation," de Lux remarked. "Few persons are ever truly lost, but the person who attempts to call back or guide the lost must be very clean and clear."

de Lux was referring to an elaborate ceremony called the Lux Clarus rite. Its performance was the domain of very high-level magi, such as de Lux's wife, Sofia La Maga Magus, and a very few crossover sorcerers, such as Roger Tau and Aurelio Zosimo. It was used to guide the newly departed to appropriate afterlife realms. The rite also was used to retrieve persons who had been disappeared and awaken people who had been put into cataleptic paralysis as a form of capital punishment.

de Lux commented that if Bobby's family had been aligned with the Lions of Light, he might've been able to intercept the tragedy. He had learned about the Fludds and their work long after the fact. "Too many factions riding a wave of discontent," he mused. "It is a relentless and violent game. Lust, power, oppression, and the will to freedom make the world go round relentlessly," he said.

de Lux produced a bottle of scotch whiskey and poured out a shot for Bobby after inviting him to take a seat. Bobby gulped half the shot and watched de Lux swill his own. de Lux refilled both glasses. Bobby observed the man transform his own glass into a tumbler within which two ice cubes formed. The Master pointed to Bobby's glass as if asking whether he would like the same. Bobby figured that he should humor the man and, thus, found himself sipping scotch on the rocks.

Bobby fidgeted. Then he asked de Lux to tell him why he had been summoned.

de Lux shrugged. A corner of his mouth twitched as did his eyebrows. He opened a clasped hand within which was a Lion of Light medallion. It was a thin gold disc on which was embossed — in a thin platinum thread — a glyph of a leaping lion in a sun circle.

de Lux placed the medallion and its chain beside Bobby's glass. He gave a reassuring nod and a wink. Bobby quietly grasped the medallion.

"You need to resume your intrigues with the fairy business. I don't want to lose what's his name," de Lux said.

Bobby pursed his eyebrows, not knowing who the Master meant.

"Your mentor's partner. The other encryption expert," de Lux announced.

"Paleologos Sortiar?" Bobby uttered incredulously.

"Yes. Him. The both of them . . . sharing Solaris Sortiar's fairy," de Lux tsked. "They're 'double-sided,' you know. Him and Lundragon. You did know that, Robert? Men in love." de Lux rolled his icy white-blue eyes and shrugged. "Solaris Sortiar's uncle Reggie was the same way — but love had nothing to do with it. The man had five wives all at once besides. A bit of a satyr. He was my best and oldest friend before my own transformation," de Lux mused and returned back to the fairy business.

"You see, Robert, I'm a little troubled," he said. "I got it from a very close and infallible source that the fairy materialized a cone snail at the Orion Club as a threatening gesture toward a sorceress who poses as a maga. A cone snail," de Lux stressed. "It was witnessed by very many people—that and a rather provocative transfiguration."

Bobby merely pinched his eyebrows, looked perplexed, and waited for more of the story.

"She transfigured into a mythical creature—a siren complete with wings, talons, red eyes, fangs, and a fish tail—or so it was said by some accounts. And she disarmed a sorceress who poses as a maga," de Lux related.

"Regina Poinciana Magus?" Bobby questioned and rued all of the action he was missing.

"The ex-consort of that man who now consorts with the fairy and the Lundragon fellow. The siren accused the woman of being a killer, like 'Morae,'" he said slyly.

"I really don't think the guys would tell her about the Conus magus charm or put her up to that," Bobby said. "Paleologos—he might twist her up, but Lundragon would never go there. He's paranoid about not repeating what happened 500 years ago when she got too smart and killed somebody . . . supposedly."

"My thinking is that she caught the Conus magus charm from our good friend and comrade Michael Solaris Sortiar and passed it on to her new companions like an STD. It also is possible that through her own wiles, she is now privy to certain intrigues that her men may not even be aware of. You know, it's really not a good idea to fuck with fairies," de Lux quipped.

"Yeah, I've been told," Bobby muttered sourly.

"They absorb and transmit things inscrutably. Very few magical persons really know what they're doing when they start in with these creatures," de Lux said. "Solaris was an exceptional magical person, but this was his hubris. A plague might be wrought upon us now on account of it, Robert. Besides, I have it on good word that the Orion Club got wrecked after the fairy transfiguration-incident because the thing's two consorts got into a snotty tiff after noticing that she was injured in the scuffle she had had with the maga-imposter. Well, perhaps that kind of martial 'gallantry' is 'love,' but I liked the Orion Club," de Lux whined. "Now it's closed."

"Just for a week, Sir," Bobby consoled. "But neither of us can go there anyway."

"Yes, well . . ." de Lux sighed. He rubbed his knuckles against his chin and snickered ruefully. "This Terra Principalis fairy mystique is very quaint, you know." He rolled his icy eyes and grinned smugly. "It's a shame I can't pick Michael's brain about it now." With that, de Lux sighed heavily and brooded before launching into a diatribe:

"For me, there is no mistaking a thought-form from a conscious entity — not to say that there isn't an illusory, fabricated, and circumstantial thought-form–like quality to all things. True power comes from really, really penetrating this," de Lux said.

"There are all classes of creatures and words by which we define these creatures — ordinary and otherwise. What we want to believe and make others into and how we expect them to behave for better or worse shapes reality, but we don't experience reality. Instead, we experience perceptions and expectations. It's narcissistic and stupefying because, in truth, we only experience others as reflections of our minds — as thought-forms, that is — not as who and what they really are, and we pay a price for this and are pathetic because of it.

"Accidental thought-forms are dangerous. The habit of

denying reality and superimposing thought constructs over it is dangerous," de Lux said. "When things turn wrong because of this, we become confused and disappointed, angry and horrified—but then we adjust our viewpoint, revise, edit, make it fit. This is called The Grand Illusion. It causes turmoil and bewilderment and the spinning of the wheel of phenomenal existence.

"These fairy-creatures that you fellows are courting are unusual—unusual for the environment into which they've haplessly alighted," de Lux continued. "I wouldn't call them 'fairies,' though. They could be anything. Have you ever heard of a mage named Albright? He was Solaris Sortiar's mentor."

Bobby shrugged and, lying, volunteered that he had been asked to locate him but had blown off the assignment. In reality, however, Bobby had indeed found Albright Magus in a remote hermitage. He had remained with him for many months in which time Bobby had long conversations with the mage and took on magian disciplines.

"Well, I need to conference with this Albright Magus fellow, so you'll have to rise to the occasion and find him," de Lux muttered. "I can't have him hiding. If anyone, you're the man who can retrieve him." He smiled as if pleased with Bobby and arose from his chair. "Stand up," he ordered. "I'm going to do something that I don't do lightly."

Before Bobby could brace himself, de Lux jabbed his fingers dagger-like into young man's sternum and clasped his other hand over the top of Bobby's head in a rather brusque maneuver. An incredible heat surged through Bobby's body—from a point in his scrotum to the top of his head. It seemed to burst open into blinding white light. Bobby's eyes fluttered and teared on the vision of scintillation and fire.

"Seraphim," Bobby gasped.

de Lux snickered. The man loosened his grip and positioned Bobby so that he would collapse into a large upholstered wing chair when he let go.

Bobby sat with eyes closed, breathing gently and feeling so contented and physically uncontained that he thought he should panic. He felt like a helium balloon that was giddily floating away to the stratosphere after having escaped from the grip of a child.

It had to have been the Pyr Sacra empowerment. Bobby had heard of it. It was only transmitted by very high-level magical persons to those they deemed exceptionally deserving. It unleashed the secret fire that then seared through all the personal limitations of consciousness — the instilled neuroses and unfortunate complications — that sabotage expression of an underlying jewel in a person.

Bobby had assumed that mercurial Lundragon was incapable of transmitting such an empowerment. Bobby never figured on being the recipient of it although he expected that Lundragon would eventually break down and give him some kind of special something. After all, in their last "heart-to-heart," Lundragon had explicitly told Bobby that he would be the sorcerer's lineage holder if he got his act together, which he had except that he had abandoned Lundragon in the process.

"Clean and clear," Bobby heard de Lux mutter. The man was patting Bobby's shoulder and chewing on an apple. "But an expert sorcerer maintains his glamour. Don't lose that edge that your mentor has become so fondly exasperated with. A sorcerer is no good unless he's a bit wily and irascible. Otherwise, he may as well take up magianism," de Lux scoffed.

Bobby uttered that Alba Sandalphon was his mentor now. de Lux winced and shook his head as if the idea were ludicrous. "There are mentors and then there are teachers who you 'sit near.' Those ancillary persons may make more pleasant company and inspire you but the villainous mentor . . . well, he is what he is," de Lux said. "I suppose it's me now. Technically. But you're going to have to go back to the encryption expert, even though it 'bites.'" de Lux then went on to press Bobby about the fairy.

"She was supposedly conjured by the occultist Lunaris Dracon back in the 15th or 16th century. You know who he is?" Bobby inquired.

"I'm aware of the story," de Lux replied gruffly. "He reincarnated as the encryption expert Tristan Lundragon. Allegedly. The fairy disposed of Dracon's wife in a beatific manner. Dracon met his end at the stake because of it."

"Yeah, well, Lundragon Sortiar created a pact with Albright Magus to basically prepare and mentor the fairy through Solaris, who fell in love with her and vice versa," Bobby recounted. "Albright supposedly is afraid of fairies, but Lundragon was trying to snap him out of it and also maybe help Albright think he was turning the screws on Solaris for what Solaris did to him with that psycho Aisa 'Moray' Eeeel-fairy who ended up getting Solaris killed," Bobby blurted. "You know what they say about the wrath of scorned women."

de Lux cracked an amused and wizened grin. Bobby continued relating the saga about Solaris and Lundragon.

"So, Solaris went and got himself killed and broke the good fairy's heart," Bobby said as if reciting a fairy tale. "Then I was recruited to step in to get her back to Ha!PPY while Albright skinned out with a hair shirt and a flailing whip in his suit case. Anyway, Lundragon was still working on the fairy—now through me, but I was just supposed to be her good friend. Then, when she got back to normal, Lundragon figured he better stick it in her before I did because, you know, I was just pushed to the edge . . .

It's her handwriting on all of those Dracon documents. That's what this is all about. But I would love her like Solaris did," Bobby blurted. "Lundragon just wants to use her—him and his fuck-friend Jason Paleologos."

de Lux brooded quietly for a while before turning a compassionate eye on Bobby and ordering the young man to keep watch over the fairy and out of harm's way for a bit longer. Bobby stalwartly told de Lux that he would do whatever he was asked.

de Lux nodded and smiled soberly. "You need to do that without getting in Lundragon Sortiar's way. I'm sure the lady is fonder than fond of you, Robert, but you're no rival in matters of coercion and amour."

Bobby huffed dejectedly.

"Lundragon and his male companion need to be preserved as well. In any case, if the 'fairy' is what she is and finds herself mixing body fluids, etcetera with these sorts, you can be sure that she will make a mark on circumstance. Who knows? She may even vindicate you. You know what the Bible says about love. It is always ready to excuse, to trust, to hope, and to endure whatever comes. It does not come to an end yet all other things must and are intrinsically flawed. But in the end, three things last: faith, hope, and love. You'll learn it. It's what's kept you alive so far."

Bobby sighed and shrugged.

Before he left the office, de Lux gave him a staff. A magician only gave a staff to a junior magician as a symbol of mentorship and transference of power. Bobby felt faint taking hold of it. Three long wands of wood: cedar, holly, and olive, were bound into the staff's filigreed bronze sheathing. Bits of different colored stones speckled the metalwork, and the finial was a carnelian statuette of a griffin, a winged creature with the head of an eagle and the body of a lion. Carnelian was associated with vigor, the sun, Venus, and Mars. And the griffin was a symbol of royalty, heraldry, courage, and foresight.

de Lux made Bobby recount the three things he had been asked to do: find Albright Magus, keep the fairy out of trouble, and protect the sorcerers Lundragon and Paleologos. "You need to tell them to tread lightly. They're no longer living in the shadows . . . parading that entity around the Inner Plane—the Orion Club, no less—and instigating mayhem and destruction of property," de Lux clucked. "Not wise. Lundragon's ambitions will be the death of him. Again."

"Gotcha," Bobby said.

"If he cherishes his 'fairy,' he will mend her set of broken wings and let her fly again—for his own good. Five hundred-odd years is a long time to hold onto something. Perhaps you can communicate this to him."

Bobby reluctantly nodded. The only appealing thing about reconciling with Lundragon was that he could stick it in the sorcerer's face that he was Leo de Lux Sortiar's man now. The playing field would be leveled. Quite quite. In fact, Bobby would have the upper hand.

As he strolled from the office sidled beside his good friend and mentor, Leo de Lux, Bobby realized that his anatomy had changed. He was not limping, and he was no longer in pain.

18

[The Moon]
Samekh

Y ou're looking 'dapper,' Bobby," Tristan grunted cautiously.

The younger man flexed an eyebrow at the senior sorcerer.

"It's been a long while. Word is you've left me for another man," Tristan jeered. He stoked the fireplace and offered Bobby a seat across from him among the settee and chairs surrounding a small coffee table in the solarium.

"Scotch or tea these days?" Tristan asked Bobby. Wincing, he passed his hand over a festive plate of baked goods and confections. "They're laced with alchemical elixirs, I'm sure. Consume them at your own risk," he grumbled. Bobby would know from whom the darling edibles came: Bellaluna.

"I haven't considered that I've 'left' you, Lundragon Sortiar," Bobby said dryly. "But I've been initiated . . . officially." Bobby propped up a beautiful staff. It was made of three woods and bronze sheathing and was topped with a ruddy, crystalline figurine of a griffin. A happy feeling that Tristan tried to smother sparked in him. He thought Bella would be very proud of Bobby.

"And who is this new master, Robert?" Tristan asked.

"Leo de Lux Sortiar," the young man replied.

A brief but woozy shock seized Tristan. "Really?"

"Yeah. Really," Bobby uttered impudently.

Tristan nodded.

"He's known about you for a while," Bobby remarked. "The Work. He's well DIS-posed with you." The fellow then announced that he was ready for the scotch. He requested that it be served in a snifter with a few drops of water, as if he had become some kind of whisky connoisseur. He took an almond-laden chocolate biscuit from the tray, snapped off a bite, and mentioned that a "hit" of espresso might be nice as well.

Tristan sat contemplating the news and observing Robert Fludd Sortiar. All cleaned up, stalwart, and cocky. He was far beyond Tristan's control now. A veritable "Lion of Light" and yet more—allegedly taken under the wing by the Lion of Light himself, Leo de Lux Sortiar.

de Lux probably had thousands of apprentices, all lined up cult-like at devotional gatherings to receive group "initiations" and "empowerments." Tristan assured himself that this was it for Bobby. But then, Bobby had endeared himself to that expatriated magistrate, Alba Sandalphon Magus. Tristan wondered whether he might have shot himself in the foot by lending Bobby out to the maga.

"Last I remember, you were asked to locate Albright Magus. That hasn't happened, has it?" Tristan remarked.

"Oh, I found out where he was, but he had already left when I got there," Bobby fibbed.

"Yes, well finding out where a person was and where he is are two different things, aren't they, Bobby?" Tristan cracked.

"I think he'll POP up," Bobby said.

"Do you, now?" Tristan challenged.

"Considering the circumstances," Bobby said.

Tristan bristled impatiently now and waited for the next shoe to drop off of this kid. Robert Fludd, a young man who in a past life might have been the youthful apprentice who had been tied up with Tomas Ladon at the roasting stake and was now, centuries later, detaching.

"This is it: the fairy's under surveillance—and so is anyone who's penetrated her—you and Paleologos

Sortiar."

"This is a truly remarkable revelation," Tristan yawned facetiously. "Tell me, how long have you been asleep since I last saw you, Bobby? The world has truly passed you by. What a shame."

"If Solaris Sortiar passed the Conus magus to her —"

"I would know," Tristan declared. "As far as that goes, he was guarded and miserly with her. He gave her nothing but a very nice fling and a broken heart. And they were not together for that long, as you know."

"Yeah, but she's under sur-VEIL-lee-ance and so is everyone who's been in her. They're marked. I'm not one of those people — but not for lack of trying," Bobby quipped. "de Lux Sortiar–who is very impressed with you for the fine work you've done for the Cause — wants you to lie low for a while," Bobby continued in a jaunty tone. "Like, don't go parading the fairy-siren-queen around in a freak show in every sorcerers' watering hole and meat market from here to the Terra Mysticus. de Lux doesn't want you to get killed or anything. You should've just left her alone and let her be an ordinary person," he added.

"The message is duly noted, Robert — or is it Fludd Sortiar?" Tristan said placidly.

"I guess she likes Jason better if he's the one they want to kill first," Bobby said. "Or maybe it's not Hipparchus Gorgon's folks or Jason's ex-girlfriend who want to do him in. Maybe you want to get rid of Paleologos. That's what I think. That's what I told de Lux," Bobby said.

"Did you now," Tristan smirked, regretting that he was no longer at leisure to duly chastise the young man. At least every word out of the imp's mouth was bald-faced lie except the part about de Lux.

Bobby shrugged. "It could happen," he said.

"Frankly, things were going quite smashingly until you showed up, Bobby," Tristan snapped. "Frankly in kind,

Paleologos Sortiar and I have a bond and an agreement, which we've kept, unlike you and me. It's been trying at times but neither Jason nor the fairy has seen fit to break my heart, but you have."

"Better your broken heart than my broken bones," Bobby quipped.

Tristan motioned toward the back door, gesturing that perhaps Bobby ought to leave. "I know I'm to blame. I was not kind; I was miserly; I was stingy in tenderness and support, considering your circumstances, your need for a surrogate father. However, I wanted to make you into someone with great force. But now you have de Lux Sortiar to tell you what a fine man you are, what a great magician and white knight," Tristan blithely blathered.

"She's been seen in the company of the 'Moray' Eel Lady. And the Lizard King is still trying to figure out how to become her favorite panty liner," Bobby remarked. "Jason and The Lizard have had it out a couple of times—but you don't go into the Outer Plane to keep after Bella's goings on anymore, do you? And when she gets really frustrated, she sprouts wings and a fish tail and jumps off the turret at the back of your house. She flies around. Usually just before sunset. I hear the neighbors find it very disturbing."

"Keep your distance from the fairy," Tristan finally barked, having lost his temper. "You've outworn your welcome."

"I'm just saying," Bobby shrugged. "But why shouldn't she be running amok? With you and your butt buddy teaching her how to be a little monster."

Tristan called Bobby an insolent pest. As if he were utterly world-weary and without time to banter with this kid, the sorcerer asked him again to leave.

"It's not as if she's 'consorting' with The Lizard," Bobby stressed. "If Jason'll just back off and leave her alone with Sauros, she'll probably kill the guy. Don't you think? Then we'll be done with it."

Tristan sat with his hand on his brow and rested for a while as if in an empty-mind state, but he actually was fuming over the exploitative schemes these Lions of Light folk had about Bella. "Thank you for your time, Fludd Sortiar," he sighed wearily. "You've provided a wealth of salient information. Farewell."

"I'm bound, according to a directive, to remain in your mentorship and service," Bobby said upon rising from his chair.

"It does not seem necessary or appropriate, Fludd Sortiar," Tristan uttered.

"I think I should stay on, Lundragon Sortiar. I think I should," Bobby insisted. He nodded. A tender gravity came over him. "Understand me for once."

"What am I to understand, Bobby? You've crossed me and come here vomiting up spite and telling me I have to sell out my fairy to the Lions of Light because they can't manage to avenge their closet-magus fallen hero, Michael Solaris, all on their own. Aren't de Lux and his son supposed to be expert assassins? Is the task too lowly for them now?" Tristan questioned.

"You and Jason are in peril, and we can't have that," Bobby said. "I know one or both of you has the Conus magus. I know it. They think Jason has it, and they're gonna' get him like they got Solaris, and then they'll go for you. And the fairy—you can't be treating her like a thing because she's got more of a mind than any of us. She's going to do something."

"She is going to avenge Solaris and, ultimately, Jason and me. Obviously. If she does it, she will do it for herself, not for your Cause," Tristan said plainly. "I need that Albright Magus to intervene to help her help herself and help us who love her as nearest and dearest and seek to protect her. Otherwise, if she is crossed through serious threat to our welfare, she may bring it all down regardless of who's who."

"Yeah but I don't think she will," Bobby said. "I think she'll fix everything."

Tristan shook his head and chuckled in an exasperated way.

"Have some faith. You know what they say about love: it's always ready to excuse, endure, hope, trust, whatever," Bobby rambled.

"Are you finished yet? May I dismiss you?" Tristan asked.

"Can I come back to work and hang out with the fairy?" Bobby requested in the guileless tone of a nine-year-old boy scout.

Tristan threw up his hands. "Why, 'sure,' Bobby. Come back anytime. My house is yours. After all, you are my 'nephew.'"

In the end, Tristan was not angry with Bobby. He was proud of him. Tristan felt that he had succeeded in his mentorship of the younger man. Bobby had liberated himself from Tristan and had surpassed him. Tristan would now regard him as a deft and ingenious young sorcerer who had a remarkably punchy and irritating glamour.

Once Bobby had departed, Tristan lurched up to the master bathroom and lugged the looking glass from it into the hidden anteroom annexed to the master bedroom. The room was small and situated behind an old-fashioned, trick wooden-panel. Bella didn't know about it—although she probably did.

The room had a white marble floor on which a gold circle was inlayed. Glass-door cabinets lined the walls and displayed containers of powders and elixirs, desiccated body parts of animals, herbs, vials of brackish tinctures, crystals, stones, ceremonial weapons and accoutrements, candles, waxes and gums, reference books, plates and parchments on which mystical diagrams were etched, and figurines of deities and power creatures. It was Tristan's inner sanctum.

Tristan flipped the looking glass sideways and splattered water and some other substances on it. He had to find out where Bellaluna was and what she was doing. He tilted the mirror this way and that and inspected the streaks and beads of liquid and patterns of the soot on it.

"Come on, come on," he urged as if he were coaxing his number to win at a roulette table.

Bella was in her old Outer Plane haunt in the woods, sulking in yet another brisk and barren New England year-end cold. She was bundled in a thick, black cashmere coat that Tristan recognized was his. She was wearing one of his good scarves and a fur hat that belonged to Jason.

She was crouching on the frosty earth in the mouth of the cave where Tristan, Jason, and Bobby had first seen her with that the deranged Aisa Morae. Tristan tenderly touched the image. Bella startled and fell back, but it wasn't because of Tristan; someone had come upon her. A man crouched down to meet her face to face. It was Albright Magus.

The mage startled, turning to meet Tristan's occult gaze. Albright expressed a knowing sneer. Then the image in the mirror dissolved.

Φ

"Do you know who I am?" Anderson asked. He tried to get a look into the fairy's eyes to determine her overall condition.

She winced and blinked. "Are you Albright Magus?" she hesitantly asked.

Anderson smiled faintly to reassure her.

She took in a deep sigh and laughed at the irony. With head bowed, she became teary. Her gloved hands inclined towards the mage's feet, touching them. Anderson wasn't sure whether this was an intentional reverential gesture or whether the fairy was trying to steady her crouching stance.

"You know that Michael did not abandon you but was taken away by very grievous circumstance," Anderson muttered.

"Yeah," the fairy sulked.

"Are there any passionate sentiments left in you for him now considering the years past and your new involvements?" he asked gently.

"It would've been a lot better if he could've stuck around and not left me to what happened," she said angrily and gasped that she was way "down a rabbit hole."

"A good analogy," Anderson quipped.

"Who or what is Conus magus, besides a snail?" the fairy asked. "They killed Michael about that, not about a neurotoxin or anything real about a government or 'terrorism' or anything that makes sense."

Anderson flung a canvas blanket into the cave and coaxed the fairy to scoot in and nestle on it. Once he entered the space, it would become warm. He propped up and ignited a small, round kerosene heater and placed a kettle on top of it. Anderson announced that he was preparing tea. He produced a satchel from which he drew apples, wheat bread, and jars of almond butter and marmalade, cheese, and marshmallows.

Once she was settled and seemingly solaced — what with a gentle sprinkle of snowflakes wafting about outside the cave — Anderson explained, plainly, that the Conus magus was a lethal magical charm. It was more of a rare and special ability through which the empowered person could instantly paralyze and absorb the life force — that is kill — another creature.

"I've seen Paleologos Sortiar do that," the fairy admitted. "You know who he is?"

Anderson grit his teeth and tried not to blanch. "On humans?" he asked.

"No. Animals on his property. He says he's doing something else, but I know it's not true—and it's my fault," the fairy stated grimly. "I supposedly did something deadly a very long time ago, and I'm paying for it now. I have 'things' in me that they take. Well, I take back, too," she said abashedly and raised an eyebrow.

She explained that she had come to be content with her situation, except that it went along with all sorts of attacks—mostly from outsiders. There was occasional infighting, too, she said. She related the incident in which Tristan and Jason came within a hair's breadth of seriously fighting each other, duel-like with staffs in hand, because Jason had essentially kidnapped her for a few weeks.

"At least they went and got me a ring instead of a collar," she added glibly. She withdrew an oversized glove from her left hand to flash a rather ornate, jewel-studded ring.

Anderson nodded sympathetically. "You've done a great service to these men in a number of ways and in so doing have atoned for rash behavior committed in a distant past. This life time is for atonement, closure, and transformation, but it will be no good if you or they are provoked to carry out dark acts. This is the fateful challenge. You do know that," he stressed to which the fairy nodded emphatically and as if it were elementary.

"You obtained the Conus magus empowerment from Michael and passed it on to at least one of your new consorts," Anderson explained. "Do you think Paleologos Sortiar is intending to use it on persons?"

"Jason knows how to do a lot bad things," the fairy admitted. "But besides a little spite or mischief, he'd just as soon keep the peace and be left alone. Me, too," the fairy said.

Anderson did not express alarm. Rather, he nodded thoughtfully and went on to explain that most of those rare persons who had the key to the Conus magus charm were not fully aware of it until some onslaught pushed them to the wall and forced them to use the power. Such incidents tended to occur during early adulthood for a magician and were generally singular. One adept who was known to use it repeatedly out of necessity was a young man named Leonard de Lux Junior, a mage and head of a revolutionary political movement that Michael had been closely aligned with, he told her.

"Michael was the only known person who knew the breath of the Conus magus charm. He knew how to use to it to heal, help, hinder, harm, or kill. He was teaching the young mage how to apply the nuances of the charm," Anderson explained. "Certain people of power and influence within a land that you now know is not a part of the ordinary world saw fit to eliminate our good friend. They used a scorned woman to accomplish this."

"The eel lady," the fairy grimaced.

"She is thought to be an entity like you but a bit demented — and some say, past her expiration date," Anderson remarked.

"But I'm not a 'fairy'; I'm a monster," the damsel said.

"You are a siren, sister to the Fates, brimming with power and wisdom, and maligned and misunderstood in time and space by puny mortal men," Anderson said. He pointed to the magical letter that remained as graffiti on the wall of the cave. Samekh. "Do you understand what that is? You know your Cabalist alphabet, don't you?"

"Samekh is associated with the western quarter, the crucifixion of Christ, the energies of transformation and regeneration, the grail, and the nature of form, spirit, and space," the fairy recounted.

"'He caused the letter Samekh to reign in wrath.' What is this wrath? Is it the shadow?" Anderson asked.

"It's the ferocity of justice and order and of the spinning of the wheel of time," the fairy replied.

Anderson nodded. He liked the notion.

"Yes. That's what you are," he told her. "It might be coming to that. Are you familiar with goddess lore? The dark mother, the warrior queen whose blessing and vengeance are the circumstances that cause a person to experience transformation?" Anderson asked.

The fairy grinned at the implication.

Anderson nodded approvingly. He confessed that he secretly had been and would now resume being her mentor. He also told her that he would teach her how to commune with Michael even though Michael had assumed a new form and resided in another plane of existence.

In all, the mage felt content. He had found a real "fairy." Indeed, he had found the Fairy Queen.

19
[The Sun]
The Fairy Queen

t was very early on a Thursday morning at the beginning of April when a legion of law officers, dogs, and trained volunteers began canvassing a woodland park that everyone knew was Bellaluna Drago's favorite place. All entrances to the park had been closed off and the few friends she had left and her parents, brother, and the brother's wife and ex-wife pined and prayed at the barricades. There was talk of dredging the Mianus River, and there was an APB out for two foreign men who Bella had been going around with for quite some time. Both men also were mysteriously missing. They had no records of existence whatsoever, which made them even more sinister and mysterious than the first man who Bella had been involved with who also had disappeared.

The inspection of Bella's home suggested that she may have been living elsewhere anyway. No peculiar items or leads could be found although her kith and kin had informed the FBI what it already knew: Bella had some bizarre interests in the occult and her apartment was chock full of arcane artifacts.

No trace was left. There was nothing but a tidy, furnished apartment that hardly bespoke the existence of an inhabitant although the mortgage and utilities had been paid up until that month.

Bellaluna Drago had disappeared. Whether intentionally or as an effect of foul play was the question.

She was in hiding, though, and was being sheltered by Anderson Albright Magus in an unremarkable ranch-style house at the back of a private driveway at the far end of a cul-de-sac within walking distance of the woodland park. The fairy and the mage spent most of their time in meditation. In that endeavor, they had become intimate but not in the same way as the fairy had been intimate with the sorcerers. The basis of their intimacy was the nearness, the energy, and the direction of that energy in the steady silence and concentration of the vision of the Work. It drew the fairy into a kind of love-bond with the mage that was not based in carnality or desire.

The mage emitted an aura of consolation and tenderness of a caliber that only a very ancient, experienced, and wise entity could express. It was sweet and somewhat pitying. Bella would sit in his presence not for the sake of the Work, but to feel that poignant kindness. It would make her tearful because she would feel rather small. She would feel vulnerable and insubstantial in the shadow of that sentiment. She would laugh ruefully about how frightened and annoyed she once had been about the man—a sentiment that the mage confessed was mutual. This fact was a contemplation in itself.

The flavor of the mage's presence was like that of the calm sea at the break of dawn when the world is silent except for a squawking gull and the rustle of reeds on a sand dune. Everything in that place has a golden and bluish tinge to it and is slightly brisk and balmy.

In that way, the "taste" of the mage's proximity differed from that of the other men Bella had known from that world. Those men were all fire and lightening and exploding stars. But those men were not as mature as Albright Magus, and they were not magi or even particularly spiritual.

The mage had been performing a kind of meditation called the Lux Clarus rite. Bella very much wanted to learn it. She had attempted to teach herself, but her technique was flawed. She assumed that Anderson would eventually transfer the empowerment needed to perform the rite and that he intended to teach it to her. She learned to be patient. In observing Anderson, she realized that the Lux Clarus was no simple thing. The process of perfecting it would be long and challenging.

Anderson was performing the rite for Bella because, having made the leap to officially cross into the Inner Plane, she was now cut off from her Outer Plane familiars: family, friends, and the patients she had worked with. It was a traumatic event; she would have to deal with the guilt about disappearing, without a trace, on kith and kin who would have to live with the torturous mystery for the remainder of their lives.

However macabre and seemingly cruel, it was often better to fake the death of the person passing from the Outer to the Inner Plane than have him or her just vanish. It didn't leave so many loose ends, but then people disappeared mysteriously every day. Such horrors were naturally occurring events in the Outer Plane however much they were treated as unnatural ones.

Persons disappeared all of the time in the Inner Plane as well. None other than Jason Paleologos had done so shortly after the New Year. He had not been well. Indeed, it was obvious that the magical attacks he had been contending with had changed from taunts lodged from the outside to something virulent that had infiltrated his body. His memory and concentration were scattered, his coordination unstable, he fatigued easily, his breath was labored, his hair was graying, his complexion was sallow, his aura was dull, and he seemed to be shrinking.

Although he resided on property in the Outer Plane, no one could find the site anymore. It, too, had disappeared. It was a horrific and inconsolable thing. People felt badly for Tristan, but they felt worse for the fairy. After all, she had lost two consorts: Solaris Sortiar and now Paleologos Sortiar.

Jason had been sought via scrying, divinatory techniques, even necromancy with no luck. Sympathetic, high-level magi had been recruited to perform versions of the Lux Clarus rite to reach him. Meanwhile, Bella had been advised by the Lions of Light people to take refuge with Anderson. They told Tristan to depart for the Principalis. Tristan didn't much like that. He refused to abandon his long-time friend or be separated from his consort but Leo de Lux Sortiar insisted that the sorcerer go where he could better preserve himself. He claimed that Tristan was already also besieged by a magical attack and needed to take steps while he still was in his right-enough mind. He also insisted that the fairy would be safer in Anderson's company, with de Lux adding that he himself wanted access to her.

Tristan did not like this at all. He broke off communications with representatives of the Lions of Light—Bobby Fludd included. He was showing signs of being not quite right, though. At first, those close to him, such as Roger Tau, thought he had become very calm and knowing in temperament, but this was inaccurate. He was becoming flat and depressed. There was something blank about his presence, as if he, too, were disappearing

Concerns erupted that Tristan might kill himself in his grief and take the fairy with him. Phoenix Dionysus had sought out Anderson to relate how deranged, desperate, and despondent Tristan had become. He said that Tristan was trying to figure out how to absorb the fairy back into himself and then die and start all over from scratch.

"We are aware of the situation and have a plan in place," Anderson assured Phoenix Dionysus. "The Lion of Light himself Leo de Lux Sortiar has something in mind. I've been asked to participate if it comes to that."

Leo de Lux, with the help of his wife Sofia La Maga Magus and Anderson Albright Magus, was on the brink of casting a spell to put the uncooperative sorcerer into a kind of anesthetic sleep so that he would not be aware of his sorrows and not hurt himself or anyone else. It would be a temporary death, like a coma, similar to but not as torturous as a form of corporeal punishment used in Terra Novit. The punishment was called the Lock Penalty because its victim would be "locked in" himself. It was an extreme measure, the antidote of which was the Lux Clarus rite, which was where the mages La Maga and Albright came in. They would undo the spell de Lux cast on Tristan at the appropriate time.

But as Anderson had hoped, the fairy and Tristan established an understanding before it came to that.

As the fairy told it, she had been sitting in the damp cold by the pond in Tristan's yard. Despite the cold season, she was spending an inordinate amount of time outdoors, as if she had become a sylph meant to live in a tree. She said it was hard for her to breathe in enclosed spaces, and although she longed to be close to Tristan, she feared him as well—because he wasn't "inside" himself anymore. She admitted that she sometimes feared that he might hurt her.

She was tossing gigantic materialized roses into the pond's icy murk until she became too frustrated in the contemplation of her plight. She churned up the pond and sunk the roses with a beech tree bough she used as a staff instead of the beautiful silver and gold implements that she had acquired from Michael and Jason's nasty ex-girlfriend.

When she returned to the house, she sensed that Tristan was not at work at the Bythos Academy but in the home. It took a while to find him, which in itself was unnerving, because she didn't trust what he was up to from one minute to the next given his mind-state.

On her third sweep of the bedroom, she slid open the

panel to Tristan's secret anteroom, and there he was. Still alive but not at all content.

His looking glass, which was smeared with liquid and gunk, was akimbo and cracked. A jagged, triangular piece was dislodged from it. Jars of liquids and powders, desiccated body parts of animals, stones and crystals, waxes, and various magical instruments were all about in disarray. The room had a bitingly pungent odor because of it. Tristan was huddled at the far end of the perimeter of the circle that was inlayed on the floor.

A trio of conjured gremlins or thought-forms — or whatever-they-were — cowered in a dark corner opposite where Tristan sat brooding or weeping with his head pressed against his knees. Although they were creepy-looking, the creatures responded to Bella's gaze with pathetic and penitent expressions. Rather than act as if she were repulsed, she angrily told them that they had failed the task for which they were summoned and were good-for-nothing slackers. She said that they shouldn't expect to get any more offerings from Tristan and should go back to wherever they came from really fast, or else.

She told Anderson that she and Tristan then had talked about everyone and everything. She reported that she had declared her devotion to the sorcerer and insisted that the trials they were facing were nothing more than the purifying flames of an alchemical kiln that burns off the dross of an element so that the brilliant, adamantine gem hidden within it may be revealed. She vowed to avenge them all — that it was already in the making — and promised to transform her host of struggling sorcerers, living or not, into light-workers who had fiery seraphim as pets.

Once the sorcerer became calmed, the fairy gently told him that he should do what that man, Leo de Lux, had said. The spell muddling his mind having been broken by love and sense, Tristan complied. He delivered the fairy to

Albright's new doorstep and departed the Terra Novit.

Φ

It was Bobby Fludd's job to escort the fairy and Anderson Albright to the New York office of Leo de Lux. As the young man had mentioned, the place was chock full of decorative insects, birds, and tropical plants such that Anderson found it a bit repulsive. Besides de Lux, the visitors were also met by de Lux's attaché, Victor, and de Lux's son Leonard, and other kin embroiled in the Cause, including de Lux's brother, who was a mage, and a man who, having married one of La Maga Magus' apprentices, was regarded as a son-in-law.

When Bella-the-siren-fairy entered de Lux's presence, he exuberantly exclaimed, "Fairy Queen!" which made her eyes blush pink. She startled, of course, because of the man's commanding and eerily winsome appearance.

"He's married but, you know," Bobby whispered to her, but she seemed too distracted to react to the jibe in any way.

de Lux was sitting in a large, throne-like wing chair upholstered in red leather and velvet. Everyone else was standing, including Leonard Junior.

de Lux waved an impatiently shooing hand at Bobby when he positioned the fairy before him. The young man reverently scooted away and watched de Lux scrutinize Bellaluna. He rose to his feet and circled the fairy while glaring with his disturbing white eyes and pinched brow.

Bella merely stood there, eyes lowered and faintly smiling as if afraid a rude giggle might escape. She did not seem intimidated or distracted until de Lux simply uttered Michael Solaris' name.

The fairy's mood suddenly changed. She cringed as if someone had forced her to bite into a grapefruit. She pressed her hands into her eyes to sop up the tears. Anderson shrugged slightly when she glanced at him.

de Lux nodded at Anderson and uttered the word, "quite nice," as if pleased by her poignant reaction.

"There's an alchemical adage that goes like this, 'the dragon only dies when he is killed by brother and sister at once, not by one alone, but by both, namely by sun and moon,'" de Lux said. "Sol and Luna. But that was grievously interrupted, wasn't it? It's a bitter thing. And now they want to wrest you from your new, replacement gentlemen-sorcerers," he said. "A fiery triangle rather than a watery one," he added provocatively. "You do know why they — and you — are under siege. It all goes back to Michael — and to me, I'm afraid."

Bella inclined her head slightly to assert that she was aware of the details. "Something about a snail," she said.

de Lux produced a sparrow by opening a fist. The bird remained placidly perched within the palm of his hand. "Can you dissolve the life force of this creature into yourself?" he asked the fairy.

"I don't know," she replied.

"Whether you can is the point of contention in all this," de Lux huffed.

"Or whether other people can because of me," the fairy responded, looking pained and miserable. She anxiously asked de Lux not to do anything bad to the little bird in front of her.

de Lux set the sparrow on his desk and, with a twitch of a finger, made it, with a piteous squeak, dissolve into a faint blue mist.

The fairy breathed hard and dejectedly. She glared with weepy ruddy eyes at where the bird had been.

"'The ability to express tenderness is a laudable trait,'" de Lux remarked. Then he turned to Bobby and Anderson to complain that the fairy was acting awfully namby-pamby for someone whose consorts were allegedly dark and ruthless sorcerers.

"Knowing how to do something and doing it are two different things," she remarked.

"My point exactly," de Lux plaintively replied. He flopped back into his throne-like chair and told the fairy not to be upset with him. "The bird wasn't real anyway, but it's not as if most things are." He rematerialized the creature. It looked like the self-same sparrow. de Lux coaxed it to fly away to mingle among all the other birds and colorful insects that were flitting around the office.

"I can suck the life force out of thing just like that," de Lux boasted and snapped his fingers. "So can you," he told the fairy. "Whether we choose to do such a thing is another matter. But you have a couple more tricks in your pocket than I do." He reached out and tugged at the fairy's skirt to pull her closer to him, but she resisted.

"I did do something recently," she cautiously declared.

"Did you now," de Lux replied.

Bella nodded resolutely. She glared at Anderson while de Lux studied her, his face brightening into a sneer. He huffed a sigh of satisfaction. "Aisa Morae." He turned to Anderson and said. "She's gone."

Anderson blanched and tottered on his feet.

"I had to," Bella protested. "She was hanging around the property. She was looking mangled and monster-like. I just told her something. I didn't know whether what happened was actually going to happen. I was trying to protect you," she told Anderson.

"That's more like it," de Lux gloated, but Anderson was shaking his head and looking ill.

"I fixed her and sent her off out of this world," Bella pouted.

Anderson had to sit down, but de Lux scooped the fairy into his lap and hugged her. "My fairy queen," he purred repeatedly and nuzzled the dolorous damsel such that the other men blushed.

"How did you do it?" he whispered.

"I told her something special," Bella replied.

"It was a bit overwhelming for her, huh?" de Lux smirked.

Bella sadly nodded.

"Can you tell me something like that? 'What's to be known through which all things are known?'" he asked.

"No," she said.

"How about Albright Magus here," de Lux taunted.

"No," the fairy responded.

"Bobby?"

"No. Especially not," she said.

"'Especially not.'" de Lux snickered and winked at the young sorcerer. "Would anyone be able to hear this news and live to tell the tale?" he asked the fairy.

The fairy shrugged.

"Paleologos Sortiar?" de Lux asked.

The fairy winced as if it were an uncertainty.

"The other one?" he asked incredulously.

With a subtle nod of the head, the damsel basically affirmed that the noxiously brittle sorcerer Lundragon Sortiar could hear the call of a siren and not waste away from it. This also meant that he was privy to an exceptional truth about the nature of existence and the transmigration of souls.

"Very interesting," de Lux mused. "Let me ask you this," he continued. "Did you torture the harpy for what she did to Michael?"

"No," the fairy gasped.

"You sent her to a nice place then?"

"I don't know where she went," the fairy muttered.

"Good enough," de Lux said. "Like us all, she was a product of circumstance. A pain body begets pain," he solemnly told his audience. "And who made that pain body but fellow creatures made of pain: ogres, vampires, opportunists, and those bent on self-aggrandizement, domination, manipulation, and cruelty. Our friend here tried to turn that poison into ambrosia with the best, most noble intent." de Lux motioned toward Anderson. "His efforts were roundly deterred. But after long years, he has acquired a wondrous antidote, which is to give refuge to an entity that has the key to the process of transformation. Our lady here: turning killers into saints and 'vampires' into angels and ferrying foes to realms of light, peace, and consolation."

The luxurious chair within which de Lux sat with the fairy on his lap swiveled around then as if it on a swivel plate. With his back to his compatriots, de Lux continued to seemingly cuddle the fairy and confer with her in barely audible tones that sounded pointed and serious.

When it seemed the conversation was done, de Lux cupped his hand over the top of her head and braced the other against her chest. He and the fairy locked eyes.

"Empowerment," Bobby mouthed to the others.

The only sound was that of the fairy's gasp.

The sorcerer kissed the fairy's forehead when he was through and muttered, "my fairy queen" a few times as if absorbed in song.

20
[Judgment]
On the Death of Lunaris Dracon

Jason Paleologos found himself fatefully confined to the Outer Plane. He was debilitated, rendered impotent, stripped of powers, and wrested from even the simplest and most basic means of communication. He could not physically move beyond the confines of his country estate. Eventually, he would not be able to move beyond a narrow perimeter of the house itself. Then the circle would close tighter until he was confined to his own paralyzed body. He was slowly being "locked in."

He wasn't sure why certain thugs within the political structure of Terra Novit and their corporatist lord, the young heir of Gorgon enterprises, Raimondo Sauros, hadn't arranged to simply ambush and kill him like they had Solaris. Why the prolonged taunts progressing to torture to slow death? Or were Jason's self-styled opponents more afraid to get close to him than they were to Solaris? Jason realized that, from the start—beginning with the petulance he endured from his break with Regina—the annoyances and perils he had endured were part of an insidious ruse to wear him down. Now he was completely overcome.

He continually wondered why he was a threat. It became known that he had the Conus magus proficiency, but unlike Solaris, he had never been involved in covert political operations. He was not sharing warfare expertise with rebels and revolutionaries; he was exterminating nuisance wildlife from his property.

He was making art, coauthoring the never-ending drivel about Dracon lore, and being in love with a fairy-siren who he had to begrudgingly share with an age-old friend who he liked enough in a certain way to love (in a certain way) on occasion. That was his life. It was relatively innocuous. He couldn't understand why he couldn't be left alone with it.

At the onset of the locked-in process, Jason had left numerous messages for Tristan through various means—none acknowledged. Whether this meant that Tristan also was debilitated or had met his end, or that he was unable to resist passion and rivalry with a shared consort and had finally turned on Jason was unknown. And the fairy was not coming around. Jason was sure her absence was not by choice. She was in peril, but he could not help her because he had been neutered.

He was waiting to die. He had the time but not the energy to prepare for it. He should have been thinking sublime thoughts—or perhaps no thoughts—or atoning or envisioning the passage through the spheres and forging a pathway to a desirable other plane or incarnation. His mind was distracted, mumbling, and static, and his emotions were merely anxious jitters. A numbness in thought developed so that he could hardly manage to fear lapsing into the void.

As if it were his last willful act, a day came when he spent several hours repeating the phrase "Come for me." He didn't know who should come for him, only that the person should. He had managed to bathe and shave, and attempted to comb a knotted outgrowth of long gray hair.

He attired himself in a crimson and sapphire-blue dalmatic, chasuble, and jewel-studded cope. He cradled his matching miter headdress in the crook of his left arm as if it were an infant although it had the feel of a severed head.

He used his diamond-studded gold and platinum staff as a cane with which to hobble down a staircase and then out through his sun room to a windswept patio, down tiers of what had been a rock garden to another, wider patio that now had a dried up and weedy fountain as its centerpiece.

He collapsed onto a bench and leaned forward, bracing himself against his staff. He contemplated the irony of its finial. Why had he been paired with the image?

Many persons assumed that the finial depicted Icarus, the youth who, with artificial wings made of feathers and wax, flew too close to the sun. The wing-contraption that Icarus' father, Daedalus, had outfitted him with, melted. The youth tumbled from the sky to his death in the sea. It, like similar Greco-Roman myths, was a tale about the consequences of overweening ambition.

Jason, as he matured, thought it best to have persons think that the finial crowning his staff was Icarus and that the image was a reminder to maintain mindfulness and temperance in his endeavors.

The staff had been bequeathed to him by his primary mentor, not the aforementioned artist Dorrie Auriel Magus, but an eerie old sorcerer named Ouranos Apokryfos. He did not choose Jason as his lineage holder. Nevertheless, the staff that Jason was in possession of had been passed to his mentor from his mentor, a magus. Indeed, the staff was an heirloom that had been passed from mentor to apprentice for generations.

The finial did not represent Icarus, though. It represented Lucifer falling from Heaven.

Lucifer originally was a name of the morning star — the planet Venus, which was the third brightest light in the sky after the sun and moon. But, as myth told it, Venus, in the guise of a Roman goddess, was exiled from the night sky as a punishment for her lack of humility.

A figurine of the goddess Venus topped the staff that had belonged to Regina Poinciana Magus, which now was the possession of Bella-the-fairy-siren. Jason never disclosed that his and Regina's staffs were similar, but

Regina's possession of such a signature piece was one of the things that drew him toward her, and it was fitting that it was wrested from her by Bellaluna.

The figurine on Jason's staff alluded to a different, more well-known version of the Lucifer story: a Judeo-Christian story about a war in Heaven.

Of course, as a youth Jason found it fashionably sinister to own a staff depicting a notorious fallen angel — a devil. The Devil. But Jason was not given the staff for it to be a testament to his dark ambitions even though it seemed so at the outset. It carried a message that Jason took too long to realize. It was woeful that, having finally come upon the realization, it could not be acted upon now that he was being locked in. Perhaps Jason was dying a slow death as a kind of strange grace for the damned; once death came, circumstances might worsen.

Lucifer, according to Judaic lore, was the foremost of the heavenly hosts and a hard task-master, brutally enforcing the rule of law and jealously brown-nosing the Lord God. When God ordered the angelic hosts to bow to and serve his new creation, mankind, Lucifer balked and went into a jealous rage. He rebelled, inciting a war in Heaven.

For that, Lucifer was cast down by the archangel Michael. His hubris was said to be — not overweening ambition — but pride. The moral of the story, however, was that to align oneself with the highest power, one had to see and serve it in mankind. Otherwise the attachment to a divine ideal might prove empty and, indeed, destructive. Having realized this, Jason cried about Lucifer because the being was so pathetic and so Commons.

He further sank into a stupor as he sat on his patio waiting to die. He was only distantly aware of feeling bitter that no one was coming for him in his last moments.

He startled then. He apprehended the sound of car

wheels slowly crackling over the gravel driveway. He heard the vehicle's door opening. The visitor's footfalls lightly crackled over the gravel pavement, paused, and started again, retracted, hesitated, and then proceeded as if the visitor was inspecting the home's condition and wondering where to begin.

After a time, Jason assumed that the visitor was in the house. He waited, seemingly patiently. His mind had become so foggy and blotted-over that he did not feel time so much anymore, merely moments of awareness, glimpses of lucidity that flashed in and out of a twilight realm of static noise, distraction, and void. When he heard the person slip through the sunroom's showcase doors and alight onto the upper patio, Jason pulled his posture up and angled his staff diagonally across him.

When he heard the fairy holler his name, he felt as if an inner star had burst that would burn him up right then. The fairy clamored down the tiered incline and slate steps and rounded the promenade surrounding a fountain to face Jason. She naturally gasped and blanched at the site of him. She was piteously wailing, "Oh God," as if she had found him dead already. A prayer to Jesus Christ even came out of her mouth.

"Don't die!" she commanded, as if furious with him.

"How . . ?" Jason rasped in a bare whisper and wriggled a finger to finish the sentence.

"I figured it out," she snapped.

"Guide me over," he requested.

"No," she remarked.

He managed to huff out a rueful laugh. It was all very sweet that she didn't want to let him go, but he told her that he was gone already. If she didn't help him pass over, he would sink into dispersion and nothingness or else end up in Hell. Didn't she know that she had come in the nick of time to help him ascend along a lighted path to another realm of being? He asked through grunts and twitching gestures whether Tristan were alive or not or had turned villainous.

"They made him go into hiding. The Lions of Light people. Something bad had gotten to him, too. He was thinking about killing himself because of it. I talked him out of it," Bella said. "He was crazy desperate to figure out what happened to you."

Then she embraced Jason. She cradled his head against her breast and wriggled her fingers in his outgrown and matted hair. She was all heat and the smell of roses and rosewood. The taste of black cherries whetted Jason's mouth, and he bristled with a scintillating and luminous sensation.

In his inner vision emerged the image of a Chiastolite stone, notable in magian lore; for when cut a certain way, the tan and brown mineral revealed the image of a formée cross. In the center of the cross in the stone that appeared in Jason's mind was the letter — tau — embossed in pale gold. The letter denoted a mark or a seal of ownership. It represented the sacred center and was said, in the mystical texts, to reign in beauty.

In a polyphonic tone, Bella began chanting the names of letters of various mystical alphabets in quick and flowing succession. As she did so, the letters appeared in Jason's mental vision. However fleeting each was, it was enough to grasp the letter's mystery. With it came unique knowledge about the self and the world.

As the letters emerged, they took their places in respective stations of mandalas — one mandala super-imposed on another until Jason was engulfed in a resplendent field of numinous parallel ideas that were the basis of name and form. He ascended through these images into light until he felt he was becoming unfettered breath and joy. Then the imagery faded like that of a very nice dream that one is disappointed to awaken from.

And he did awaken. Alive. In the embrace of his fairy, with his head resting against her breast. He could hear her heartbeat, smell her sweetness, and feel her life and power.

He felt that he could breathe. He felt that he could see. He felt lucid and solid, virile. Alive.

"Did you ever wonder why you and Tristan are so close?" she quietly asked. "Why you are so involved in his work?"

"Tristan and I fancied ourselves to be on the dark side in our youths — boys of 15 or so," he admitted. "In dabbling in the kind of things we imagined dark sorcerers did, we discovered that we were fonder than merely fond of each other — not of other men generally, but of each other. Dependent in a way . . . solaced," Jason mused. "I had thought it was an aspect of my libertine spirit, but now, I ask myself why I should be bonded to the reincarnation of Lunaris Dracon and covet his fairy-creature so tenaciously that I might choose her over him."

"Trauma sometimes binds people together," Bella remarked.

"You and I were bound before 'trauma' set it," Jason scoffed. "For me at least."

"I don't mean us. I mean you and Tristan," Bella responded.

But Jason didn't understand her. He went on with his story. "We were carousers, happy miscreants, and academicians of distinction; marauders, lotharios, pirates, and 'vampires.' People feared us. They aspired to be like us, craved sexual intimacy with us, and coveted what we had earned and captured. It was the lead up to a hard lesson. He and I are together for that lesson. The work is secondary."

Bella smiled in a wise way and asked Jason to tell her how Lunaris Dracon had died.

"You know the story," he said with a wrinkled brow, but she prodded him to go over it again.

"He was burned at the stake along with his young assistant, who the accounts leave nameless," Jason sighed. After a stuttering hesitancy, Jason admitted that the assistant had reincarnated as Bobby Fludd, which was why Tristan was so melancholic when the rascal abandoned him. "But do not tell Bobby this," Jason stressed. "In truth, we abused the fellow. He had more of a right to you than I—and perhaps more than Tristan. He was your protector and friend then and now; Tristan—Dracon, that is—was your lord, a benign despot is all."

"Yes, but Bobby wasn't the 'sorcerer's apprentice,'" the fairy said.

"Yes. Yes, Bella. We're quite certain of this," Jason assured her.

"No," she countered. "Bobby has his own trail of tears."

"Does he now?" Jason replied, realizing that Bella had something to disclose.

"He was busy being a troubadour back then and he still is," she said. Bella smiled and laughed in a demure but patronizing manner as if she thought Jason was silly not to "get it." She recounted the last moments of Lunaris Dracon's—that is, Tomas Ladon's— life in detail.

When they brought him out to the stake, he was resigned, she said. He had assumed a kind of detached and meditative state, like a trance. His captors were trying to break him from this mood because they feared that he wouldn't feel as tortured and sorry as they thought he ought to. For this reason, they did not garrote or hang him before the burning or fix a tether to his neck so that he might be strangled while burning and die faster. Rather, it was decided that he and his assistant should die torturously rather than quickly.

Unlike Ladon, the assistant was violently resisting. "His face was bloody and so beat in that you couldn't recognize him," Bella said. He was hunched over and moved like a rag-doll because he was just so beaten up. It was amazing that he had the energy to fight and resist the way he did. Otherwise, he had been a very handsome fellow. "Some people thought that his beautiful looks were an evil thing about him. But anyway, he was hollering and resisting all the way however much he was beaten." They finally restrained him and bound him to the stake back to back with Tomas Ladon.

"The assistant began to cry then," Bella said, "because he was helpless, and he was afraid to die in an incredibly painful way."

Ladon dislocated his shoulders and cut his wrists as he squirmed through the ropes and chains that bound him to grasp the assistant's hands. The younger man flinched at first but then took one hand and struggled to get hold of the other. It calmed him. He lowered the intake of breath from the top of his chest to his belly, and he moved his attention up to a space just over his head as if attempting to entrance himself and be released from his physical prison before being unnaturally wrenched from it.

"Consoling the younger man was the last wise, kind thing that Tomas Ladon did before he died, and maybe he was helping the assistant remember that his Work had to be perfected and engaged at that very moment. That's what it was for, and there was no other choice anyway. But the executioners didn't like the holding-hand thing," Bella said.

They poked at the men for doing that. Ladon hollered something in an unknown language. It caused his killers to retreat and some onlookers to faint. They called him a devil and a sodomite and of course begged him to repent before they lit the pyre, which they were going to do either way. Neither man said a word, but each submerged into trance as best he could and gulped in the kindling smoke to suffocate before the fire cooked him alive.

Bella retold the story as if relating a fairy tale, as if it were all a quaint melodrama but her mood abruptly changed. She clasped Jason and pulled tight on his hair as she sulked with her head buried in the crook of his neck.

"I didn't mean for that," she whimpered. "I was trying to protect you. I wanted you for myself. Because I would be good to you, and I knew you were great. I'm so sorry," she sobbed.

Jason bristled. "Now what are you saying? Who was Tomas Ladon?"

"You were. Tristan was the other man, the younger one," Bella whimpered. "Everyone thinks Tristan is Lunaris Dracon so much that it's as if it were true, but he isn't. But you can't tell him that. He'll . . . figure it out," she stuttered. "Don't tell him. Alright?"

Jason laughed at the irony of it—ruefully. To be self-effacing. Literally.

"Do you really want to be Lunaris Dracon again?" Bella asked.

"No," Jason replied.

"But Tristan really wants to be. That's his tribute to you. Think of it like that," she said.

Jason was agreeable. He gently asked Bella if she remembered her own end or where she went after Ladon lost his life.

"I lived in your head. Where was I going to go?" she whimpered.

"Perhaps we were once one person and I made us into two," Jason reasoned.

Bella shrugged.

"What's all this inane talk about fairies and sirens, then?" he snickered.

"Reality isn't about reality," Bella said. "It's about

belief. Best to just play along."

Jason was in agreement with her, realizing that wisdom was a very lonely state of mind. He wanted to be away from that place, to be quiet, to make art from expansive ideas, to be joined with the woman who had emerged from his soul, and to feel tender about his long-time friend with whom he would soon reunite. That was all simple enough.

"He was very upset that you did not favor him with the Conus magus charm," Jason confided. "I wondered whether you were sparing him and leaving me to fate. I was a two-faced sort at the beginning," he confessed.

"You both got what you most desired. I'm not sure I had much to do with it except for existing in the first place," Bella muttered. "You thought you might attain something through me, and you did. Good for you. That's called faith."

"Who's turning you into a lady mage? Not Tristan?" Jason quipped.

"Albright Magus found me," she grinned.

"Ah! Albright Magus," Jason exclaimed. "How is the old man?"

"He freaked out a little when he learned that I made the Eel Lady disappear," Bella admitted.

"Did you?" Jason felt full of pride. He thought the news was the juiciest, most sorceress-y thing he had heard in years. He called Bella a chip off the old block and a beautiful dragon.

"Was avenging Michael Solaris a practice run then?" Jason asked.

"In a way," the fairy asserted.

"What happens next?" Jason asked.

"Something," the fairy quipped nonchalantly. "It always does."

21

[The World]
How the Story Ends

Jason Paleologos Sortiar, who—even though he came off as a nice guy—was only "in it" for himself, flipped off the Lions of Light even after all the crap he had been through. That was Bobby Fludd's view. The sorcerer had the gall to refuse to meet with Leo de Lux Sortiar even though de Lux sent Jason a really nice staff crowned with a silver, gold, and platinum figurine of Pegasus and Phoenix both springing up to fly out of lapping flames. de Lux also bought a few more pieces of Jason's artwork. (The sorcerer especially personalized one of the pieces for de Lux and gave it to him for free. So, that was his "thanks, K, bye," Bobby figured.)

The sorcerer supposedly spent a few days with Anderson Albright Magus—probably messing around with Lux Clarus rites, but there was innuendo about "confessions" and "guidance." The word "tears" also laced the gossip, and people wondered what transformation of consciousness occurred in Jason Paleologos during his brush with obliteration.

The sorcerer had become a bit of an enigma, but they all had after the fairy got through with them. Maybe it was that the more they became authentic and clear within themselves, the more they became mysteries to others because in being more "themselves," they were a little removed from the automation of things. Their gears didn't turn as a matter of course or reaction; they turned because they felt like it. This threw everyone else off and either rankled them or forced them to wonder how and why they themselves were turning and churning.

Jason was going back to the Terra Principalis to get it going again with his buddy, Tristan Lundragon. Bobby knew that Tristan was hiding in the same place that Albright Magus had been. Bobby could hardly imagine Tristan being holed up like a monk in a Hyperborea. He wondered what he was doing with his time—conjuring up more fairies and fucking them maybe. He could do that now that he really was Lunaris Dracon, Bobby supposed.

Jason said he had had enough with the Dracon shit. He was leaving all that to Tristan and the fairy while he dedicated his life to art and ideas and "light." Whatever.

He was taking the fairy with him to the Terra Principalis, of course. He asked Bobby to come along. Bobby had intended to go back because it had become home, but he had no intention of hanging around with the sorcerers and their fairy-siren-queen. Then Jason quietly whispered that the fairy needed him. "You have to help her find Sauros Sortiar." He gave a provocative nod of the head. "You'd find that interesting work, wouldn't you?" he asked. "Then you and your Lions of Light people will have a notch up on things, hmm?"

So, Jason wasn't such a self-involved loser maybe—but then, you know, he only wanted the fairy to go after Lizard Boy Sauros because of what he did to him. It had nothing to do with the Cause. It definitely would work, though. So Bobby agreed.

He found himself accompanying Anderson Albright Magus to prepare Tristan about what had gone on. Meanwhile, Jason and the fairy went on a honeymoon or something. In any case, as much as Jason said he was in a rush to get back with Tristan, he really wasn't. He obviously wanted that fairy all to himself, having disappeared with her for nearly two weeks before reuniting with Tristan. Bobby didn't quite get what the fairy saw in either of the sorcerers, but they were her men; that was for sure.

Then Anderson explained to Bobby that Jason and the fairy were "soul mates," that Tristan was the fairy's "sweetheart," and that in some potential future a few lives hence when she and the two sorcerers managed to more clearly set boundaries from one another, the fairy and Michael Solaris Sortiar would have another run-in to get on with what they had started. Anderson warned Bobby that if he didn't figure out what he and the fairy and also what he and the sorcerers were doing in the same melodrama, he would find himself in similar straits again. It would not be as if Bobby would remember it or even be the same person, but it would be like a loop in a hologram.

"We're merely waves on the top of the sea," Anderson said. "One must understand how to revel in being both the wave and the sea."

Yes, Sir.

When Jason and Tristan did have their reunion, it was a strange sight for Bobby. Their emotional display was intense. They gripped onto each other's arms and shoulders and necks as if testing whether the other was really real—familiar, solid, robust, and in the flesh. Then there was all this hugging, sobbing, sentiments of remorse—and kissing.

They sat gripping hands and pawing at each other, their bodies tightly slumping against each other. Their demeanors were as doleful as they were ecstatic. Tristan, of course, was dragging the fairy to lean against him on the other side. It was a strange sight. The three of them huddled together, crying and sighing with relief and not knowing whether they were happy or sorry to have arrived at that moment of their lives.

Then Tristan gripped his head with his hands, one of which was enmeshed in Jason's, and became really broken up. He told everyone that during his long repast in seclusion, he had realized something about himself. He wasn't the incarnation of Lunaris Dracon.

"I've become that. I've become that in this life in every way — in all my art and work and skill — as if it were true, but it isn't. Things are confused and convoluted in the passages through time. We make up stories to make sense and purpose of our lives and to validate the continuity of them. But what our purpose and continuity really are and what we imagine them to be are different mostly. For this reason, there are perhaps truths that are not to be known and when known fully remove us from this sphere and force us into another."

Jason hugged and bolstered his friend and told him that he had become aware of the situation and that it was a remarkably sweet thing. He said that they certainly had succeeded in the Dracon work and that it was remarkable and great that all their efforts would lead them to the point to which they came — self-revelation and transfiguration. "How does that go, Albright Magus?" Jason asked. "That passage about seeing dimly? From the 'Good Book.'"

"'We now see as if viewing a dim reflection in a mirror; then we shall see face to face. What I know now is partial; then I will know completely — as completely as I am known,'" Anderson orated.

Bobby followed the passage through to its end in his head — the one that Leo de Lux had uttered tongue-in-cheek and Bobby had shrugged at, being bewildered to hear the man utter it.

Our knowledge is imperfect, and our prophesying is imperfect, but when what is perfect comes, what is imperfect will cease.

When I was a child, I spoke like a child, I felt like a child, and I reasoned like a child. Now that I am a man, I have no use for childish ways. We now see as if in a dim reflection in a mirror; then we will see face to face. Now my knowledge is incomplete;

but then I will know as completely as I am known. Ultimately, only three things last: faith, hope, and love, and the greatest of these is love.

Φ

It took about two weeks before things got back to normal—"normal" being the squabbling between the two sorcerers over who was monopolizing the fairy's attentions and affections and what she should be allowed to do for her own good. Tristan did not want her to go back to the Terra Novit to have a little "chat" with Lizard Boy. Jason did. So there was a lot of arguing to the effect that Jason was a selfish, opportunistic bastard for putting the fairy up to avenging him. Jason insisted that, no; this is what the fairy had a mind to do.

Bobby didn't care about the motive; he wanted to get into it. Life was so boring otherwise. After Lizard Boy was gone, half a dozen like him who were twice as toxic would spring up to keep the ball rolling in the revolutionary struggle anyway. It would just go on revolving like that, which was why they called it a "revolve-a-Lution," Bobby thought.

Then Tristan insisted that if the fairy and Bobby were going back to the Terra Novit, he would go back too. They needed his protection, he argued. It was an insult and idiotic, but Bobby grit his teeth and held his tongue. Of course, Jason said that if Tristan was going, then he would go, too. So they all went back and dragged Albright Magus along to be their spiritual counsel and referee.

Finis

Other books in the series:

Book 1: La Maga A Story about Sorcerers and Magi

The Sorcerers and Magi series begins with the life and times of a lady mage named Sofia La Maga. Upon returning to her hometown in her magical world after long years of exile in the Himalayas and thereabouts, she befriends, mentors, and rehabilitates the troubled teenaged son of an imposing and elitist dignitary, the high sorcerer Leo de Lux. Strongly averse, then curious, then acquiescing, and ultimately exhilarated, de Lux both falls for Sofia La Maga and also embraces a portended predestined role as the leader of a utopian movement—the Lions of Light--that seeks to overturn an oppressive social system that not only gratuitously exploits magical persons of lesser status but persons like you and me who inhabit the Outer Plane. Magical fantasy is woven with insights from Eastern mysticism and Western esotericism in this first installment of

Book 3: The Savior at the End of Time

Chaos Magic meets Jesus Christ Superstar. The Savior at the End of Time, the third book in the Sorcerers and Magi series, is a veiled take on the Christ-story in which the unassuming and disheveled but oddly charismatic iconoclast, Professor Aurelio Zosimo, introduced in book one, is haplessly rendered into a new messiah for the Lions of Light agenda and the "Immanentization of the Eschaton." The novel references the post-modern magical counterculture current of Chaos Magic. In this installment of the series, Leo de Lux and Sofia La Maga are at odds about their designs regarding Aurelio Zosimo. Both find themselves in over their heads as plot line of the series progresses toward an apocalyptic showdown and the revelation of portentous secrets.

Nonfiction

The Seal of Secrets of the World Adventures in Astral Magic

The Seal of Secrets of the World is a diagram described in a medieval magical book called the Arbatel. The Arbatel is a treatise on how to live in harmony, ease, and intimacy with the energies of the Multiverse. Behind the Christian piety is a more ancient, Pythagoric and Neoplatonic spiritual paradigm that views the world as a multilayered place full of spiritual beings: some elemental, some celestial, some angelic, and some demi-godlike, archonic, or patriarchal. In the spring and summer of 2010, the author, Soror ZSD23 explored the content of the Arbatel and, in the context of solitary and group workings, evoked the so-called Olympic Spirits described in the text. The book notes the author's experiences and insights in working with the Arbatel, provides guidance on practicing and simplifying evocation magic, and includes auxiliary essays related to her studies in magic and mysticism.

www.ingramcontent.com/pod-product-compliance
Lightning Source LLC
Chambersburg PA
CBHW072216170626
46813CB00003B/966